FIRST
FRIDAYS

FIRST FRIDAYS

CHERLYN MICHAELS

HYPERION

NEW YORK

Library of Congress Cataloging-in-Publication Data

Michaels, Cherlyn.
    First Fridays: a novel / by Cherlyn Michaels. — 1st ed.
        p.   cm.
    ISBN 1-4013-0814-7
    1. Female friendship—Fiction.   2. Young women—Fiction.
3. Dating (Social customs)—Fiction.   4. African American
women—Fiction.   5. St. Louis (Mo.)—Fiction.   I. Title.

PS3613.I344F57 2007
813'.6–dc22   2006041112

Hyperion books are available for special promotions and
premiums. For details contact Michael Rentas, Assistant Director,
Inventory Operations, Hyperion, 77 West 66th Street, 12th floor,
New York, New York 10023, or call 212-456-0133.

DESIGN BY KAREN MINSTER

FIRST EDITION

10   9   8   7   6   5   4   3   2   1

FOR
BABEE SORSE

For lending your energy, pulling me up,
and helping me to vibrate at a higher frequency.
You are my soul . . . I'll follow you anywhere.

ACKNOWLEDGMENTS

FIRST AND FOREMOST, I'd like to thank all those who purchased and read a copy of my first novel ever, *Counting Raindrops Through a Stained Glass Window*. Putting your creativity on paper and baring it for the world to see and judge can be a scary thing. Thank you for receiving it well, enjoying it, and telling me about it. That book and your reception to it will always be near and dear to my heart.

I'd like to thank my mother and father (Barbara and James) and my sister and brothers (Gerald, Kim, Tate, and Chris) for their support through their constant encouragement and through telling any and everyone they knew to purchase what they considered to be "the best book ever written" in their biased opinions. I was cool with it.

I'm grateful to my agent, Jenoyne Adams, for her constant enthusiasm, encouragement, and general friendship. Sometimes, I truly forget that you're my agent.

I couldn't do without the constant support of my down-to-earth fellow authors Carla Curtis, Shelia Goss, Linda Dominique Grosvenor, Peggy Eldridge-Love, and Alisha Yvonne (also owner of Urban Knowledge—Memphis). Thanks to Kimberla Lawson-Roby, Gloria Mallette, JD Mason, Karen Quinones Miller, and Rose Beavers for your support of my first novel. Thank you, Nancey Flowers, for your everlasting support of my writing career from self-publishing until now. I am ever so grateful for each act of kindness.

I would like to especially thank Demetrius Johnson for giving me airtime to share my novel and for "bragging" to listeners and Monday Night Footballers on how good it is. Had me ready to run out and purchase a copy myself! See you next football season at Gary's!

Special thanks to my special friends who have supported me by attending my book signings, buying, reading, selling, and telling others about my book: Angelia Anderson, Tracy Williams, Nolan Ferguson, Josette Houston, Shawn Smith, Romeo Payne, and Yolanda "Yogi" Jerry. Thanks to my supporters and fellow enlistees of Vic's Funk-Soul-Steppin' class. Glad you found the energy to read between our workouts. Also thanks to the ladies of Delta Sigma Theta Sorority, Inc., for your support and for a few of you selecting my book for your book clubs and inviting me to the meetings to discuss. Each one has been a pleasure and a joy.

Thanks to all at Hyperion for your enthusiasm and support of my writing: Ellen Archer, Leslie Wells, Beth Dickey, and Miriam Wenger.

And always a thanks for continuing support of my books and all African American books to Tee C. Royal of Rawsistaz.com and fellow St. Louisan, LaShaunda Hoffman of Shades of Romance Magazine (SORMAG). And a special thank-you to Faye Childs of the Blackboard Festival and soror Robilyn Heath of Urban Knowledge Bookstore in Baltimore.

At one with you always,

Cherlyn Michaels
www.cherlynmichaels.com
cherlyn@cherlynmichaels.com

FIRST
FRIDAYS

ONE

"HE IS SUCH AN ASS!" I YELLED IN A WHISPER TO MY best friend over the phone. "I don't think it's even possible for anybody to be any more stupid than he is." I clicked ALT + TAB on my work computer to quickly change the screen from the company document to the draft of my personal entrepreneurial plan for my own business— an Internet café. I peeped over my shoulder to view the doorway to my office. "I'm just going to put up with his crap for nine more months, then, in September, I'm out of here. I already have my resignation letter cued up and ready to be printed."

"Don't you think you should hold it down, Naja? Somebody could be listening. The situation seems tense over there. Anybody could be snooping to get a tidbit of info to bust you." Vlora's usually serene voice was frantic. "Or your phone could be tapped or something."

"Screw them. I'm not worried about any of the idiots that work here, either." I said that with confidence because Formix was a small company, and I knew they weren't up to date on employee spy technology like many of the larger companies. If they were, I probably would have been fired a long time ago. "They're all walking zombies around here. Ass-kissers."

"Like you said though, you want to work nine more months before you can strike out on your own, so you need to chill. Don't get so antsy like you usually do."

I smacked my lips into the phone. "Mr. Benton can kiss my ass. He's a joke, and so is this job. All he has is a title and a little bit of power, and the only thing he does is try to make the rest of us fear him. He's obviously suffering from preemie penis syndrome."

I looked out of my office window at the St. Louis snow that was starting to stick to the sidewalks. Ever since I was a little girl, I have loved fresh fallen snow, and I still get that giddiness that I did back then. Feel like I just want to call it a day and go outside to make snow angels.

I snapped myself out of my two-second trance. "Every day he insists on sending his little assistant around at whatever time of the day to summon me to his office, where I'm to give him a run-down of what I'm doing. Fiber optics is not that interesting, and it's not like this job is challenging anymore. I've lost more than half of my subordinates, and I can manage them all in about three hours throughout the day. I spend the rest of the day working on my business plan and searching the Internet. And they're still praising me and telling me what a wonderful job I'm doing." I reached for my sandwich, which sat on top of a pile of desk clutter, and took a bite. I ran my hand over the pooch of my stomach.

"I hate micromanagement. That's why I can't wait to be my own boss. I've been wanting to do this for years." I pulled the phone away from my ear and peeped over my shoulder again. The sound of footsteps and rustling papers signaled me and in one swift movement, I changed my computer screen back to a work-related document just as Mr. Benton passed my office door. His toupee lay firm as he looked up from the documents in his hands and pressed on a fake smile as he passed. I nodded my head, but didn't return the smile. I clicked the keys again to return the computer screen to my plan and put the phone back up to my ear to a still-talking Vlora.

"So are you going it alone, or are you getting partners?"

"I still want to get partners, but I haven't had time to network." I searched for my water bottle and finally found it behind a stack of folders.

"You should come on out to First Fridays this week and network with people there. You might find potentials. This month, it's going to be right downtown where you are. At the Vanguard Lofts." The sound of ice rattling from a cup to her mouth came through the phone. She chomped.

For months, Vlora has been trying to get me to go with her to these monthly First Fridays events. But the last place I wanted to be was in a room full of stuffy suits with people talking over my head about financial matters, the trade deficit, or the global economy. As it was, I'd been working on my business plan for five months now, and I was using *Business Plans for Dummies* as my reference guide. Even still, I was feeling befuddled.

"I don't think I'm ready for that."

Vlora laughed. "What's to be ready for? What do you think it is?"

"I don't think I'll be able to hang. I'm not up on any financial terms, and I can't discuss any details about financial matters beyond savings, mutual funds, or a 401(k). I haven't acquired a taste for caviar or Brie. And I really don't think I can stand a whole night of MBAs and other overachievers. I'd be bored out of my mind, listening to elevator music or Beethoven or something."

Vlora continued to laugh. "See, that's the main reason you need to go. You don't even know what you're talking about. First Fridays is nothing like that. You've been watching too many . . . well, based on that description, I don't know what the hell you've been watching."

"Yeah, that's what you say," I replied.

"The people who go to First Fridays are just like you. You got your management types, lay workers, business owners, political figures, athletes . . . it's a mixture of people, and it's all about networking and professional presentations. And then you can get your party on afterward."

"Oh, yeah. Partying with a bunch of overachievers. Sounds like . . . fun."

"Don't let the suits fool you. It can get wild up in there. You should bring Allie. You know how she likes to party."

"Yeah. My little sister is always down for a party. But she'll have to find a babysitter."

"Oh, you know she'll find a babysitter. Allie's not missing any parties." She blew a short breath, and I could feel her smirking through the phone. "And I can help you find a man, too. Now I'll admit, you really do have to look beyond the glitter to find a gem, because everybody will be blinging. Fake bling. But the gems are there, and you need one. Maybe then you wouldn't be so uptight. You need to be stretched out a little, if you know what I mean."

We both laughed. Vlora knew that the last thing I was looking for was a man, yet she kept trying to find one for me—something she'd done ever since we met in college at St. Louis University. But doing research and planning for a business were taking countless hours of my time, and I had nothing left to devote to a relationship. The last thing I needed was some man getting on my nerves and throwing me off track from my goals.

Footsteps sounded in the hallway again, and from the way the heels slid across the floor before each step, I knew it was Mr. Benton's assistant, Heather. I hit ALT+TAB. She leaned her upper torso in the doorway of my office, as if she feared full frontal exposure. Her lids blinked over her green eyes and she cleared her throat. "Ms. Rodgers? Mr. Benton would like to see you in his office right away."

"Thank you, Heather."

She gave the doorpost two taps with the fingernails of her right hand and flashed a mouthful of colorful braces. Her blond hair swung around as she turned to go from whence she came, dragging her feet behind her with each step. Why she couldn't just call, I never knew. Perhaps she was as bored out of her mind with her job as I was.

"Gotta go. Mr. Boss has summoned me to his office again for my daily report." I took a bite of my half-eaten sandwich, located my chips, and shoved one in behind it.

"All right. But hang in there. Watch your back and don't do anything stupid." She reloaded her mouth with ice.

"I won't," I said. "I'm saving that for the day I hand in my resignation letter. I'll be telling all these bastards to go to hell and kiss my ass on the descent down."

I told her I'd think about First Fridays before I said good-bye, even though I knew I wouldn't go. At least not this month. I didn't care what Vlora said; I could use a good party, but I wasn't going to be caught there looking clueless.

I used my fingers to rake life through my dark brown kinki curls and freshened my copper-colored lipstick before grabbing my notepad and going to Mr. Benton's office.

I walked into his office, ready to go through my normal routine. I'd tell him how I'd placed another call to supplier A or followed up on a call from customer B; that I'd made the changes on document C and was ready to send it out.

Mr. Benton sat at the round table in his office along with two other audience members. Mr. Benton's boss, Dave, sat on one side of him, while Amanda, the head of Human Resources, sat on the other side. There was an empty seat opposite the three of them. They seemed bunched up together as if the person to be seated in the lone chair opposite them was stricken with the plague and about to be quarantined.

Performance review time, I thought to myself. This would be easy. I relaxed my shoulders and took a seat in the chair that was obviously meant for me. We exchanged unpleasant pleasantries. Despite their intention to look like a firing squad, this was always a good meeting. I wouldn't have to talk much. I'd just answer a few questions about how much I loved my position and this company, then sit back and listen to the asshole's—I mean, Mr. Benton's—straight-faced praises for a job well done, get the nod from Dave, and the letter from Amanda showing the bonus and the raise that I would see on my next pay stub.

"Do you know why you're here?" Amanda asked me as she swooped her long red hair behind her dainty pearl-studded ear.

She'd never asked me that before. I felt a slight rise in the room temperature as I wondered if they had indeed come up with funds to install employee spyware on our computers and had observed me surfing the Internet or working on my business plan.

"Evaluations, I assume?"

They exchanged eye contact with one another before looking everywhere but at me. The back of my neck began to itch under the heat.

"Well, no," Amanda stated. She shuffled through papers in front of her before she stopped abruptly. "Your performance has been wonderful the entire time you've been working here."

"She's been an outstanding worker," Mr. Benton said to Dave and not to me.

Dave gave an abrupt nod before Amanda continued. "I know you're aware that Formix has had three consecutive bad quarters.

Unfortunately, we've had to make changes. This has never before affected management."

I felt a lump in my throat. "Am I about to be transferred?"

Mr. Benton looked at Dave as if asking who was going to be the one to answer my question.

"Transferred? Well, no," Amanda said.

I felt as if I should have breathed a sigh of relief; however, the tension didn't seem to leave the room.

Mr. Benton finally decided to take over. "Basically, Naja, the company has decided to do some restructuring in order to alleviate some of the loss, and to improve our chances of recovery. We feel that these changes will minimize the damage already done, and put us in a better position for future growth."

Dave grunted.

It was obvious that this change would be something that I wouldn't like. Perhaps I would have to take on the job of another manager, and would have double duty at the same pay, which meant I would actually have to start working for a change. Whatever it was, I wanted them to just spill it. It wouldn't matter anyway, because I wasn't here for the long haul. Even if I didn't like the change, all I needed to do was chill until September came.

Amanda decided to take the reins again. "We've combined some management positions and eliminated some."

Her lips stopped moving and Mr. Benton took over.

"We feel that your position is really unnecessary, so we've eliminated it," Mr. Benton said. He formed his hands into a steeple and rested his chin on them as he awaited my reply.

"So, what are you saying?" They were ticking me off.

"I'm afraid we're letting you go," Amanda said. "Permanently." She proceeded to pull papers out of the stack before her and place them in front of me. "Don't worry, you'll receive severance pay. We appreciate all that you've done for us." She slapped a pen on the papers for my signature.

I swallowed my disbelief. "I'm fired?" The hot room was still quiet except for the sound of more papers shuffling.

My left hand went to my chest as I started to feel a shortness of breath. This was not in the plan. I looked at Dave, then stared hard at Mr. Benton.

I stood up. "If you're restructuring and getting rid of unnecessary jobs, then tell me what Mr. Benton does that's worthy of keeping *his* position?"

"Neither Mr. Benton, nor anyone here, needs to explain his position to you, Ms. Rodgers," Amanda spoke sternly.

I paced before the table as my superiors were becoming unnerved. Sure, I hated my job and I hated my boss. But it was better than no job and no boss at all. I wasn't ready to strike out on my own just yet. I needed time to build up more of a cushion. My business plan wasn't complete, and I didn't have a partner yet. As much as I hated to admit it, I really *needed* this job.

I tried to get a grip.

"I . . . I . . . I'm sorry. My apologies. I'm just getting a little emotional here." They seemed to ease up a smidgeon as I reclaimed my seat. "What about another position? Anything. I'll take it, no matter what the pay." I looked up at Dave.

Dave mumbled something inaudible before speaking. "All positions are filled now."

I could only guess at whose jobs were safe. My arms were folded tightly across my chest and I tapped my foot rapidly. I eyed the framed "Teamwork" picture on the wall.

"Naja, as I stated before, you'll receive severance pay—one month's salary for every year that you've worked here."

I gave up as I looked at their united front of solidarity.

I allowed them to finish out the rest of the meeting, then returned to my office.

"Oh, this is unreal," I said to myself as I examined my raided office. The computer processor had been snatched, leaving exposed wire connections hanging everywhere. An empty box had appeared on top of the clutter on my desk, presumably for me to pack my things. I could think only of my business plan, which I had spent months on, and which was on the company hard drive. Even though I knew better, I had never saved it to a disk and didn't have a copy of it on my computer at home. There was no use in even asking to use the computer to retrieve it; I'd have to start over.

In disbelief, I sat back down at the desk and took a bite of my unfinished sandwich and ate a few chips while I figured out my next move.

Mr. Benton appeared and stood in the doorway awkwardly without saying a word. I stared back at him blankly.

"Oh," I said as realization set in. "You want me to leave *now,* right?" I felt dumbfounded.

Mr. Benton stood motionless in the doorway for twenty minutes while I meticulously went through the desk clutter and all my drawers for my personal items, then packed them in the box they graciously provided for me. Then, without saying a word, he escorted me down the narrow hallway, which seemed three miles long.

"Good luck" was all Mr. Benton said as he opened the back door. He quickly closed it behind me, pulling it tightly.

The new-fallen snow compressed under my feet as I loaded the box into the trunk of my car. I got into my car and waited until I had pulled myself together before I turned on the wipers, and then drove home in thought. I needed to do something and do it quickly; otherwise, I'd find my butt out on the streets in a few months. I was now without a job or a business plan, or a path forward to start my business. I couldn't do it alone. I needed a partner. And maybe even a drink. I might have to consider First Fridays after all.

TWO

I STIRRED MY CARAMEL LATTE AS I LOOKED OUT AT the intersection of Twentieth and Market, while sitting across from Vlora at the Rosebud Café. A light dusting of snow blew across the sidewalk beneath the setting sun. Four high school kids claimed the corner of the café closest to the video games, and feasted on ketchup-drenched French fries and sodas. Black Hole Incident, a local jazz band, was performing their daily happy hour gig on the other side of the café, and the music flowed toward us.

Vlora had gotten up and now sat on one of the red barstools at the counter, waiting for her drink order while talking to the owner, Chaney. I could tell by the way they stole quick looks at me that Vlora was tactfully explaining my sullen mood to our friend, whom we had come to know over several years by patronizing his café. With hot coffee in one hand and a cup of ice in the other, she crept across the black-and-white-checkered floor to the window table we usually chose.

"Easier said than done, I know, but you gotta get out of the funk that you're in. We're not leaving here until we map out a plan of what to do next," Vlora said as she tapped an ice cube into her mouth. She took a napkin and dabbed the tip of her nose, which had gotten wet when she tipped the cup. While many in her predicament would have considered rhinoplasty, Vlora was proud of

her oversized nose, and thought it brought an alluring unique-
ness to her face, which was true.

"With all due respect, Vlora, I don't feel like making a plan
right now," I said with a flat voice as I leaned my forearms on the
table. "I want to sit here and mope. Some of us actually do mope
as a part of the process, you know."

Vlora wasn't one for negative emotions. To immediately
bounce up and make plans and goals for continuing on with life
was her answer to things like breakups, divorces, firings, and
death. Sometimes, I thought, she really did have a heart of stone.

Vlora sucked, then began to chomp on ice, before she swallowed and said, "Unh-unh. See, me myself personally, I don't believe in moping." She held her hand up to her mouth. "You start
moping, then you never stop. Next thing you know, you're in
your apartment every night going to bed to blues records, a case
of wine, and with a cigarette dangling from your dry cracked
lips. And you don't even smoke."

"A little dramatic, don't you think?"

She tilted her head. "Starts with moping."

A loud cheer erupted from the kids in the corner. They
slapped the back of one kid standing in front of the video game,
who held up his arms in apparent victory. Chaney came over to
the table and placed two large slices of red velvet cake on the
table. He wore an apron over his L.A. Lakers throwback and
baggy jeans. A diamond earring sparkled in his left ear. "Compli-
ments of the Rosebud Café."

I lifted a smile to Chaney as I ran my hand back and forth
over my stomach at the same time. "You know this is my favorite.
Especially yours," I said as I picked up a fork and slid the cake
closer to me, promising myself to do extra crunch work on my
abs later. I plunged into it and let the moist fluff melt in my

mouth and the creamy icing coat my tongue. I was starting to feel better already, instantly forgetting the extra layer of insulation surrounding my belly.

"Mmmm . . . misery loves calories," Vlora said as she took a bite of her slice as well. She licked the icing off the fork.

"Thank you, Chaney," I said with my hand covering my mouthful of cake.

"May I?" Chaney asked as he touched the back of the chair next to Vlora and across from me. His light and neatly trimmed mustache glistened over his warm brown skin.

"Oh, by all means. Please join us," I said, dipping into my cake again.

He turned his St. Louis Cardinals baseball cap backward and seemed to grapple for words as he turned his deep-set eyes to me. "I hope you don't mind. Vlora told me what happened with you and your job. . . ."

I reached my hand across the table and placed it on top of his for a brief moment. His hand felt warm and solid. "Vlora knew I wouldn't mind you knowing. You're like a big brother to me and a lot of others in this community. I know you got my back."

Chaney leaned his head to the side a little and gave a one-breath chuckle. Vlora's eyes darted back and forth between Chaney and me as if she were watching the beginning of a love scene in a movie. She was always trying to get something going with me and somebody. Anybody. Even a brother figure like Chaney. She took another bite of cake and licked the fork.

Chaney ran his eyes over my face and spoke as if he couldn't say what he really wanted to say. He said, "I just wanted you to know that I'm here for you. You know, if you need anything, I'm here for you."

"Awwww," I purred at him. "Thanks, Chaney." I reached across the table and patted the backside of his hand again, the way one pats the head of a cute puppy. "I'm fine, though. I've got six months of severance pay. It's not the end of the world; I'll be all right. I really appreciate your concern though."

His smile was crooked. "Well, like I said. If there's anything you need, don't hesitate to call me." He emphasized "anything." Vlora's eyes volleyed back and forth.

He slapped the table with his hand. "Let me go take some orders," he said. He got up and moved the chair back underneath the table. "You ladies enjoy your cake." He winked at me before he headed over to the table where a group of guys were reviewing menus.

"What's up, Black?" Chaney said to each of them as he shook their hands, then proceeded to talk to them and take their orders.

Vlora gave me a swift kick to the shin with her pointed-toe shoes. "What's with the 'you're like a brother to me' crap?" Vlora asked. She whined an imitation of my words.

"Ow!" I reached down to rub my leg while giving her my best mean glare. "What do you mean?"

She leaned on her forearms on the table. "Chaney would be so good for you. And here you come with this big brother crap. He's cute, too. At least, underneath all that ridiculous hip-hop gear, he is."

"Chaney?" I looked over at him with the boys before I waved my hand at her in dismissal. "Chaney's our friend. He's everybody's friend. He doesn't think of me in that way. He *is* like a big brother."

"He didn't wink at *me*."

"*You* didn't lose your job."

"I swear," she huffed, "you can be so difficult at times." She leaned back in her chair.

"Anyway, you know that I'm not looking for a relationship right now. Especially now. I need to get myself together and try to figure out what I'm going to do about this business. And if I open my Internet café, the last thing I can focus on right now is a man. That'll have to wait until later." I threw my napkin on top of the empty plate and pushed it to the side. I inhaled and released in satisfaction.

"This isn't from your feminist routine, is it? It's been about a year since your last relationship. Me myself personally? I think you need a balanced life, and that includes a love life. All work and no play for you means hell for those of us who have to be around you," she scolded.

Truth was, my love life hadn't been anything to shout about in quite a few years, which was one reason I wasn't anxious to jump back into the dating scene. My most recent involvement, about a year ago, had lasted nine months. It was with a relationship therapist named Layton, who I had met through a work associate who was seeing him with her boyfriend in an effort to get him to take the next step. Since he was counseling others on their love lives, you would have thought that he was an expert at love himself. But he turned out to be a dud who put absolutely nothing into his commitment to keep it going. First, we began going out less and less often, then talking less and less, until we just stopped talking at all. He got busy. I got busy. And from there, it simply fizzled out and we drifted apart until we didn't call each other anymore. It was no one's fault, really. I guess we just weren't that into each other. To me, it was a better route to go than a twenty-thousand-dollar wedding ceremony, and then splitting up five years later.

I had gone out on a few dates after Layton, but seemed only to run into men who never wanted to take me out; they wanted to skip the formalities and take me to their place or come to mine. That's when I decided to put on the brakes. Finding the right one was going to take an investment of time. I hadn't turned my back on love or men; rather, I was putting my love life on temporary hold, just until I got the business up and running. Whenever that might be.

Black Hole Incident's first set ended as the door was opened and another round of January breezes chilled the room. I shivered and took a sip of my latte, which was rapidly losing its heating power. My sister, Allie, stopped at the counter and placed an order with Chaney before walking over to our table with a wrapped bundle in tow behind her. I pulled Andi close to me and began to strip off her layered outerwear.

"And who do we have here?" I said to my four-year-old niece as I peeled off her designer coat, revealing her Tommy Hilfiger overalls outfit, complete with Reebok socks and Nike kicks. I looked up at my little sister. "You know you are too much with this name-brand wear. It's such a waste. Kids grow out of clothes so fast, and you're spending all your child support money on designer clothes for her?" Disgust filled my voice as I pulled out a chair for Andi and laid her coat on the back of it.

"I get all of her clothes at a thrift shop. You just go to the ones in the rich neighborhoods. That's the secret," Allie said, grinning at her own cleverness. "And her entire outfit cost less than a brand-new one from Target. So step off." Her tiny diamond nose ring sparkled with every move of her head.

Allie had taken off her own coat to reveal a tight pink and white sweater with BEBE written across the chest and a V-neck that dipped so low that her tattoo was clearly visible. Her Apple

Bottoms jeans displayed both way too much apple and bottom. I'd always been disappointed in the fact that her apple actually went to her butt, while mine had gone to my gut. I hadn't even had kids yet, but I had a pooch like Mom had had when she was alive.

"Still, don't you get tired of you and your kid being walking billboards?" Vlora asked as she eyed Andi's coat.

Allie stopped what she was doing and wagged a long finger-nail at both of us. "Look. You two are childless and only four years older than I am. This is *my* daughter. When you all get children, then you can tell me how to raise mine."

Allie put Andi in the seat next to me, and she plopped down in the chair next to Vlora. Chaney brought over two mustard-only hamburgers and a bowl of soft-serve vanilla ice cream, and water for Allie and Andi.

Allie broke off a piece of burger, dipped it in the vanilla ice cream, and took a bite. Andi followed suit with hers.

The lines in Allie's face relaxed and her voice went from stern to soft in an instant. "Oh, uh, Naja? I need to hold a few hundred bucks, just until Haven sends his next child support payment," she said as she smiled sheepishly.

Allie was raising a child, but somehow I always ended up paying right along with ex-fling Haven. Allie had had a difficult childhood, which resulted in her not getting her GED until she was twenty-two, and then she went off to college. But even then, her head was all over the place. After changing her major ten times and colleges three times, at twenty-five she dropped out a year before completing her business degree to give birth to a beautiful baby girl. Haven, the father, was a much older single man who traveled a lot and wasn't about to give up his freedom or his career as a sports agent to play daddy to the result of their casual relationship. But to keep the government out of his pockets and his life, Haven promised to make a healthy child support payment to Allie every month, and he faithfully did. Allie's problem was that she tried to live off it, instead of using it to supplement an income she would earn. That wasn't working for her, although she kept on trying.

Vlora rolled her eyes to the ceiling. "How about 'Hi, sis, how are you today? How has your week been?'" Vlora said to Allie. "If you at least start with that, you'd find out that your sister lost her job a couple of days ago."

Allie's head shot up from her hamburger sundae. "What?" She paused. "You hated that job anyway, right? And that saves you from quitting, right?" Andi tapped Allie on the arm and pointed to the cup of water on the table that she was unable to reach. Allie passed it to her.

"I didn't plan on quitting until September. I wanted to rack up nine more months of pay for a bigger cushion before I quit."

"Well, with the severance pay you're getting, you're just three months short. Me myself personally? I think you should count your blessings and go ahead and start your business now," Vlora said.

"That three months of pay is a lot. Suppose I end up needing it to cover bills while getting the company off the ground? You know they say it takes about five years for a new business to break even. And now I have to start my plan from point zero because it was on my work computer; I didn't save it to a disk. And I still don't have any contacts or partners. I'm just not ready yet." I shook my head and dropped it into my open palms.

"Excuses, excuses," Vlora replied, unmoved. "And that's all the more reason for you to come out to First Fridays tonight. You still haven't said you are definitely going to go." She looked at

Allie. "You should come, too, Allie. We can make it a girls' night. Can you get a sitter?"

"Hells yeah. I've heard about First Fridays, and I've wanted to check it out. I need to snatch me up a rich and successful businessman." She pointed to a busily eating Andi and mouthed exaggeratedly, "She needs a father." Then aloud, she said, "It's kinda late notice, but I should be able to get my usual sitter. She's a homebody of a teenager and doesn't seem to get out much on the weekends, poor thing. Zits. Overweight. Flat-chested," Allie said, shaking her head as if this was the greatest human tragedy ever. She and Andi took the last bites of their hamburger sundaes and washed them down with water.

"Great. Then it's official. If we leave now, we can meet up there at the Vanguard Lofts in three hours."

"I never said I was going," I said uselessly as I pulled out my checkbook to write my little sister a check. Vlora guffawed.

"You're going. See you in a few hours." Vlora gave her mouth a final swipe with a napkin before she got up. She gave my arm an assuring rub before putting on her coat and leaving.

"Thanks, sis," Allie said to me as she put the check in her purse and proceeded to bundle up Andi again. "I'll see you tonight." She kissed me on my cheek before she flipped open her cell phone and walked back out into the cold, tugging Andi behind her.

I watched Chaney serve fries and sodas to a few kids before I put on my coat to go. He winked at me one final time and smiled his crooked little smile as I waved to him on my way out, with the hip-hop sound of A Tribe Called Quest from the jukebox pushing me along the way.

THREE

SOULFUL SOUNDS OF CONTEMPORARY JAZZ GREETED me as I entered the spacious lobby of the Vanguard Lofts. Dimmed overhead studio lights softened the room, sophisticated paintings dressed the walls, and artful sculptures on posts were dotted across the floor.

I checked my coat, picked up a complimentary glass of Hpnotiq, one of the night's sponsors, then slowly walked around, taking in the sounds, observing the scene, and eavesdropping on conversations.

I continued to weave through the lobby and spotted Vlora as she was finishing up a conversation with a fashionably dressed older woman. Vlora had changed into a smart but sexy short pinstriped skirt and a sleeveless stretch blouse. Her high-heeled strappy sandals accentuated her freshly shaven legs. The woman handed her a business card while her mouth seemed to move a mile a minute. She gave Vlora a soft pat on the shoulder and walked across the room and linked arms with a man. I walked over to Vlora.

"Ah, you made it," Vlora smiled.

"What? You didn't think I'd show?"

"Wasn't sure. I like that outfit," Vlora said, speaking of the plain black pantsuit I wore with a large-collared white blouse. "But it's for the office. Next time spruce it up a bit. You look like a walking stiff."

"Gee, thanks."

"Well, what do you think?" Vlora asked as she gestured at the room.

I glanced around. "I admit, it's not as bad as I thought. It actually seems like an easygoing atmosphere, although I can't see partying with these people later. They don't look like partiers to me."

Vlora laughed a laugh that said that the devil was yet to come.

"How'd all this come about? How long has St. Louis been doing First Fridays?" I asked.

"It's not just here. They host monthly events in about thirty other cities and in Jamaica, too," Vlora said. She explained that First Fridays was the largest African American networking organization in the country, and that they were also a part of national events like the Essence Music Festival and the National Brotherhood of Black Skiers. "They even had an annual cruise. And there's always a complimentary drink or gift from one of the national or local sponsors like Budweiser, Busch, Bacardi, Martell, or Hpnotiq." She sipped from her frosted glass of Hpnotiq.

"I didn't know all of that," I said, impressed. "This is bigger than I thought."

"So, have you made any contacts yet?"

"Not yet. I just got here, and I've been scoping things out. Trying to get a feel for things."

Vlora let out a long, hard breath. "You don't have time to leisurely scope out the place. Get out there. Mingle. Go meet some people and make some business contacts." She shooed me away with her free hand.

Vlora has a way of being pushy and blunt, and sometimes it irritates me to no end. She doesn't believe in beating around the bush. It wastes too much time and life is too short, she would say. And often she's right.

"Remember, you don't have a job, and you need to get your

business up and running pronto," she said to me as if I were her child.

"Ah, look who's here," I said as I spotted Allie walking toward us. I was especially happy to see her now because this would shut Vlora up and get her off my case. For the moment.

Vlora's berry-stained upper lip met the tip of her nose as she viewed Allie from head to toe. "Wow. You look . . ."

"Nice," I jumped in, finishing her sentence for her.

Allie's slender frame screamed "hot sex on a platter." She had outfitted herself in a tight black leather miniskirt with black fishnet stockings. Her slinky, sleeveless V-neck blouse exposed the edges of her braless tattooed breasts, which jiggled freely with each step she took. Her feet were fitted with platform sandals that showed off her French-manicured toenails and her sparkling cubic zirconium toe ring and matching ankle bracelet. Her jet-black weave curtained her back to her shoulder blades. She was a far stretch from business casual.

Vlora tsked. "Okay now, see, I was going to say a 'hot mess.' But you can insert 'nice' in there if you want to."

"Careful. Your jealousy is starting to show," Allie said to Vlora as she rolled her shoulder. Her heavily bangled arm clanked noisily as she brought her drink to her dark red lips.

"You can't be serious," Vlora said. She expelled disgust and scoffed. "Look at you."

"Whatever, bitch," Allie said as she rotated on one heel and swung the front of her body around to me and her back to Vlora, throwing out her hip as she came to a stop.

Vlora clenched her teeth and leaned down close to Allie's ear. She talked through a tight, pressed-on smile. "I told you about calling me 'bitch.' I don't care if it's a term of endearment between you and your little friends . . ."

"Lighten up, Vlora, dang," Allie said in exasperation. "You're not *that* much older than me. Only four years. You act like we're a generation apart."

"I'm not going to tell you anymore to not refer to me as a bitch. That's all I got to say." Vlora's forced smile became more natural as she waved to someone across the room. She gave Allie an evil stare to indicate that she meant what she said, then returned to her smile again.

Allie sighed and did a slow three-sixty to scope out the room. "Ooh, la, la! These men look rich," she said in pure excitement. Her eyes twinkled with what looked like joy as Vlora rolled her eyes upward.

I smiled at my little sister. She'd been a handful in years past. She still had a colorful personality, but she was slowly coming into her own, I felt.

I was six and Allie was two when our father fell asleep behind the wheel of a car during one of his frequent business trips, so Allie hadn't felt the pain I felt in losing a parent. At least not until we lost our mother twelve years later to breast cancer. And even though there had been a rift in their relationship because Allie didn't take to the feminist bedtime stories that our mother used to tell, she was fourteen, nonetheless, and this time she completely fell apart.

After Mom passed, each other was all we had, and I refused to allow us to be broken up by Allie's being sent to a foster home. So at eighteen, I convinced the state to let Allie live with me while I worked and went to school and provided for both of us. I didn't have time to grieve—I didn't have that luxury.

Allie showed out. She gave me as hard a time as a child could give a parent. Only I wasn't her parent, and she had no intention of treating me like one. So Allie proceeded to show me that she was the stronger and the smarter sibling by hanging out late, smoking first cigarettes, then marijuana, drinking, and partying. She did have sense enough to calm down a little and change her crowd when she got arrested with her friends for shoplifting. It took me a while to come up with bail, and Allie suddenly found our one-bedroom apartment to be a resort compared to jail.

But even then, the damage had been done. Allie tried to straighten up, but with my trying to learn the world my own damn self, I didn't have the proper tools to guide her correctly.

Allie ran her hand down the front of her skirt as if to smooth it out. "I'm definitely going to meet an intelligent, rich man tonight. Excuse me, ladies. I'll catch up with you both later." Allie tossed her straight and newly purchased hair at us before she took off to mingle.

"Okay, now it's your turn," Vlora said.

"Would you stop being so pushy? I'm going to mingle in a minute." I wrinkled my brow at Vlora's assertiveness.

"Let me tell you what to watch out for."

"Oh, you got mingling instructions now? This ought to be good."

"There's a lot of genuine and serious people here, but watch out for the shysters."

"Shysters?"

"Yeah. There's always a few mixed in. You'll know them when you see them." Vlora caught sight of someone she wanted to talk to. "I gotta go. There's Raj Shabazz. I've been meaning to follow up with him on some insurance policies." She rubbed my arm and started to rush off, then she turned back to me. "Go. Mingle." Again, she made a shooing motion with her hands.

I ignored Vlora, which was usually the best way to handle

her pushiness. I would get around the room and network in my own time, not hers.

After lightly touching my face and determining that it was dry, I cruised the room and took in conversations as I passed:

"Give me a call on Monday and we can discuss in more detail," one well-dressed man said to another as he handed him a card from a gold-plated case.

"How about lunch next week? Give my secretary a call and . . ."

"That's interesting. We're actually looking into something similar. You ever heard of . . ."

"Geneva Hamilton," a beautiful woman in a masculine pantsuit firmly stated as she vigorously gripped the hand of the man she spoke to. By the look on his face, I was sure that he couldn't wait to turn his back to her and massage his fingers after she finally decided to let go. Whenever that might be. Geneva appeared to attempt to trade her cover-girl looks for the respect of her fellow businesspeople. Her shoulders were squared, her hooded eyes were locked on his, and her face was taut as her voice boomed, "I'm president and CEO of . . ."

"Nice place, isn't it?" said a refined male voice from behind me. I looked over to my right and brought into focus an exquisitely suited slender man with well-trimmed facial hair and buffed fingernails. He sipped a cocktail in a stubby glass, and I tried to figure out why he was wearing shades since the room was dim and the sun had long since gone down.

"Yes, quite nice," I stated as I gave the room a quick once-over to show that I wasn't just agreeing for the sake of agreeing. Allie was floating around the room and seemed to have no problem socializing, while Vlora had moved on past Raj and was now talking with a young man. No doubt she was grilling him in order to determine whether he was legit or not.

The man before me stuck out his jeweled hand. "Let me introduce myself. I'm Shadique Patterson, founder and CEO of Diamond Entertainment." I shook his hand, and he retrieved a business card from the pocket inside his coat jacket. "And you are?"

"I'm Naja Rodgers," I said. There was an awkward pause, and I felt like I should have presented him with a card as well, or at least added a title to my name.

"Are you a business owner?" He looked at me intently.

"Not at the moment," I said, embarrassed. I bit my lip. I was already starting to feel as if I didn't measure up to the others here. "But I'm hoping to start one," I quickly added.

"What industry?"

"I'm looking to open up an Internet café."

Shadique lifted his shades to reveal a wrinkled brow, so I explained further. "It would be a place where people, especially those who don't have a computer at home, can come and access the Internet in a cozy atmosphere. There'd be a bar with flat-screen monitors, tables and plush chairs, and couches with computers alongside them. Soft jazz and neo-soul would be piped in, and they could order their favorite alcoholic or nonalcoholic drink or coffee beverages."

He stroked his chin and nodded his head. "I see, I see. Sounds quite interesting," he said. "How far along are you?"

"Well, I was almost finished with my business plan, but, um . . . well, let's just say I have to start over from scratch. What business are you in?"

"I dibble and dabble in quite a bit. I'm in entertainment, and I have investment properties across the country. I'm a board member of several organizations. Basically, my business is a conglomerate."

I felt as if I was supposed to be impressed.

"Tell you what," he said casually as if he was about to do me a huge favor. "Why don't you give me a call next week and we can talk more. I can go into more detail about what I do, and perhaps I can help you get your business off the ground. Give you some pointers or direction. I like the sound of what you're doing. I may even want to invest in it." His face was serious, and I could tell that he thought my business might be a worthy investment.

I threw my shoulders back and smiled on the inside. My confidence was starting to build. I looked down at his card again and noticed a P.O. box for an address, his cell phone number, a pager number, and an e-mail address.

"Where's your office located?"

"I'm on the go all the time. The best way to reach me is on my cell. If I don't pick up, you can page me. Oftentimes I can't pick up because I'm out to lunch or dinner with high-profile clients, or in meetings regarding major deals. Lots of major deals. It's a rough life, but I love it," he said as he flipped his thumb across the edge of his lower lip. "But don't get me wrong, I'll be sure to make time for you." He gave me a wink and made a clicking noise with his mouth.

I was feeling grateful. He was obviously a big shot, and he was willing to help someone on my level get established. A surge of energy raced through me. I was ecstatic. I shook his hand vigorously. "I will definitely give you a call next week," I said excitedly. "Thank you so much. I really appreciate your making time for me." I became embarrassed when I realized I was still shaking his hand. I loosened my grip. "Sorry, guess I got a little carried away."

Shadique chuckled. "That's quite all right. I look forward to hearing from you next week." His big shiny ring glistened on his right hand as he brought his drink to his lips. After taking a sip, he nodded his head and walked away.

I felt empowered now. I was still at the beginning stages, but I felt like I fit in. I was a young woman with an idea, and I was here because I was moving forward with it. I was making a way for myself, and I wasn't putting my fate in the hands of corporate America. I spotted others who were standing alone and introduced myself. I engaged in small talk, inquired about their businesses, and talked about my venture. I explained that I'd been so busy that I had run out of business cards, but I took theirs and promised to send them mine. After I had some made up, of course.

Later, I came out of the restroom after blotting the oil from my face. I spotted Allie taking a card from one man and bidding him farewell before she tapped the shoulder of another, batted her eyes, and smiled. Out of nowhere, I locked eyes with a handsome man with curly black hair across the room. It dawned on me that I'd seen him at several points throughout the night, and if I didn't know any better, I'd say that he'd been following me around the room. Confidence consumed me now, so I decided to walk over and introduce myself. But before I could take a step in his direction, I was approached by an ebony-toned man with light brown eyes and trimmed facial hair.

Adrian introduced himself to me, and we talked about his business ventures, which included partnerships and investments in small retail operations. Then I gave him the rundown on my planned business before I explained that I was here looking for potential investors, contacts, or collaborators. After talking for about forty-five minutes, I had gotten Adrian's card, and felt that he might indeed be the partner I was looking for. He had the expertise I needed, as well as the interest, and he was looking for another business opportunity, too.

The night was going extremely well, and by the time I met up with Vlora and Allie again, I was ready to kiss Vlora for making me come to First Fridays. We found a couch and took a minute to rest our feet.

"How's it coming?" Vlora asked me right away. "Made any contacts yet?"

"Actually, yes. I've made quite a few." I pulled out all the business cards I had collected, and Allie did the same.

"I've met a lot of great people, too," Allie said in total awe. She went through her stack of cards, calling off names and titles: president, CEO, founder, director. She put the cards into one stack again and said, "I can't believe I met all these heavy hitters in one night. This is, like, unbelievable. I am about to be spoiled rotten." She smirked. "It's about time. I'm tired of going out with broke men. I feel like I'm president, CEO, and founder of the Broke Men's Club."

"Did you say Shadique Patterson?" I asked Allie.

She sifted through her cards and pulled one from the stack. "Yeah, Shadique Patterson. Owner of Backlash Productions."

I sifted through my cards and pulled out the card Shadique gave me. "I met a Shadique, too."

Allie shrugged. "It's a networking event, so we're bound to meet the same people as we go around the room. No big deal."

I shook my head. "No, that's not what I'm saying. It's the same name, but a different business. They can't be the same person."

"Let's see," Allie said. We put the cards side by side to compare the info. Same P.O. box for address, pager number, and cell phone number, but different business and title.

Vlora leaned in to look at the cards. She calmly sat back. "Oh, I see you've both met Shadee."

"Shadee?" we both asked.

"Yeah. Shadique Patterson? That's Shadee. Shadee's a regular. One of those shysters I warned you about. He's here every month with a new business and a new title, trying to impress women. He's harmless. Just looking for either a sugar mama or, at best, some easy panties to slide into."

"So, he's not a business owner at all?"

Vlora laughed. "Shadee? Please. Shadee is a barber in the hood. He preys on all the fresh faces that come every month." She laughed again. "Looks like he found two this month."

"What? But he told me to contact him next week about my business," I said, still not wanting to believe what she was telling me. And with all that bragging he was doing, talking about high-profile clients and major business deals, he had to be legit.

"Girl, the only thing Shadee can help you with is a good lining if you need one. You got a lot of people in here frontin'. Trying to make it seem like they're bigger than they are. Let me school you."

Vlora took the stack of business cards from my hands and started going through them. "Take Shadee's card." She held it up. "P.O. box. Translation, no physical business location, so business is probably out of the trunk of his car—if it exists in the first place. And these titles, president *and* CEO, founder *and* director. All these are fancy ways of saying a one-person operation, again, if it exists at all." She slapped the cards back in my hands. "Y'all better learn to read these people."

Allie's face sank. I was crushed. I'd been walking around, first feeling inferior, then gaining the confidence to talk to these people, only to find out that some of them were barbers, or worse yet, unemployed.

I found Adrian's card and went over his information. He had a downtown address; office, cell, and fax numbers; and a Web site address listed. I showed the card to Vlora. "I know Adrian. He's legit. Very business savvy. You can learn a lot from him."

"Great. At least all is not lost," I said.

Allie went through each of her cards and reviewed the information on them. She began ripping the cards up one by one with a scowl on her face. Vlora laughed.

The double doors that led to the other side of the room were opened, and a blast of hip-hop mixes began to lure everyone in.

"Here comes the fun part," Vlora said.

"I still can't imagine these people dancing. They look too stiff."

"I want to go home," Allie said and pouted. She was pissed.

"Ah, quit your bitchin', and come on." Vlora bounced her shoulders to the beat as she got up and pulled us off the couch. "You're here and the night is half over. You might as well get your groove on."

We went into the darkened room, which was set up to give a club atmosphere. Colored lights flashed on the walls to the beat, and people had already begun to fill the dance floor. A crowd of observers, mostly women, formed around the dance floor.

The three of us decided to make the night a good one. We went out onto the floor together and began to dance. It wasn't long before someone came up behind Vlora and invited himself to become her dance partner. Soon, a partner came to claim Allie, who had shaken off pissivity as she found her groove.

Even though I was in the crowd and I'm sure no one was paying attention, I didn't feel comfortable dancing by myself, so I started to head off the floor.

"Hey now! Where are you going?" Adrian said as he grabbed

my wrist. "Come on. I know you're not going to waste this song."

I giggled and began to dance with him. Vlora looked over and mouthed, "He's a cutie," and she gave a nod.

Vlora seemed to think that any man she saw me with was a cutie, I had long since noticed. I think she just had that girlfriend itch—if any one of her friends are single, she feels it her duty to make sure they're hooked up. No matter how grotesque the man may be. He would just be a stand-in until someone more decent came along, after which I would be questioned about what it was that I saw in the grotesque guy in the first place.

We danced for about twenty minutes before the crowd became lively. Suit jackets came off, ties were loosened, and skirts were flying. These same mild-mannered walking stiffs were now whooping it up on the dance floor.

Shadee was bumping and grinding behind Geneva Hamilton, who seemed to have dropped her tough-woman exterior and was letting it all hang out. Her father must have been a preacher because she appeared to have stripped from the masculine suit she had modeled earlier to reveal the ho dress she wore underneath.

The crowd began to go into hysterics over two women who had somehow gotten into a "drop it like it's hot" dance-off with each other. They danced with their backsides a few feet apart, and competed over who could stick her derriere out the furthest and drop it the lowest for the longest time. The crowd whooped and cheered, egging them on. They danced closer and closer to each other until their backsides actually touched. One of the women began to shake her thighs and butt at breakneck speed, and the other followed suit, each looking over her shoulder to see who was vibrating the fastest. The crowd went into a frenzy as they alternated shaking and dropping. Then they stopped, laughed, and exchanged high fives.

I signaled Adrian for a time-out, and we headed for the edge of the dance floor.

"Thanks again for talking to me earlier," I said to him. "I'm really anxious about talking to you about my business in more detail. My girlfriend told me you were savvy."

The whites of his eyes stood out as he grinned and stroked his chin. "Well, I do my best. What location are you planning for your Internet café?"

"Mill Creek Valley."

"Mill Creek Valley?" He looked perplexed.

"Yes. Anything wrong with that?"

Adrian frowned, then made a face as if he'd just eaten something sour. He gestured to go back to the other side of the room where we could have a conversation. "The most important factor in starting a business is location. You need to make sure that there's a need in the community and that they will support you. Be *able* to support you."

"I've researched that," I said with assurance. "Fewer than three percent of the homes in Mill Creek Valley have computers, and a lot of their money is spent in that neighborhood. I have the sources at home. We can go over that next week."

Mill Creek Valley is a unique, self-supporting community in St. Louis. The people there are working class to poor. Most lack transportation, but find that they really don't need it because everything they desire is in walking distance: restaurants, Laundromats, grocery stores, post office—whatever they want. They also have their own little neighborhood bars, clubs, and churches. It is a town within a town.

"No, no, no. I believe you. It's just that"—he paused to search for words—"it's just that I can't see those people supporting an Internet café."

Those people? What did he mean by *those people?*

My shoulders slumped. "What are you saying?"

Adrian treaded carefully. "I'm not saying anything bad about the people there. Hell, I grew up in Mill Creek Valley. It's just that, well, I'm wondering if they would have an interest in computers, that's all. You've got to give the people what they want. That's the key to being successful in business."

"Just because they can't afford their own computers doesn't mean they're not interested. They're lining up in libraries, and taking turns at Kinko's trying to use one. My business will give many of them access that they may not have had otherwise."

"I know what you're saying. But you can't run a business off an emotion," he declared.

"Emotion? Who's making decisions based on emotion?" He was bringing me to a boil, and my tone was starting to rise.

"Hold on now. I'm just saying, for Mill Creek Valley, maybe you should consider another line of business. Matter of fact"— he leaned in closer and said to me as if he were giving me the inside tip of the century—"I can get you in on a couple of other business opportunities. You seem like a smart woman, and I would love to have your expertise."

"I'm really interested in my Internet café."

"So am I. But not for Mill Creek." He raised his hands in the air. "Just hear me out. I know a couple of different groups that are trying now to bring businesses to that area. But something that the community will support. We're planning on two liquor stores, and even a Lincoln dealership. Now, I can help you out with getting your own liquor store there, or even get you in as a partner for the car dealership."

"That community doesn't need another liquor store. They can

hardly afford brand-new cars. Most of them ride the bus or trains."

"Personally, they may not be able to afford them, but they will buy them anyway. And they'll always buy liquor. Cognac. Whether they need it or not." He flicked his eyebrows up and down twice and flashed a sinister grin.

Adrian was making my stomach turn. "So your method of doing business is to bring into the community the things they want but can't afford? Like dangling a carrot in front of a rabbit?"

"Nobody twists their arms on what to buy. I don't put a gun to nobody's head."

"But you're going to take advantage of their weakness and take their money?"

"Didn't your friend tell you I was business savvy?"

I was disgusted, and now I was fuming. Adrian's form of business dealings had become unsavory to me, and I didn't want to be a part of them. More so, I didn't want to share my dream with anyone who had that train of thought.

I extended my hand to shake his. "It was nice meeting you, Adrian, but no thanks. I don't think I'm interested in working with you."

Adrian shrugged his shoulders as if to say it was no skin off his back. "Suit yourself. I got mines."

I started to walk off, but a thought nudged my brain. I had to ask him a question that I already knew the answer to. "Adrian?"

He looked at me with raised eyebrows.

"Just wondering. With all your success, how much do you give back to Mill Creek? You know, the people whose money you're taking while you're looking down on them for buying from you?"

Adrian answered my question by not answering. Instead, he

gave me his back and returned to the dance floor. He found another young lady partying by herself and began to dance with her.

My jaw ached as I clenched my teeth together and walked out the front door. I pulled his card from my purse and ripped it into small pieces before I tossed them to the cold air. I felt that the entire night had been a bust.

FOUR

It was two in the a.m. when I put the finishing touches on the operations section of my business plan. I had only five more sections to go. I wasn't listening to that nonsense that Adrian was talking about three weeks ago at First Fridays. Mill Creek Valley was a thriving and self-supporting community, and I knew they would support my Internet café, which I planned to call Exodusters 1879. I decided on that name because I wanted it to represent the great escape to a whole new world of information and opportunity, much like the great migration from the south to the north after the abolition of slavery. I had done my homework and there were a lot of young people and adults who wished they had access to a computer and were excited by my idea and expressed interest. The more I thought about it, the more pissed I was by Adrian's implication that working-class people were not interested in stimulating their minds or building themselves up, but only in bling bling and Hennessy.

I got up from the kitchen table and turned off the hanging overhead lights. The streetlights poured into my living room through the oversized and undraped windows and landed on the brick walls. I passed folders and soon-to-be-organized stacks of papers that I had on the breakfast counter, couch, and tables, as I walked over to the window and peered out over the empty downtown streets below. I thought I was the only one up at this hour working. I wiped my eyes and yawned before turning and trudging up the carpeted steps of the loft to the bedroom to finally get some sleep.

VLORA AND CHANEY did me the honor of offering input on the different sections of my plan, which was all good. But I wanted to find a permanent business partner.

"You can't let one person stand in the way of going after what you want," Vlora said over coffee at the Rosebud Café. It was Sunday afternoon, and she had agreed to meet with me to help me think some things through for the next section. She was also trying to get me to agree to attend the next First Fridays.

"First Fridays is not the only place where I can network," I said to her.

"True. But where else are you going?"

I shrugged my shoulders and said nothing because I had nothing lined up at the moment. It was tough to randomly meet people who were into business ownership just walking around on the street, mainly because they were in seclusion somewhere working. And right now, I had no other venue.

Chaney had been walking from the back room to the front constantly, directing three of his workers on what to do. They were setting up for their weekly Sunday night poetry set.

He made his way over to our table when a sudden rush of cold air burst into the room as two teenaged boys came in. They took a seat at a booth on the opposite side of the café from the other kids, and said nothing to each other as they took off their coats and skullcaps to reveal their faces. They looked like the rest of the kids in the neighborhood. One pulled off the baseball cap he wore under the skullcap and revealed blond cornrows over his wide-set blue eyes, while the other sported dreadlocks. They both wore slouchy baggy jeans, long white T-shirts, and white athletic shoes. They sat in the booth and their eyes roamed every inch of the café. They took in everything from the black-and-white portraits of Josephine Baker, Ethel Waters, and Bessie Smith, to the paintings of the Washington Theater, the St. Louis Stars, and James "Cool Papa" Bell that were displayed on the various walls of the café. Chaney's attention went from us to the boys.

"Something wrong, Chaney?" Vlora asked as we watched his facial expression move to uncertainty. She whipped out moist towelettes and wiped off her hands.

"No, nothing's wrong. It's just that I've never seen these kids before. They must be new to Mill Creek Valley."

Chaney did a lot of community service work with kids in the area, so he knew just about all of them, and they knew him. His Rosebud Café had become the hang-out spot for all ages in the neighborhood. The kids liked him because he dressed like them and could talk like them when he needed to. They could identify with him. When other store owners shooed them away for fear of thievery, Chaney welcomed them into his shop to play video games, and provided platforms on the weekends for them to display their verbal talents through singing, rap, and spoken-word performances. And he often gave them discounts or even free French fries when he believed that seventy-five cents equaled a hundred dollars to one of them.

Chaney believed that making the café a haven kept kids out of trouble, and he considered it giving back to the community he grew up in. As a result, he could call just about all the kids by their names: the names they were known by on the streets, as well as the ones that were recorded on their birth certificates. So whenever someone came in from outside of or was new to Mill Creek Valley, Chaney noticed.

"Let me go take care of them," Chaney said. "Be back in a sec."

Vlora started giving me more tips and after a while Chaney made his way back over to where we were sitting. He loved shooting the breeze with his customers whenever he had the chance.

"Hello again, ladies," he said with a mile-long grin. "Naja, I love what you have so far in your business plan. When do you think you'll have it wrapped up to move into motion?" He whipped the towel out of his back pocket and playfully snapped it in my direction, but didn't hit me.

"Well, I'm more determined than ever now," I said, internally referring to my conversation with Adrian. Negativity had a way of stirring up something within me. Fueled my fire even more, and made me want to show what I could do. Made me more determined to prove them wrong and myself right. "But I prefer to find a partner. Someone experienced. It would make things so much easier, and it's great to have another mind to bounce ideas off of."

"I agree with you. I loved being in business with my wife. It was the greatest thing." Chaney looked at me, but I watched his mind drift to the past. Back to the days when his wife was alive. He and his good friend, Melinda Soule, had opened up the Rosebud Café together, then they fell in love and married two years later. Melinda had been the heart of the café, and one of the reasons that everyone loved coming here. She had lit up the room, and always sparkled when greeting customers and hosting events. She died suddenly after a vein exploded in her head, two years after the wedding. An aneurysm, they said. It wasn't until then that Chaney found out that she never knew she was seven weeks' pregnant with their first child.

Chaney had closed the café for about three months, and we all wondered if he'd ever open up again. But he did. Ever since then, the place had been his life, and he immersed himself even more in helping the kids of the community. We all guessed that he looked at them as the kid he had lost. Since Melinda's death eight years ago, he'd left no time for anything else.

"We're sorry, Chaney. We didn't mean to . . ." Vlora started to say.

Chaney halted her with softened eyes. "No, it's okay. I'm okay with everything now. I was blessed to have had such a wonderful person as my wife and business partner. I'd do it all again if I could," he said, his eyes landing on me.

Vlora wiggled and straightened up in her seat. "Maybe you can help me then," she said to Chaney.

"What's that?" he asked. He leaned on his folded arms on the table, his hands covering his well-defined biceps.

"I'm trying to convince Naja to come back to First Fridays for networking. She had a bad experience last month, and now she doesn't want to go anymore." Vlora picked up her ice cup, only to find that it was empty. She made eye contact with one of the waitresses.

"You can't let one bad experience stop you in anything," Chaney said, turning to me. "I went out to First Fridays a few times a while back. Met some great people there. True, you have to kinda wade through people. Feel 'em out. But I came away with some helpful contacts. Some who I still work with today."

"See," Vlora added. She supported her chin with her hand.

"Okay, okay," I said reluctantly. "I'll give it another try. But if I meet more Shadees and Adrians, I'm out and I'm never going back again." I took a sip of my drink.

Chaney laughed. "Shadee? Shadique Patterson? Is he still showing his face there? Let's see, the last few times I was there, he was president, CEO, and owner of an interior design business, a multimedia company, and a marketing and advertising firm. Think I still got all his cards. What's he now?"

"Yes, that's the one. And you don't even want to know," I said. A laugh went around the table.

"Hey, Chaney, did you find out who the new kids were?" Vlora asked, changing the subject.

"Yeah, they're new to the neighborhood. Manny and Jarvis. They don't hang out with the other kids. Probably feel out of place, but I'll make them feel comfortable. I'll introduce them to the other kids."

"I know you'll make them feel comfortable. You always do," I added. Chaney smiled, the right side of his lips rising slightly higher than the left and showing half of his perfect set of teeth. It was charming.

"Chaney," one of his workers called from the other side of the café. She held a clipboard and tapped it with the pen in her hand.

"Hey, I got to get back to helping set up for tonight's show. I hope that you ladies will be here."

"I'd love to, but I can't make it tonight," Vlora said.

"What about you, Naja?"

He caught me off guard and my tongue stumbled. "Well, I hadn't thought about it."

"Come on back. Be my special guest. I'll even have a slice of red velvet cake just for you."

The mere mention of red velvet cake made me rub my middle again. "I don't think my midsection could take another slice of your cake."

"What are you talking about? You and your midsection look great. See you tonight at seven?"

"Yeah. I'll be here tonight."

Vlora kicked me under the table. She always did that to indicate that the man in closest proximity was someone whose bones she'd recommend that I jump. I promised myself to take off the shoe she kept kicking me with and beat her with it later.

ALLIE SIMPLY REFUSED to be outdone. She stormed into First Fridays, this time at a club called Seven, with a vengeance, dressed in an elegant and sexy business suit, with a low-cut camisole and a matching clutch. Her makeup was light and natural, and her extensions were up in a French roll with wispy curls falling down both sides of her face.

"You like?" she asked Vlora and me, as she did a little spin at the bar.

"Very nice," said Vlora while sucking a bar pretzel from her back teeth. "If I didn't already know you didn't finish college, I'd approach you to see what business you were in."

Allie rolled her eyes at Vlora and blinked her false lashes in slow motion. She snapped open her clutch and retrieved a stack of business cards and shoved one in my face. "Boo-yah!"

I took the card from her hand and read it: Eboni Enterprises, Inc. Allison B. Rodgers. Owner/operator. "You can't be serious," Vlora said as she read the card over my shoulder.

"Hey, don't hate the player, baby. Hate the game," Allie said as she snatched the card out of my hand and clucked her tongue. "I need this back. I could only afford to make fifty, and I've got to distribute these carefully."

"So what are you going to do if they ask you about your business?" I asked.

"Got it all planned." Allie picked up one of the complimentary cognacs that the bartender placed before us. "I've been practicing all week." She brushed her right shoulder off. "Watch me in action, haters."

Allie strutted with confidence as she went around the room introducing herself to men, and just to look legitimate, some women, too. She tossed back her head in fake laughter occasionally for dramatic effect, took some business cards, and selectively gave out hers before shaking hands and moving on. She was on point.

"That girl is a trip." Vlora laughed. "I'm going to walk around a bit, too. I'll catch up with you later, okay?" She lightly kissed my cheek before moving on.

I was a little lax this time around. I wasn't exactly anxious to meet fake people, so I decided I would just enjoy the complimentary appetizers and drinks, and listen to the music.

I met up with Vlora again sooner rather than later, and she introduced me to various people she knew, and they, in turn, introduced us to people they knew.

Vlora was tough and discriminating as we mingled. She didn't just take a business card. She scrutinized it. She asked for physical locations, how long they'd been in business, and other questions that seemed to be a test of whether they were legitimate or not. If she felt they were legitimate, she'd keep the card. If not, she'd almost flick it back at them and say something like, "Nice meeting you," and move on. It was clear to them and everyone around them that they had just been called a fake, and dissed.

Geneva Hamilton stood right next to us, talking to no one, so I thought it would be the perfect opportunity to introduce myself. I had spoken mostly to men, and was hoping to network with powerful women in the community, as well. By overhearing her conversations, I knew that Geneva was president and CEO of her own professional executive coaching firm.

I wiped my palms on my suit before turning to shake her hand. "Hello. Geneva Hamilton, right?" I looked up what seemed like two stories.

Geneva slowly turned to face me, looked down, and searched my face for recognition. "Do I know you?" She left me hanging.

"No. I'm, uh, introducing myself now." She still didn't take my hand so I faked a wave, then wrapped it across my waist. "I'm Naja Rodgers. I saw you here last month. Didn't get a chance to introduce myself to you then, so . . ."

She examined my hair, then moved to my ears and my suit before reaching my shoes. Then she worked her way back up again. "Mmm-hmm."

The woman left me speechless. Silence and an uncomfortable feeling settled in the space between us, and I didn't quite know how to remove it.

"Are you a business owner?" she finally asked, raising one eyebrow.

"Not yet. I'm working on it now."

I grinned. She didn't.

"I'm president and CEO of my own company," she snarled. "Did you even go to college?" An icy breeze seemed to come off her body to chill my bones.

Was she insulting me? No. Maybe she was feeling me out like Vlora does.

"Yes. I went to SLU. Bachelor's in Business. Summa cum laude."

"Harvard. MBA," she stated. "Magna. Cum. Laude." She tapped her wineglass with the tip of her acrylic nails. If it was even possible, she seemed to turn colder. Her eyes looked through me like I no longer existed. Like I never existed. Her head oscillated as she examined me from head to toe again, before she said, "Excuse me, dear," and strutted to the other side of the room to stand alone.

"Did you see that?" I turned and asked Vlora, who still stood next to me.

"Saw the whole thing." She took a swallow of her drink.

"What's her problem?"

She put her hand on my shoulder. "You don't know? She's a bitch. A real one. You'll run into some women like her, who feel the need to compete with other women. They'll size you up and determine your worth, and if they don't think you measure up to them or are in a position above them, they move on. Some of them network up, not down. Usually means they're insecure. It's their problem, not yours." She patted my shoulder as if to say, another lesson learned.

All these rules in reading people and their little quirks and nuances were getting to me; I needed a stiff drink. You had the good mixed in with the bad, and I knew it was grounds for a headache if I wasn't careful.

I was headed to the crowded bar again when I saw the same handsome guy I'd spotted last month. The yummy one whom I kept locking eyes with inadvertently, and whom I was going to talk to before I was stopped in my tracks and had my time wasted by Adrian. This time, I would make a point to meet him. If this turned out to be a bust, I was going to just give it all up.

Putting on my best professional face, I glided over to where he stood and said, "Hello. I remember seeing you here last month. I was going to talk to you then, but never made it over to you."

"Yes, I remember. I saw that you got caught up talking with Adrian Wellston." He offered his right hand. "Russ. Russom King."

Russ's short stature produced a voice that was as deep and smooth and mellow as the tailored suit he wore. His dark skin appeared silky under his curly black hair. He had sexy, heavy-lidded eyes with lustrous long lashes, and his cologne gave off a lustful scent that made my knees buckle.

I introduced myself.

From there, the talking was easy and the spirit was light. As he spoke, I must admit that I had to force my mind to stay on business. I talked to him about Exodusters 1879, and he told me about his career. Somehow, I was able to hear that he was from Atlanta, where he was into commercial real estate. He had come to St. Louis for residential real estate, because the market was good here, especially in the city, he said. He would buy old homes in the city, rehab them, and either turn around and sell them or rent them out.

"I'm also looking for new opportunities." He brought his glass down after taking a sip. His right hand covered his left, which held the glass. "I'll be honest. I'm really interested in your business, and would like to talk to you about it more."

His lips almost seemed to pucker beneath his light mustache after he spoke, and they glistened after he licked them.

Vlora joined us and I made the introductions. She gave her usual eyes and planted a smirk across her face that I knew meant "He's a cutie." Somehow, she managed to hold her peace while we finished our conversation.

"I'd love to talk to you more about my business. We can certainly arrange some time," I said.

"How about lunch this week?"

Excitement tingled down my spine, but I didn't want to be excited. No. Overexuberance was the wrong emotion here. I mentally calmed down and kept a certain professionalism about myself. "That would be great, Russ. We can meet at the Rosebud Café. It's in the community where I'm planning to open my business, so that will give you a chance to see the location and get a feel for the neighborhood as well. Do you know where that is?"

"I'm sure I can find it. Then it's a date?"

My lips parted and waited for an answer to pass through, but none came. I avoided Vlora's eyes at all costs, but felt them burning cupid hearts in my face.

"I'm sorry," he said. "Date is the wrong word, right? It's just that you're so beautiful, I guess I lost myself there. My apologies. It's a meeting? Monday at noon?"

I smiled coyly and fluttered my eyes. "Monday at noon would be fine."

Russ shook both our hands and said that he was calling it an evening.

"Now that's a hottie," Vlora said, after he left. "He had it right the first time. It should be a date, not a business meeting."

I watched Vlora as her eyes danced. "Don't get excited. It sounds like he might be a potential business partner, and that's what I'm looking for most. I'm not even thinking about his looks." I tried my best to keep a poker face while I made that statement.

"Get out of here. Don't you even stand there and try to tell me you didn't notice how handsome that man was. And did you see how broad his chest was? His shoulders? Hmph!" She bit the middle of her right index finger. "I can tell he works out. Don't you want to know what he looks like outside of that suit?"

"Vlora!" I said like I was shocked, but she was reading my mind. "You sound just like a man saying that."

"You know, that would work out great if you and Russ became business partners. Then you could start a relationship, then get married. Like Chaney. It'd be like killing two birds with one stone."

I shook my head. "I definitely wouldn't be doing that."

"Doing what?"

"Mixing business with pleasure. Too dangerous. If it doesn't work out, you got problems in the workplace, or even worse."

"Not necessarily."

"Not a chance I'd want to take."

"You are so scary. Lots of people are in business with their spouses or boyfriends. You heard Chaney's story."

"That's one success story. There're a lot of other people out there whose business suffered because of a good relationship gone bad. That's not going to happen to me."

Vlora slid her lower jaw left and right and smacked her lips. "You know what? I'm not even worried about it. Because I saw the way you were eyeing that man. You'll probably be knockin' boots before you can say, 'cha-ching.'"

I rolled my eyes and tried my best to throw her off track, but Vlora was good at sniffing out situations. Damn right, I noticed how fine he looked and how smooth he talked. But the bottom line was that I needed a business partner only, and didn't want anything to get in the way of that. Didn't want to ruin my business before it got off the ground. And relationships, especially new ones, had a way of doing just that. Screwing everything up. My business meant everything to me, and I wasn't going to let anything get in the way of that. No matter how fine Mr. King looked, or how delectable he appeared to be. I'd planned on this business for too many years to have it messed up by possible drama. When I got it up and running and was ready for a relationship, I'd look outside the business, and not within.

"You don't know what you're talking about."

Allie approached us with a "mission accomplished" smile on her face. She pulled out a stack of cards and handed them to Vlora. "Read 'em, girl!"

Vlora searched through the stack and read the names, businesses, and titles, and reviewed them for authenticity. "Very impressive." She flipped the cards over and noticed that Allie had even jotted down keywords from her conversations and any plans made to call or meet. She handed the cards back to her.

"Now tell me. What are you going to do when you call them or they call you, and they find out that you don't have a business? Better yet, you don't even have a job. What then?"

Allie snatched the cards out of her hand and jammed them in her clutch purse. "I'll figure something out," she grumbled. "It's all in the grand scheme of things."

The curtain that divided the club was pulled back, and a flow of people poured from the bar to the dance floor.

"Shall we, ladies?" Allie asked as she looked hungrily in the direction of the crowd.

We dipped and bopped on over to the club side. Evidently, people had been waiting all night for this. By the time we got there, boogie-land was already full, jackets disappeared, and skirts were swinging. We made our way onto the crowded dance floor and danced together until one by one, we were each claimed by a partner to dance the night away.

FIVE

CHANEY WINKED AND SMILED HIS DIAGONAL SMILE as I sat at my favorite booth that overlooked the intersection. He was walking around with his water bucket, watering all fifty million of the plants he had around the café. Guess you could say he had a green thumb.

I began to de-layer myself before my meeting with Russ. The February winds were always the coldest, and the new snow had only seemed to enhance it. Wearing a big heavy coat hardly seemed to do any good. St. Louisans had learned that the trick was to put on clothes in layers that would tire the wind out before it got to your skin. Of course, it tired you out by constantly taking them off and putting them back on every time you went somewhere. But that was just how you dealt with midwestern weather.

"What's up, Black?" Chaney made his rounds and said to all the males, young and old, who were present and who entered the shop. Even if he didn't take your order, which he liked to do, too, he made sure to greet all of his customers personally.

Russ entered the shop looking sexier than he had the night I'd met him, even before he had a chance to pull off his coat and reveal himself. He didn't have to. I knew it was him by his short stature and broad chest. The snow in his mustache began to melt into little water droplets within seconds of closing the door behind him. He began peeling off clothes after he spotted my waving hand and began walking toward me.

A funny feeling hit my middle. It was like rushing water pulsating against my internal walls, trying hard to escape. I must have been feeling hungry, because I knew it shouldn't have been the sight of my potential business partner, Russ, who was making me feel this way. Didn't want it to be that. He was going to be my business partner, not a love interest.

Chaney had finished watering his plants, and he threw a towel over his shoulder as he watched Russ take a seat at my table. Somebody paid for Black Star to rap consciousness to the café from the jukebox as the smells of savory soups and various spices floated in the air and teased our nostrils.

"I don't know if this Atlanta brother can get used to all this cold and snow," Russ said as he draped his clothing over one chair and sat in the other. His soft eyes sent a weakness to my knees and caused my insides to flutter all the more. I attempted to focus.

"Aw, it's not that bad. It's all in how you look at it," I said as I stared at the folders he'd brought and not directly into his eyes. I beckoned him to look out the window. "If you just follow a snowflake from the sky, and watch it find a peaceful resting place on the sidewalk or the grass, then it looks absolutely beautiful. Has a calming effect."

"Yeah," Russ said with skepticism in his voice. "Until you have to walk in the stuff or try to drive and stop your car in it and go sliding across the street." He laughed, displaying a gorgeous set of teeth.

I smiled with him. "Like I said, it's all in how you look at it."

My eyes focused on Russ's folder of information, on the table in front of him. We seemed to lock eyes for a minute without anything to say. Only a jolt of electricity could be likened to the feeling. His large dark brown eyes stared without blinking. I shuddered as a chill went through me.

"Cold? Me too," Russ said with a grin that instantly warmed me.

Chaney made his way over to our table. He looked at Russ and tipped his head back. "What's up, Black?" He held his hand out and up for the standard brotherhood handshake, but Russ didn't seem to know what to do. His eyes appeared to question whether Chaney was speaking to him or some other person—or you'd have thought Chaney had spoken to him in some derogatory kind of way.

I spoke up to fill the awkward silence. "Chaney, this is Russom King. I met him at First Fridays last weekend, and I'm *hoping* we're going to be business partners." I introduced Russ to Chaney.

Russ stared uncertainly at Chaney as Chaney's hand moved from the upward to the more familiar horizontal handshake position, and Chaney's smile slowly fell. There appeared to be some unspoken communication taking place between their bodies. Russ hesitated and searched Chaney's eyes before taking his hand and giving his head a quick upward nod.

"Russ," Russ said. He took his hand back and folded his arms across his chest, tucking his hands tightly against his sides.

"Yeah, right, my man," Chaney said in a cautious tone.

Chaney didn't say it, but I could tell he was offended. He wasn't used to this type of response. He had offered Russ brotherhood, and instead was given a yardstick in the chest and told to keep his distance. The air stiffened between us as Chaney took our orders. Coffee with cream and sweetener for me, but Chaney knew that, and Russ's facial expression seemed to ask why. Straight black for Russ.

"So, Russ, have you thought more about my plans?"

He tilted his head forward and widened his eyes seductively, or maybe I was reading into that, as they seemed to move over every inch of me. He softened his voice when he spoke. He placed his hands on the table, putting one on top of the other.

I tried to empty my head of the personal thoughts to focus on the business plan that I'd brought along. Russ flashed a smile as if he sensed the battle that was going on inside me. But he opted to get to the business, as well.

"You've got a great start here," he said as he flipped through his copy of my plan. "But I think you need to strengthen your Executive Summary in order to attract investors." He turned to that section, discussed what I had, and what he recommended I add to it.

I somehow was able to jot down notes on a pad, but I was mesmerized by the strong, take-charge tone of his deep voice. His mustache danced over his plump, brown lips with each word he spoke.

"How do you feel about that?" Russ asked after we had been meeting for about forty-five minutes.

"Huh?" He had snapped me out of a fantasy that involved me and his lips, and I hadn't heard the last two minutes of what he'd said.

He leaned back in his chair and smiled. "You need a break?"

I tapped my pen on my notepad and stared at it like I was pondering a thought. "N-no, no," I stammered. "I was just thinking . . ." I paused.

"I'm listening."

I felt like an idiot. My mind went blank and I couldn't find the save that would keep me from looking utterly ridiculous, so I decided to fold. "Look, I'm sorry. My mind drifted off and I didn't catch the last few things that you said."

"Am I that boring?" Russ asked with a chuckle.

"You? Boring? That would be a no."

"Okay, why don't we take a business break from here. Why don't you tell me more about yourself?"

"Me? Between First Fridays and now, I feel like me and my business are all that we've talked about. What about you?" I leaned into the table and dropped my chin on the backs of my hands. "What's your life story?"

Russ laughed at my look of anticipation. He obliged me and said that he was the only child of two business-savvy parents. His father was a city developer and his mother had sold her interior design shop to became a stay-at-home mom who catered to him and his father.

"What about relationships?" I asked. "Are you in one right now?"

"You applying?"

I blushed. My face got hot.

"Sorry, I couldn't resist. No, I'm not in a relationship at the moment." He paused and lowered his voice. "But I would love to be. With the right woman." He stared into my eyes as he took a slow, deliberate sip of coffee. He lowered his cup and licked the wetness from his lips, all while keeping his eyes on mine.

My stomach stirred and my thighs tingled. I swallowed. "Well, now. I guess that answers my question." I took a sip of coffee as well, hoping to cool myself down. "Ready to get back to work?" I asked.

"Only if you are." His long eyelashes seemed to wave at me as he blinked slowly.

We went back to the business plan as I continued to struggle with my focus.

SIX

RUSS AND I MET UP AT THE ROSEBUD CAFÉ AGAIN A few days later to talk business. He hadn't yet agreed to be my business partner, but with all the input he'd given, I was sure of his expertise and wanted him to jump on board. So I was trying to impress him.

As we had discussed, I had strengthened the Executive Summary and given more details on the need for my business and why I was the best qualified to bring it about. We sat at a booth and talked details over the coffee that Chaney had sent over by his waitress.

As I flipped a page, the two teenagers new to the area, Manny and Jarvis, sauntered in. Chaney glanced up from the counter where he was wiping down the area of a departed customer, checking the clock, which read 10:30 A.M. The boys took their places by the video games. They removed their coats, retrieved quarters from their pockets, and began playing.

The dark-skinned boy began bopping to a beat in his head, then he pulled rhythmic lyrics from the sky to etch a portrait of the thuggish lifestyle that he wanted others to believe he lived. He had flows. The blue-eyed boy latched onto the rhythm as it came his way and the small shell that dangled from one of his blond cornrows began to get crunk.

"What's up, Black," Chaney said to them. They gestured acknowledgment and kept playing the video game while grooving on their self-created beats.

"Yo, it's kind of early, Black. Shouldn't y'all be in school?"

The dark-skinned boy chewed on a toothpick and mumbled, "Snow day." He started rapping again as the black-inked tattoo on his arm did a ditty.

It took a lot for schools to be closed for snow, and Chaney knew that. For anything under eight inches, you'd better have your butt in school. Anything over that or a blizzard constituted a day off.

There was only about three inches of snow on the ground now, which was hardly a reason to close any St. Louis school. And as a better indicator, no other kids were around. On snow days, the Rosebud Café was filled with loud kids and bustling with activity.

"Damn kids," Russ scowled under his breath as he turned from the kids back to me. He waved to the waitress for another cup of coffee. "They all aspire to be lowlifes and thugs." He folded his arms and twitched his lower jaw. "I say let them. They'll learn. Or get shot and die. One of the two."

Skipping school was something that Chaney didn't take too kindly to, and the last thing that he'd be was an accomplice to truancy.

"You sure about that?" Chaney asked the boys. "They usually announce snow days on the radio and local TV. I didn't see or hear anything." Chaney kept his cool as he walked toward the boys.

"Jus' our school," said the blue-eyed boy as he leaned over and continued playing the video game.

"Jarvis, right?" Chaney asked the dark-skinned boy, who jerked his head upward. "True dat," he confirmed. His lips parted and revealed a gold grill.

"And Manny?"

"Fa sho," Manny confirmed as he continued to play. His grill was silver.

Chaney persisted. "It's just strange. Usually the other kids come here on snow days."

"He said jus' our school, man," Jarvis said, getting agitated.

"Whasit to you, dude?" Manny asked. He straightened up and stepped back from the video game and swayed. He towered over Chaney.

My heart quickened in my chest. Russ took another sip of his third cup of coffee.

Chaney didn't flinch. He stood at attention and folded his arms across his chest. Jarvis took a couple of short steps over and posted up behind Manny as they faced Chaney.

My heart leaped up to my throat and I got up from my seat. I had no idea what I would do if something jumped off. But I wasn't about to just sit there and let these little thug wannabes try to take Chaney out. Russ remained seated, looking unmoved by the possible turn of events. He flipped through my documents and took yet another swallow of coffee, peering over his shoulder. He turned back, retrieved a cigar from his jacket pocket, and puffed it to life.

"Relax, bruh. I just don't want to appear to be supporting kids skipping school. You both have been here a few times. You should know a little bit about me by now." He extended a closed fist for a dap.

Jarvis completed his dap. "A'ight. We cool, man. We cool."

"Ay yo trip. We got this. A'ight?" Manny said as he pounded the top of Chaney's closed fist, then hit it head on. He went back to playing the video game as Jarvis watched over his shoulder. Chaney left and disappeared to the back of the shop. I took my seat again.

"I thought we were about to have some trouble up in here," I chuckled, feeling relieved.

"Wouldn't have surprised me," Russ said. "That's what you get when you try to be friends with these kids instead of being an authority figure."

"The kids respect Chaney. They can relate to him and they know he's got their backs. Long as they do right."

"That's what I mean. They relate to him as one of them. Look at the way he dresses," he nodded toward the counter where Chaney had gone. "He looks like an adult version of a thug, trying too hard to be like them. All they see is someone they can dupe and run over." His voice rang firm. "I bet they wouldn't have stood up to me that way. Nobody disrespects me."

"Why? Because you're wearing a suit?"

He leaned into the table. "You have to show these little thugs how to be a real man. Not try to be their homey and prove to them that you're down. You have to be ready to break a foot off in their asses if they step to you wrong."

Funny, because for someone whom these boys would have respected, he sure didn't stand up and show this type of manliness that he said he had. And being every bit of about five foot seven or so, which was a good three inches shorter than Chaney, I didn't understand how he thought the kids would fear or respect him more. But I decided to let him roll with that thought.

Russ and I went back to discussing business. The boys had ordered French fries and had just saturated them with ketchup when the police came in. They walked around, then nodded to Chaney, who had abruptly reappeared behind the counter and seemed to signal them with a simple nod of his head and a heightened brow. Policemen of the community respected Chaney for who he was and what he did.

The officers walked up behind the boys, who were knee-deep in French fries and soda. "Well, now, look who we have here at a little after eleven. And on a school day at that," said the officer who wore the name BROCK on his badge.

"If it isn't Jarvis and Manny," said Officer Dotson. "Tell me, boys: Why am I not surprised?"

Jarvis dropped a French fry and Manny wiped his hands down his white T-shirt. He grabbed his coat and his legs got set to run from their seated position.

"Don't even think about it," Officer Dotson said as he stepped closer to the table and stood in Manny's path. He put a hand on his holster for a brief moment, just enough to let reality set in.

"What's this? About the fifth time this month?"

The boys put on prison-faced stares as they stood up. Their eyes turned cold as they looked with grave disdain at the officers. Jarvis lifted up his T-shirt and put his hands in his front pockets. Manny shifted his weight from foot to foot as he stared the officers down.

A tired-looking woman forced her way through the door and brought in a burst of cold air with her. Her heavy military-style coat was topped with a burlesque scarf that seemed to choke the life out of her face. The bags under her eyes were dark. She removed her wool cap and didn't bother to fluff out her matted-down hair. She found Jarvis's eyes, and hers filled with tears.

"You know I just got off work, boy. Why you keep doing this to me?"

Jarvis winced and wobbled from side to side. He rolled his eyes and turned his back to his mother. His head dropped and his shoulders drooped.

"You turn 'round when I'm talking to you, boy," she demanded.

"Yes, ma'am," Jarvis said with sudden remarkable enunciation. He turned around to face her.

She moved her head from side to side as she began her performance. "I don't know what I'm going to do with you. I just don't know." She looked at the officers, then spoke with great intensity to the ceiling. "I don't know what to do with him anymore. I do the best I can." She shook her raised fists.

Officer Brock was unmoved by the performance, as if he had seen this all too many times before. "Well, unfortunately, Mrs. Taylor, he's a minor and he's your responsibility. And you do stand the possibility of jail time if you can't keep his little a—um, if you can't keep him in school."

Mrs. Taylor put her fist on her hip and extended the other arm to waist level. Her jaw tightened and her breathing quickened as she talked to the officer. "I can't do everything. I work three jobs just to keep a roof over this here boy's head, food in his mouth, and clothes on his back. I teach him right from wrong. He knows." She turned to Jarvis. "Don't you know right from wrong, boy?"

Jarvis quickly and obediently nodded his head.

Mrs. Taylor walked over to Jarvis and slapped him in the back of the head. "What's that? Speak up, boy. You know I don't do no sign language."

"Yes, ma'am," Jarvis mumbled. Embarrassment took over his face as his thuggish façade faded away.

"Maybe if you talked to his father and got him involved—" Officer Brock tried to suggest.

"Father? What father? Officer Brock, as much as you called my house, have you ever known a daddy to pick up the phone? Have you ever seen a daddy come to see about this boy? Naw. All you see is me. This boy ain't got no daddy. None that's worthwhile anyway." She scowled and her chest heaved. She looked at Jarvis and flashed her teeth. "But he's smart. He gets As and Bs in school. When he goes."

Jarvis winced as if that was the last piece of information he wanted revealed to the world. Didn't want that on his record. Looked like he had just been Tasered, which he might have actually preferred.

Manny took a seat out of harm's way and sat with a gangsta lean.

Officer Brock tried a different angle. "I know you may not like his father, but maybe if you found him—"

"*I'm* his daddy," she asserted with clenched fists. Officers Brock and Dotson responded by taking two steps back.

"Well, ma'am, I hate to do this, but I'm afraid we're going to have to issue you a summons for truancy court," said Officer Dotson.

Her hand jetted to her heart and her performance went into high drive. "Oh lawd! You see what you doing to me, Jarvis? All I do for you and you can't even go to school? I just got off my job three hours ago and I get home and try to get some sleep, then I get this officer calling me and I got to get my tired ass up out of bed to tend to you? And here I might have to go to jail because you won't go to school? What's wrong with you, boy?"

Jarvis shrugged his shoulders like he didn't give a damn. And I guess that was all it took because the next thing I know, I see Mrs. Taylor all on top of the boy, wilding out and going crazy, having an Ike Turner moment. She looked like a Muppet on a mule as she threw closed-fisted punches at his head and upper body. Jarvis bent over and used his arms to cover his face.

Manny began to laugh. He put a closed fist up to his mouth and laughed. "Oh, shit." His legs bounced as he sat.

"I don't know what you laughing at," Mrs. Taylor said before she started pummeling Manny. Mrs. Taylor went back and forth between Jarvis and Manny, issuing punches and laying blows.

Chaney and I ran over to them. Officer Brock had stood back long enough, then I guess he figured that he should do something about it, only so he wouldn't be accused of not doing his job. But it was apparent that both officers were more than willing to see Mrs. Taylor do what they wanted to do themselves, but couldn't: beat some sense into these boys.

Russ took another puff on his cigar and blew into the air as he watched the scene from afar.

By the time we reached Mrs. Taylor, Officer Brock had placed a light hand on her shoulder, but her arms still flailed wildly, hitting the boys. Officer Dotson stood next to Mrs. Taylor and put up one hand to appear to deter her blows.

"Whoa, whoa, whoa," Chaney said as he restrained Mrs. Taylor's arms. "Mrs. Taylor, there's got to be a better way than this."

Mrs. Taylor's whole body rose and fell with each breath she took through her flared nostrils. Except for her clenched fist, she appeared to be coming back from being overcome by a holy spirit. "I'm tired," she wailed. She picked up a menu from the table and began to fan herself. "I try so hard to be a good example for him. I don't know why he wants to be a thug. Damn 50 Cent. I can't watch him twenty-four hours a day. I just got home from work from the casino boat." Her shoulders fell hard as if she had just given her last breath.

"You're a card dealer or something?" Officer Brock asked.

Mrs. Taylor sniffed and shook her head no.

"You work in the kitchen or clean?" I asked.

Again, Mrs. Taylor shook her head no. She fanned herself faster.

Jarvis scoffed. "She's a gambler," he said. "That's her so-called work. Gambling the money that she gets from her first two jobs."

"Made five hundred this morning," Mrs. Taylor proudly announced. "And all I wanted to do was come home and get some rest before I have to get up and go to my first job." She swung her pocketbook at Jarvis's head, but he leaned backward quickly and her purse grazed the tip of his nose. She spoke to the ceiling again. "Lawd, if I don't never birf another child for as long as I walk this here earth, I swear it'll be none too soon."

Chaney and I exchanged looks of bewilderment as I heard Russ chuckle behind me. He tapped ashes into an ashtray before turning back around and flipping through another page of my business plan.

"Ma'am? You have a gambling problem?" asked Officer Dotson.

"Gambling problem? Who that? I ain't got no gambling problem." She rolled her neck and said as if she were highly offended, "I got a low income problem. And I'm trying to grow it."

"Gambling is no way to solve your income problem. Perhaps you should replace that with another job. But you've got to do something about your gambling addiction," Officer Brock tried to reason.

She turned slowly. "Y'all hard of hearing? This *is* my job. I don't *have* a gambling addiction. I don't look forward to going. I don't gamble away all my money or everything I own. I go because it's work. Just like you doing right now. Working on your job? It's a part-time job I work four nights a week." She scratched her head.

An older couple had just finished their muffins and coffee and gotten up to leave when Chaney huddled with the boys and began talking quietly. He started to do his thing. He asked them questions about where they wanted to go in life and what they wanted to be. And then he took them on a verbal journey of what it would take to get there. Jarvis and Manny looked like they had heard it all before. They stood with their heads cocked to the side and with exasperated eyes.

Unperturbed by their show of disinterest, Chaney took them on a stroll in the café and pointed to the pictures of the famous people on his walls and read the positive quotes under their names. As they stood before the portrait of James Baldwin, of whom the boys were totally unaware, he asked Jarvis to read the quote.

Jarvis hunched his shoulders and shook his head no, but Chaney insisted.

"Read the quote, boy," Mrs. Taylor chimed in from across the café. She remained alongside the officers as they gave Chaney time to work his magic. "Can't you see the man is trying to help you? Lawd knows I can't." She threw up her hands and sighed.

Jarvis concentrated on the words and strained his eyes. He puckered his lips as if to sound out the words. "Kuh . . . kuh . . . kuh-now . . ."

"Can you see it?" Chaney asked. The words were big as day from where we were standing and if Jarvis couldn't see it, he had to be damn near blind. He pulled Jarvis directly in front of the picture and closer. "Now read it."

His voice was low. "Kuh . . . kuh . . . kuh-now . . . when . . . sss . . . whence. You . . . k . . . k . . . came. Kuh-now whence you came. Know whence you came . . ."

I knew Chaney's heart was sinking. "That's enough," he said with discouragement in his voice. He removed his baseball cap and scratched his head. "I thought your mom said you get As and Bs in school."

"I do."

"Well, why can't you— Never mind."

He called Manny over to read it and Manny did worse than Jarvis.

Chaney paused and I could see his distraught mind working overtime. His face hung low as he looked down at the black-and-white-checkered floor while thoughts ran through his mind.

Mrs. Taylor was trying to negotiate with the officers as Chaney paced, then he rejoined them. "Where are Manny's parents? Did you call . . . his mother?" He asked the officers, guessing there wasn't a father there either because if there was, chances were he wouldn't be out here.

Manny laughed. "Up north, yo. So, uh, I don't think she'll be able to make it here today. She's a bit tied up. Knowhaimean?"

Chaney looked to the officers for confirmation, and they gave it—Manny's mother was in prison, serving time as an accomplice in a drug deal. He was now living with his seventy-two-year-old grandmother.

An idea exploded over Chaney's face. He pounded his right fist into his left hand as he spoke. "I've got a plan. Why don't you leave the boys in my care? I'll make sure they get to school every day." He stared Jarvis and Manny down. "And after school, they'll come to the shop, and I'll tutor them in reading."

Manny spun toward him and laughed aloud. "You must be out of your damn mind!"

"Aw, hell naw!" Jarvis shouted, as he covered his face with his hands. His mother swung and hit him on the back of the head with her purse. Jarvis released a yelp and rubbed the back of his head as he whimpered.

The excitement of life filled me. I jumped in. "I think it's a great idea. As a matter of fact, I'll help tutor."

"You will?" Chaney asked beneath his breath. His face seemed to light up.

From across the room, Russ snapped to attention. He stamped out his cigar in the ashtray and quickly rose to join us.

"I think it's a brilliant idea and a wonderful thing you want to do," I said. "After all," I continued as I looked at the officers, "so many people want to take boys like Jarvis and Manny and just lock them up. I think that it's wonderful that you want to save them. To help them make something out of their lives. Of course I'd want to be a part of something like that."

"I'll help out, too," Russ's heavy voice said.

Jarvis was startled. "Where'd he come from?"

Russ continued, "I'm Russom King. You all can call me Russ." He bowed his head to the officers and Mrs. Taylor, then retrieved business cards and passed them out to everyone. "I think it's important that fine boys like these two have positive male role models in their lives. Often, that's what makes a difference in their lives and puts them on the path of the straight and narrow. Keeps them out of trouble," he stated as if he'd be asking for their vote later.

Most of the customers had left by now and quiet swarmed the café as the officers, Mrs. Taylor, and the boys looked Russ over. He appeared to have come from out of nowhere, and they were trying to fit him into the scene and figure out what the hell they were supposed to do with his business card.

Chaney had skepticism written all over his face.

Russ cleared his throat before speaking again. "When I was back in Atlanta, I did work with a lot of troubled youth, helping to get them on the right track."

Officer Brock spoke. "Well, it's up to Mrs. Taylor, and we'll have to talk to Manny's legal guardian. . . ."

Mrs. Taylor shifted her weight onto one leg. "Shit. Y'all can whip his ass for all I care if that'll keep me out of jail." She raised her pocketbook to Jarvis's head again; he flinched and that was enough for her. She lowered her arm in satisfaction.

"I'm sure we can probably work something out," Officer Brock said. He shared a glance with Officer Dotson, who gave his approval.

"Good, good," Chaney said as he rubbed his palms together. "Tell you what. Let's all have a sit-down. I'll get some coffee over here and we can hash this thing out right now."

Jarvis and Manny looked lifeless as they sat, helplessly watching their lives being planned, and not in the way in which they would want. We went over rules for the boys before Mrs. Taylor put her hat and coat back on and headed for home. The officers escorted the boys back to school, and Chaney went back to work.

Russ and I sat back down at our table and wrapped up our business discussion. "It's going to be great working with you," Russ said.

"With the tutoring?" I asked, since he hadn't confirmed being my business partner.

"Well, that, too. But I was talking about the Internet café. I read your plan. You've sold me on it, Ms. Rodgers, and I very much would like to be a partner." He held out his hand as we stood up.

I jumped with excitement. "That's great!" I took his hand and shook it—I nearly shook the man's arm off.

"Before you get too excited, I feel that it's only fair to warn you that I can be a bit of a pit bull when it comes to business. I'm all about success, by any means necessary."

"Exactly the kind of partner I need." I was still shaking his hand. He pulled me close and hugged me. I hugged him back. Two seconds turned into five, which turned into ten. The congratulatory hug became a damn good feeling, and guilty pleasures ran through my body as his arms tightened around me. He wasn't letting go, either.

I pulled my body back, only because I felt that I probably should. It was as if that moment were suspended in time forever.

I took his hand and shook it again. This time, right proper-like.

SEVEN

"TELL ME WHAT YOU'RE THINKING ABOUT," RUSS said. He leaned back in his dining-room chair and folded his arms across his succulent chest. His luscious lips were pressed together like he was trying to hold back a knowing smile, as if he could read on my face exactly what was going on in my mind.

For the past few weeks, we had gotten together on almost a daily basis at the Rosebud Café or Russ's apartment, putting together timelines, poring over both our credit reports and determining our financial net worth, filing business registrations, considering locations, and finding funding and other resources. Keeping my mind on the business forms rather than on him was a daily task at first. I would sit there meeting after meeting, struggling to concentrate on the matters at hand, losing to the lust in my mind. Eventually, I'd drift off and get lost in his eyes, melt in his voice, and get wrapped up in his biceps.

If that wasn't bad enough, the fact that Russ had a tender and romantic side didn't help one bit. Since having my own business was my passion, it was nothing for me to work eight, ten, or twelve hours nonstop. And he could, too. But all work and no play would make bitches out of us both, he said. So, after working long stretches at a time, Russ would schedule a break, which might be dinner, when we talked about anything but business, or a jazz concert, or a history museum, and, once, he even ordered me to a day spa, where my assignment was to receive a manicure, pedicure, and a reiki massage. He ordered in my favorite foods for meetings when he learned what they were, and sometimes ordered mini-breaks, when we played "Name That Tune" with jazz songs or played his spontaneous game of "You share something about you and I share something about me." Russ insisted that all this was for us to get to know each other inside out—as business partners. I went along with it all because I needed the break, and I'd be lying if I didn't say that I didn't mind one bit being escorted around the city by a fine-ass man like Russ.

"Going into business together is like a marriage," he said once. "If you want it to last, you need to know every single thing about your partner that you possibly can. Not just the stuff on paper and their business acumen. You need to know what their pet peeves are and how they resolve conflicts. You need to make sure that you can stand them for long periods of time, and that they're able to put personal preferences aside to make sound business decisions. In other words, we both need to know each other in and outside the office."

At first, it had been hard trying to ignore my growing interest in him, especially while spending so much time together. But over the weeks, I had been able to talk myself into clarity, put my feelings in check, and listen to my common sense. And to put my business first.

But it still didn't stop the mind-drifts into fantasyland.

I began to feel hot with embarrassment. Russ's voice brought me out of my trance and I realized that I was sitting across from him over papers and half-empty cartons of Chinese food and a bottle of wine, just staring at the man. My eyes were looking in his direction; not exactly looking at him, but rather inside him.

As if my recent thoughts were of the long-ago past, I could

remember how good his arms felt around me a couple of weeks ago when he agreed to be my partner. I started to wonder if his lips were as soft to kiss as they looked. Wondered what his tongue tasted like, and how his hard body would feel pressed up against mine. And how good it would feel to have his hands stroking my back, rubbing my legs up to the inside of my hot thighs. I began to get moist.

He repeated, "What are you thinking about?"

I felt naked and exposed. "Oh, ahhhh, nothing. Well, not nothing," I stumbled. "I mean, I was thinking about something, it's just . . ."

"It's just what?" he asked, not cutting me any slack. His thick fingers stroked his clean-shaven chin. Clearly, he must have sensed my fantasy and guessed that he was the main feature. He was going to try his best to drag it out of me at all costs.

I reached across the paper-covered table for the wine and poured a second glass.

"You sure you want more of that?" He laughed lightly. He laced his fingers together behind his head and gave his prominent chest a stretch.

"Why wouldn't I? What are you saying?"

"Not saying anything. Just trying to find out what you were thinking. Because with the look you had on your face, it must have been gooood. Real good." His wet tongue glided over his bottom lip.

He saw through me.

My face flushed and I tried to empty my mind. But it was difficult because his cologne floated up my nostrils and stirred my feelings. I stretched my neck from shoulder to shoulder.

"I was thinking about expansion," I lied. Well, I actually had thought about it before, but just not at that particular moment.

"Expansion? Expanding to more stores?"

It worked.

I bounced my pen on the messy pile in front of me. "Yes, I know we haven't gotten the first one open yet. But with the feed-back we're getting from the neighborhood surveys, question-naires, and potential investors, I think we should start now on getting pitches together to gather up investors for more cafés in different neighborhoods. Over time, of course." I leaned back on the armless mahogany chair and crossed my legs.

He looked damn sexy as his long lashes hovered over his large brown eyes as he thought about my suggestion. He licked his bottom lip again and I just wanted to suck him up. "Don't you think we need to give this first one a little breathing room? See how it does?"

"I'm not saying open other stores immediately, but to go ahead and start planning for success. If this first store doesn't do so well right off the bat, which, by the way, is not going to hap-pen, then we just hold off on expansion indefinitely. But if it takes off like I think it will, then we have a plan in place to expand."

Russ took his focus off me and began to dwell on my idea. I felt like I had escaped the lion's den. Whatever he was reading on my face, he was reading correctly. And I didn't want to so much as open the door for that discussion.

"It's a thought, but I think we should hold off."

"Okay."

"Okay? Just like that?"

"Yeah. What's the problem?" I asked. I was just relieved to be able to change the topic.

Russ's delayed smile appeared. "Ahhhh. Changing the subject. I got to hand it to you on that one. That was smooth. Pretty slick," he said as he pointed a finger at me before quickly dropping his hand. "You're good," Russ said as he reached over and poured himself a second glass of wine as well.

"What's wrong with your hand?" I asked.

"What?"

"Your hand?" I pointed to his right hand, which was balled in a loose fist. "You always hide it or drop it quickly. You got a scar or something?"

Russ lowered his hands to his lap, and looked down. He paused, seemingly to consider whether he even wanted to have this conversation, or what he would say. Deciding that he would, he raised his hand up in the air. Opened it toward me and spread his fingers. It took only a second to notice that the tip of his middle finger was missing.

I lifted my hand to cover my open mouth. "I'm so sorry," I said.

He waved his hand. "It's okay. You didn't know."

It was obvious that however long ago this had happened and whatever had happened, it still haunted him today. And it was more than just the missing fingertip. It was deeper than that.

"Can I ask, um . . ."

"Happened when I was a kid. I was eight years old." He took a sip of wine, probably to muster the ability to tell the story. He expelled a heavy breath that contained more suffering than I could imagine. "One day, my mother decided that she had had enough, and she decided to leave. She didn't hate me, but she had never wanted to be a mother really. At least not yet, I guess. Turns out she had gotten pregnant with me, and my father was excited. He was older, and I was his first. She wanted to have an abortion. But he convinced her that everything would be all right. He wanted to marry her and have a family, and he convinced her."

The more Russ talked, the more pain took a toll on his body.

He appeared to slowly disintegrate before my eyes. A movie was being played in his mind. Once the reel started going, it was impossible to shut it off.

"No, it's okay. Really. I want to share this. Let me."

I sat quietly and gave him the floor.

"I loved her, and she loved me. She took good care of me. I just remember her never being happy. Don't ever remember seeing her smile. I'm sure she did; just can't remember it."

He took another swallow and rubbed his stubby finger as he continued to relive the past. "So, I guess one day, she'd had enough and she decided to give up the life she never wanted. Only, I loved her. I didn't want her to go. So I cried when she packed up a suitcase and said she was going away, and that I would never see her again. I held on to her pant leg for dear life, but that didn't help because she threw a suitcase in the car anyway. Her face was so distant and not there. It was so empty. I know she didn't feel me or hear me. She got right into the car and slammed the door, and my hand got caught in it. Dad was screaming from the porch as she was about to drive off. She stopped. She opened the door and I lay on the ground. Crying. Blood running down my hand. I just remember her looking like she couldn't see me. It was like she didn't have a soul. She told my father to call an ambulance, then drove off. And I never saw her again." Wetness filled the corners of his eyes, but he wouldn't let it fall.

His words hung in the air and swirled around the lifeless room, the trophies, the certificates, and the numerous awards that decorated the walls.

Russ kept rubbing his finger. His face was strained. "They tried to save it, but couldn't get the blood to circulate. So they had to take my fingertip off.

"I remember my father saying that she took my manhood. That I would never be a whole man again. And that's what I see when I look at my hand or what I think people must think when they look at my missing finger. That I'm not a whole man. So I've always tried to make up for it in other ways." He paused and looked around the room at his achievements. "Because I am a man."

"Of course you are," I finally said.

I reached for him. He pulled back at first. So I just held my hand out and opened it. Laid it on the table and waited for him. Slowly and easily, Russ brought his over to mine and graced it with a light touch. And that touch turned into a relaxed letting go, and the bond of trust formed between us.

I used his words. "That's the thing about being business partners. We share so much more," I said as I sandwiched his hand between mine and offered a warm smile.

"Thanks," he said. He cleared his throat. "Talking about manhood, this is uncool of me to be breaking down like this."

"Nonsense."

He slowly pulled his hand away. "How about we get back to work, partner?" His tone became more casual. "If you're really serious, let's talk more about this expansion idea."

I hadn't been, but now that it was out and on the table, I didn't think it was such a bad idea after all.

"BELIEVE ME, you will not regret this," an excited Allie told me as she hailed me with extended arms. "I am going to be the best administrative assistant you've ever hired." She squeezed out more than a healthy serving of mustard onto the last half of her tuna-and-sliced-pickle sandwich, then smashed the top half of the roll down on it, causing the mustard to ooze out the sides. I wrinkled my nose as she picked it up, took a bite, and licked her fingers.

Vlora displayed that "You done did it now" look on her face as she sat next to Allie and across from me.

"Famous last words," I said as I watched Chaney peering out the window of the front door. A new coffee shop chain had just opened a store in Mill Creek Valley a couple of weeks ago. Catty-corner from the Rosebud Café. Chaney hadn't lost any business as of yet, but I could tell that he was worried. I didn't think he should be. The Rosebud Café was more than a coffee shop; it was the vein of the community. The new shop, Mooncents, had higher prices, and didn't offer the community programs or the creative platforms that Chaney did. No video games for the kids, no live bands, and no jukebox with hip-hop music. They piped in elevator music. Frankly, I thought it'd be a matter of months before Mooncents turned tail and ran to another neighborhood to suck them dry. There was no way Mill Creek Valley would continuously support an outsider at the expense of a neighborhood landmark like the Rosebud Café.

Music streamed over from the jukebox and mixed with the low-level chatter from the handful of people who were in the café. I turned back to Allie, who was speaking to me. "We are going to work so well together. Watch. We're not going to be like those family members who work together and end up not being able to stand each other's guts. This is going to be so cool." Allie surrounded me with her arms and damn near squeezed the life right out of me. "You are the best."

"Don't get too excited. There are rules," I said, in as stern a voice as I could command. I kept a stone face as I listed out my bullet points on each finger. "You will be at work from eight to four-thirty. Half hour for lunch. Chaney's letting us use an office here in the back, free of charge, until we get our own facility together, and I already have everything set up for you. You'll be able to figure out which desk is yours when you go back there." I nodded my head toward the entryway that led to the rooms in the back of the café.

"Cool. It's not even going to be a problem." She grinned heartily.

"We start tomorrow morning. I have a stack of papers that need to be sorted properly; letters that need to be typed, printed, and mailed; and a whole host of other stuff."

"Sounds good to me. This is going to be the best thing for us, you know. We're going to have great memories. 'When me and you started this business together . . .'" Allie looked dreamily upward, then brought her thrill-filled eyes to me again. "Naja, I really do appreciate this. Seriously. You knew I really needed a job, and, well, it means so much to me that you would hire me."

"That's what families are for," I said. I held my arms open and we gave each other a tight hug. "Now get on out of here. It's about time for you to pick up Andi."

Allie pulled away, wiped the corner of her eye, and glanced at her watch. "Yeah, you're right." She grabbed her coat and began to bundle up.

"I'll see you bright and early at eight o'clock in the morning," I said to her as she started to make her way to the door.

"Ewwww. Um, about that." She sucked her teeth. "I'm going to need the day off tomorrow. The cable man is coming. He's going to hook me up with *all* the channels. Then we're going out for lunch." She winked at me. "And anyway. That eight o'clock in the morning? I'm not feeling that. I mean, I'd really like to, but I don't think I'm going to be able to swing it. I'm just being honest.

I get up at seven and go jogging in the morning, then come home and have breakfast and read the paper before I can even think straight. Or else, my ass is grass for the entire day." She almost snorted and flung her knock-off designer purse over her shoulder. "I'll see you Tuesday about nine-ish. Cool?" She waved her hand frantically and smiled hard as she whipped out her cell phone and dialed.

Vlora really didn't have to say "I told you so" because her face and that condescending smile said it all for her. I had a sneaking suspicion that this was going to be one of the biggest mistakes ever. Until the store was up and running and I could draw a salary, I was living on savings and paying Allie from the business account. What I really needed to do was to keep on her about finishing up her last year of school and making her own way, instead of always being her bank and her safety net. I knew that. It was just difficult because she had had such a hard childhood, then became a mother before she was ready. Hell, she wasn't even ready now, but I couldn't tell her that. We had been on the outs for so many years, and since the pendulum was swinging the other way, I wasn't eager to change it.

"Told you not to hire relatives. That's why my business is successful. You don't see none of my relatives working for me. Anybody with a drop of Dern blood in them doesn't get hired."

"It's for Andi."

"Honey, that's your bag of tricks and I'm not saying a word about it," Vlora said. "How's the partnership going?"

We had our coffees refilled, and I updated her on how Russ and I had been working together almost daily for the past six weeks or so, diligently mapping out structure and operations. Russ was an all-around business wizard. He had tightened up my original business plan and took the lead in executing it. What's more, we worked well together. I had no complaints. When we disagreed on points, Russ would take charge of getting both our perspectives on paper, and would lead in compromising to come to a decision. I felt as if I had chosen the perfect partner and I felt that my dream, my baby, was coming to fruition.

I also told her about how Russ had agreed to help me and Chaney tutor the boys. He hadn't been able to get started just yet, but he would join us soon.

The boys were actually responding and starting to drop their tough exteriors—Jarvis more so than Manny. Chaney had discovered that Jarvis had been getting good grades by memorizing things, rather than actual knowledge and ability. Once we made that discovery, we were able to make real progress.

"You know, somehow I can't help but detect a little extra interest in Russ on your part. More personal than business." She blew on her steaming coffee, then put it down and opted for the ice.

I tilted my head to the side. "I'm not going to deny that he's a very decent-looking man. He's a perfect gentleman, very courteous, sensitive, and a lot of fun, and . . ." My shoulders lifted with delight and I laughed out loud, then told her the story of how one night, we had worked into the wee hours of the morning and we were both tired and getting cranky. Russ just got up and went to his album collection. Yes, albums. He threw Frankie Beverly and Maze on the record player, and after thirty seconds, we were up dancing and singing to "Joy and Pain."

"Yep, that sure sounds like a confirmation to me," Vlora said as she nodded and tapped out a rhythm with her fingernails on the table.

"No, not at all. I mean, yes, he's a great guy. And I think under any other set of circumstances, he would be someone I would go for. But we're business partners," I said. Trying to reassure myself.

"Why don't you get off that and just go with the flow?"

"I am not about to risk my business on a wing and a prayer of a relationship. Relationships are so fly-by-night these days as it is. I can see it now. We get together, it doesn't work out, then either the business is going to fail because he's going to sabotage it or, at best, I have to work with a partner who has a funky attitude or somebody that I can't even stand to look at."

"You know, try as I might, and you know I always try—" Vlora started.

"Yeah, you do."

"Me myself personally? I don't know whether or not I'm with you on this one." She bounced up and down from bobbing her left leg.

"With you on what?" Chaney asked as he walked over to our table. The Sunday afternoon crowd was always pretty light, and he had more time to sit and chat with his favorite customers, or at least I liked to think we were his favorites. He pulled out the black metal chair, swung it around, and straddled it.

"Mixing business and personal relationships. Whether they work or not," Vlora said. "Could be a good thing. Or it could be in the same category as the 'don't hire family members' rule. They'll always take advantage of you and run all over you because they think you won't fire them."

"I don't know about that." He shrugged, then rested his chin on his arms. "Worked for me and my wife. I loved working with her."

"You mean to tell me you all never had problems? You never had personal problems that spilled over and affected the business?" I asked.

"No, I'm not saying we never had problems. You have that whether you're in business together or not. But no, we never let our personal problems affect our business. This café was our bread and butter, and we weren't about to let it be affected by personal matters. We kept that at home. But just like any relationship, communication is the key. You have to talk about that stuff up front."

"Would you do it again?" Vlora asked. The late afternoon sun was setting, and a shadow from her nose was cast across half of her face.

"No doubt," Chaney said. He looked at me. "Having a wife who's also your business partner? Oh, it can't get any better than that." He shook his head with pleasure.

"Well, I'm glad it worked out for you, Chaney."

"Yeah," he said. "So what's up, ol' girl?" he asked Vlora. He reached over and patted her arm a couple of times with the back of his hand. "You got somebody special? You thinking about going into business with him?" His eyes widened and he waited eagerly for the answer.

"It's actually not me we were talking about. It's Naja."

He jerked his head back and a crease formed in his brow. "Naja?" He turned toward me with a frown.

As usual, Vlora took this as an indication of some sort of attraction, and her eyes bounced back and forth between me and Chaney. She felt that she had found a nerve, and she definitely was going to do a dance on it. "Mmm-hmm. *Na-ja*," she said, elongating my name.

I rolled my eyes at her.

I'm surprised the man didn't get whiplash with the way his head went from Vlora to me. "You're getting with that . . . I mean, you and your business partner are getting together?"

Vlora made as subtle a face as she could without being seen by Chaney.

"No. Vlora here was saying how nice a guy Russ seemed to be, and how well we get along together. I was telling her that I wouldn't mix business with pleasure."

The smirk on Vlora's face was replaced by a frown before she immediately changed to neutral right before Chaney glanced back at her. He looked lost.

"No. You're right," Chaney said. "I mean, yeah, it worked for me and my wife. But we were one of the lucky couples. It's much more difficult to do today. It's hard to have a relationship with a coworker, let alone a business partner."

"Is that right?" Vlora asked, making light fun of his abrupt turnaround when he found out we were talking about me instead of Vlora.

"He may be a great guy—to you, at least—but the question becomes, how well do you know him? How much background info do you have on him? His past relationships? And, well, you just don't know him like that, and it could affect your business in the long run. Generally speaking, of course."

"My point exactly, Chaney. Thanks," I said.

"Good," he said. He looked relieved.

"You don't like him very much, do you?" Vlora asked Chaney. She placed an elbow on the table and balanced her chin on her knuckles.

He hesitated before answering bluntly, "I don't really know him enough not to like him."

A group of customers came in, and Chaney knocked on the table twice. "I got to get back . . ." He pointed to the counter, then got up and left.

"You need to quit," I fussed.

"What?" Vlora asked. She shrugged her shoulders and faked innocence.

"Don't give me that. You know exactly what."

She did a closed-mouth laugh that rattled her from within.

I looked at my watch. "I gotta go. Russ and I are working tonight."

"On a Sunday night? Umph. Well, don't do anything I wouldn't do," Vlora said. She winked at me as I got up.

"It's business, Vlora," I stated uselessly before I left.

EIGHT

I CALLED RUSS ON MY CELL PHONE TO MAKE SURE he had made it home and to let him know I was on my way over. Just thinking about working with him started my juices flowing. Any other time, Lord knows, I would have been all over him by now. But I was proud of myself for being able to keep things strictly business.

Sometimes I did wonder if Russ felt anything for me. There were times when we met when I thought I could just feel him staring at me, only to look up and see him staring at the wall behind me. Or sometimes even looking intently at a document, which made me feel like a fool. Maybe I just wanted him to look at me.

Russ opened the door wearing jeans and a form-fitting shirt. Before, if he wasn't wearing a suit, his clothing was loose and his shirt hung freely from his body. But in this shirt, his shoulders, biceps, and pecs were heavily defined, and I could see where he was starting to form a little beer belly. He must have felt me staring at it. He ran his hand over his stomach, then patted it and said, "I got to work on this a little more. Gets harder the older you get."

"Tell me about it," I said. We both laughed.

The only way to describe Russ's house is "stiff." His buttoned-down leather sofa and chairs and dark living room and bedroom furniture look like they belong in a psychiatrist's office. The air smells of nothing—no fragrance—and a small television on a side table in the dining room broadcast CNN.

We took our usual seats at his dining room table and picked up where we left off the last time. By spending a lot of time together, we were managing to get the business off the ground quickly. We were looking to open doors next month, Memorial Day weekend.

"Picking up from our last meeting, I really don't see any reason we shouldn't look at the option of expanding quickly," I said as I looked over our financial statements. I looked up to find Russ staring at me. This time, he really was staring at me.

"I'm just curious. What do you find attractive in a mate?"

"Whoa," I chuckled. "I think you've had one too many glasses of wine." I playfully pulled his half-empty glass away from him.

Russ grabbed my wrist and held it for a second. I couldn't move. I felt something like a surge of electricity move from his finger to my wrist and up my arm. By the time it reached my face, I was breaking out in a mild sweat.

"I'm just curious," he said. "I've noticed that since we've been meeting, I've never known a man to call you. Every time your cell phone rings, it's your sister, or one of your girlfriends. So I was just wondering if . . ."

I pulled my arm back slowly. And reluctantly. "Well, no, I don't have a man at the moment." My heart began to dance at the thought of his being interested in my love life. But why? Because if he were interested, there would be nothing we could do about it—because we were now partners.

A sudden shyness came over me. I felt flushed, and I continued my answer between breaths. "It's just that, with everything that's going on with the business and all . . ."

He grabbed my hand. "You're a strong black woman."

I blushed more. "Thank you." I gave a sheepish grin.

"You're ambitious, you've got drive, and you know what you want. You seem to be in control of everything and on top of everything. You've got your life together."

"You're embarrassing me," I said as I batted my eyelashes.

"There's something I've wanted to ask for the past couple of months."

I was glowing, feeling giddy. His eyes seemed to sparkle as they looked at me.

"Are you a lesbian?"

The needle skipped across the record player in my mind. *What?*

The blood in my veins quickly turned to venom, and I snatched my hand out of his with a vicious force. The handsome face that I had just wanted to smother with kisses I now wanted to slap the shit out of.

Russ's eyes widened and his mouth gaped open at my reaction. "I didn't mean anything bad by that." He skipped a breath. "I mean if you are, you are. It's no big deal. It's nothing to be ashamed of. Because . . ."

"Because what? Some of your best friends are gay?"

He looked dumbfounded. "Well, I was about to say that because it seemed like the natural thing to say, but it's really not true."

"Why would you think I'm a lesbian?"

Russ looked helpless as he shrugged his shoulders. He scrambled for words. "You got it going on. And I . . . well, it's just that . . . I've never seen you with a man, and . . ."

Sister girl leaped out of me. She donned burgundy hair, a gold tooth, large hoop earrings, and two-inch-long fingernails with a Playboy bunny on the pinkies. I rolled my neck and wagged my finger. "Oh, so a woman's got to have a man on her arm or she's a lesbian?"

"No, I'm not saying that, it's just that you're so strong, and . . . I've been flirting with you and you haven't . . ."

"And since you're God's gift to women, if I don't respond to *you*, then that *must* mean that I'm a lesbian, right? You know, you men are a trip. You all need to swallow that large ego you're nursing." I was hotter than asphalt on a sun-baked southern road in the middle of a sizzling summer.

Russ swallowed hard as he tried to figure a way out of the fix he created. "Man," he said. "How did I get here?" He ran his fingers through his soft curls.

"What you should be asking is how you're going to get the fuck out." Steam poured out of me now.

I began gathering my papers.

"What are you doing? You leaving? We still have a lot to cover tonight if we're planning to open next month."

"I think this is a good breaking point for tonight." I was pissed. I stacked papers and folders on top of the books we were using for research. The uneven stack fell over, and I began to pick up the fallen papers and folders and put them back on top. The pile kept toppling.

Russ's face softened and he erupted into laughter at my continuous cycle of slamming fallen papers and folders back on top of the pile.

He got up and pulled out the chair directly across from me. He grabbed my hand again and attempted to bring me around. "What do you fear the most?"

This man must be crazy. Throwing out thought-provoking questions was his answer to everything. I knew he was trying to change the conversation, desperately trying to salvage something, and get back to business, but I wasn't having it. There was no going back tonight. I stared at him with bewildered eyes.

"What do I fear the most?" I slammed another folder on top of the stack. It fell off. I let it fall onto the floor as I answered. "Insecure men who see a strong woman who obviously has it going on—maybe even better than they do—and feel threatened because she's not looking for someone to support her, or marry her, and since she isn't, their insecurities categorize her as a lesbian."

Russ's hand slid off mine.

"But I shouldn't say I fear them, you know. I pity them." I firmly placed both hands on the table and looked him square in the eyes. "I pity them because instead of saying, 'Hey. Here's a strong woman I could build something with,' they think, 'Here's a strong woman who makes it apparent to the world how worthless and insignificant I am as a man. That I'm weak as shit. And I can't have that. So, instead, I'm going to call her a lesbian.'"

This time, my words shook him. I knew how Russ felt about not being a whole man with the loss of his finger.

Silence enclosed us as distance came between us. Russ sat there speechless, as if he didn't realize a woman's words could be so powerful.

I felt hurt. It wasn't that I had anything against gays, lesbians, or, hell, even asexuals. But I was tired of men who apparently thought that because I wasn't all over them or all over men, period, that it meant I liked women.

"Look, I think that we should take a break."

"We're still going into business together, right?"

I shook my head in disbelief. "What? You think that just because we have an argument that I'm going to want to go home and take all of my marbles with me? You know, you're something else, Mr. King," I huffed. "I'm not in a relationship with you. You have your own personal life and I have mine. You have your own personal views, I have mine. Business is separate. Now, I get the feeling that you think a woman can't manage that, and we let our emotions rule over our logical decisions, but somehow, I can. Maybe I got an extra dose of testosterone or something, huh? You think?" I picked up my stack and headed to the door.

Russ stood up, placed his hands on my shoulders, and squared me up with him.

"Wait. Look. I'm a man. And as a man, we say some pretty dumb things."

I was unimpressed. "Yep."

"Look, I'm sorry. I was out of line. It was wrong of me to ask if you were a lesbian. To even think it."

I shifted my load to one side and tapped my foot against the floor.

"Please accept my sincerest apologies. It's just that . . . it's just . . . I really couldn't see why a smart, intelligent, and beautiful woman like you didn't have a man."

"So again," I said. "A woman has to have a man to complete her?"

"No, that's not what I mean to say."

"Then, what, Russ? What do you mean to say?"

He stepped in close to me. "I mean to say that you're beautiful. You are drop-dead gorgeous. And you're smart, kind-hearted, and brilliant."

I tilted my head to the side and sucked my teeth.

He continued, "And really I was just wondering if I ever stood a chance of getting with you."

Not what I expected.

My heart warmed. He took me by surprise. I put down my

folders and put his face between my hands. He felt soft and warm against my palms. I slowly and gently pulled his nose close to mine. Felt his light breath across my lips. Felt his glow, and it matched mine.

"No, you don't," I said with satisfaction. "Not because I'm a lesbian, but because we're business partners. And. I. Don't. Do. Business partners." I pressed on a two-second smile at the end of my statement. I spread one hand across the width of his face and pushed.

Russ slowly ran his tongue over his upper teeth. Rejection dripped from his skin. He rolled both his shoulders. "Okay, I know you're ticked about the lesbian thing."

"No, really, I think it would be a bad idea to mix business with pleasure. Seriously." I picked up my things again.

"Why?"

I stopped everything and looked at him. "Just look at us right now," I said. "We're in business together. People like us get into a relationship, then the relationship goes bad, they break up, then the business suffers because one knucklehead wants to get back together and gets angry because she doesn't. Then he tries to retaliate by destroying her business. I'm not having it," I said defiantly. "This has been my dream, and I'm not letting any man stand between me and my dream."

"What's more important to you? Finding love or pursuing your passion?"

The question perplexed me. Stopped me dead in my tracks. I didn't know how to answer.

He continued, "Don't answer that. But think about it. I mean, really think about it. And answer it to yourself."

The air swirled around us and filled the empty space that we had created.

"And anyway, what makes you think it would be me chasing after you and destroying the business?" he asked as an after-thought.

"I just know myself, and I know nothing would come between me and my business. I know me."

"And nothing would come between me and business. Business is business. Personal is personal. Two separate things."

"Um-hmm. You say that now."

"Really, they're two separate things. If I didn't look at it that way, I wouldn't be as successful as I am now. If we were to get into a relationship, and, by the way," he moved closer to me again. He put his lips within a centimeter of mine and purposely blew his hot breath across my face. "I'm feeling a vibe from you. Been feeling it."

I backed off.

Russ chuckled, then gazed at me with eyes full of intent. "If we were to get into a relationship, it wouldn't affect the business, regardless of what happened," he said softly.

I erected a barrier to prevent his penetration into my heart. "What time shall we meet tomorrow, Mr. King?" I asked, ignoring his statement.

Russ grabbed my hand and pulled me close to him.

I stared at his hand on mine. "Mr. King, I really would prefer that you not manhandle me like I'm some piece of meat, thank you."

The lust fled from Russ's face.

"What time is good for you tomorrow?" I asked.

"Six o'clock is good."

"Great, then I'll see you at six."

"Fine," Russ said.

"Good day," I said.

"Good day? Where are we, fucking England?" Russ asked as I walked out the door.

In the car, my hands shook as I gripped the steering wheel. My heart was still fluttering, regardless of how much I tried to make it subside. He was as attracted to me as I was to him.

I took deep breaths, slowly counted to ten in Swahili, then started the car and drove off.

NINE

THE NEXT COUPLE OF MEETINGS AFTER THE LESBIAN conversation were stiff for both of us, but productive. Russ had made it easier for me to keep my focus, so actually, it was just what I needed. He brought my mother's words back to me all the more strongly. After my father died and she became both mother and father to us, her trials made her want to instill in us the value of being an independent woman. She transformed from a stay-at-home mom to a full-blown feminist after getting fed up with attitudes in the workplace regarding her capabilities of performing as a single, working mother. Her bedtime stories were lessons, and her favorite authors were Germaine Greer, bell hooks, and Angela Davis.

So my determination had grown and my inner strength was renewed. I'd made a vow to myself to do all I could to succeed and to not let anything or anyone, especially Russ, distract me from that.

And so it was.

Well, for the next couple of weeks, at least. Then I began to cave. I kept a stiff upper lip while I envisioned him as a tall glass of chocolate milk waiting to be slurped slowly through a narrow straw.

All was forgiven and forgotten in a few weeks' time. After all, he had professed his undying love for me—at least that's the way I heard it. But I didn't want to come across as totally relaxed because I was enjoying watching

Russ walk on hot coals. Not that he hadn't before, but he treated me with the utmost respect now, being sure not to offend me in any way. Russ even fully agreed with my idea to plan for expansion, and was figuring out how to attract investors while I worked on the proposals and presentations.

Then he started softening and allowing his personal touches to come through again. We met at his place for about a month, until we found and leased our space for the café. Initially, Russ went out of his way to separate business and personal conversation, until eventually things got so cool that we were able to float between the two without any issues.

By the time we started planning for the grand opening in the spring, things were on point and we were dangerously back to stealing lustful looks at each other; something I knew I shouldn't be doing.

We snapped up a quaint little storefront between Imo's Pizza and a bookstore, a perfect location. It was on a block of storefronts that had living quarters above. The windows were wide and deep with sitting ledges, and the inside was spacious. We'd find a designer to have it transformed into the Internet café.

MAY'S FIRST FRIDAYS EVENT was downtown at the Renaissance Hotel. Every month since the beginning of the year, I'd gone with Vlora and Allie. It was a double pleasure now. It gave us a chance to hang out and have fun together, and I could network for business on the side. Russ came every month, too, although we didn't go together. We'd sometimes get together while we mingled, especially when either of us came across someone whom we might be able to exchange with. Through direct and indirect contacts we made at each First Fridays event, we had found a real estate agent, contracted renovators, and found custom computer builders and furniture suppliers—all of whom we were able to cut deals with.

Many of our dealings were "I can do this for you if you do this for me." And Russ was great at networking and wheeling and dealing. We worked side by side through everything: location hunting and meeting with contractors, accountants, and attorneys. Russ found the interior designer, and we all agreed on a floor plan that included a bar and a custom fireplace in the middle of the café. He also found the contractors and led the way in getting the work done. Together we went to the furniture store to pick out couches, chairs, floor coverings, and accessories for the store.

We were practically joined at the hip. But often, he commanded the conversation. I took that to come from his background of being a Realtor and a great salesperson. Those were skills I just didn't have, so I was happy to hand over the reins. I didn't know what I would have done without him. We definitely had a strong partnership.

"I really could use a raise, sis," Allie said after the professional development seminar at First Fridays. On occasion, the event host would arrange to bring in guest speakers for special seminars before the networking reception. We'd previously participated in discussions on team building, leadership skills, and effective management. This month's topic was on business finances.

A burst of laughter escaped Vlora before she was able to catch it. She cut her laughter short and apologized with her eyes.

"Beg your pardon?" I asked, hoping that my question would cause her to think again as we walked to the main room. No such luck.

"I need a raise. My cell phone is about to be cut off because

I'm three months behind on the bill." She ran her finger over her diamond nose ring.

"Why not just use your home phone until you can pay your bill and afford to get it turned on again?" Vlora asked her.

"Can't," she said. "The home phone got cut off three months ago. I was going to say something about it before, but then I thought about it. I'm a grown woman with a child, and I need to take care of my own responsibilities. And I realized I didn't really need a home phone anyway. Wouldn't need the cell phone if it weren't for Andi. I need some avenue of communication in case she gets sick or something."

"Ahhh, family," Vlora said, leering at me.

"So, can I have a raise?"

"How about I just loan you enough to take care of your cell phone bill and even your home phone?"

"A loan? I'd have to pay it back?" she asked with a twisted lip.

"That's what's usually meant by the term 'loan,'" Vlora added.

"Gawd!" Allie said. She pondered my offer and came back with, "Well, if that's the best you can do, I guess so. Can you write me a check now?"

"This can't wait?" I asked.

"I don't want to forget later. I'm going to the Lake of the Ozarks for the weekend, and I need to take care of this first thing Monday morning when I get back. My friend Malika asked me to double with her boyfriend and his old college roommate from Nigeria. Oh, that reminds me, I'm going to be late Monday morning."

"You mean as usual?" I mumbled as I wrote the check and handed it to her.

"How are you going to a resort for the weekend, when you

can't even pay your bills?" Vlora raised her eyebrow at me as she posed the question that I was supposed to.

Allie gave her head and eyes a slow roll in Vlora's direction as she clucked her tongue. "If you *must* know, Miss Thang, Malika's boyfriend is footing the bill. I'm not paying for a thing. Now. Any more questions?" Her eyes were planted on Vlora, who said nothing, but pressed her lips together firmly as she stared back.

Allie folded the check and put it in her purse. "Okay," she said. "I got to get to working the room."

"You mean you've been coming here for months now and you haven't found your rich man yet?" Vlora asked.

"No," Allie said glumly as she pulled out her fake business cards. "It's, like, half the people are legit, but they're trying to feel you out. Want to put you through the wringer. And then you got the other half who aren't even who they say they are. They dress and act like they're all that, and you get with them later and find out that the BMW they've been bragging on is, like, twenty years old, *if* they actually have one at all."

"Interesting," Vlora responded. "And tell me, what is it that you're driving again?"

Allie rolled her eyes at Vlora because Vlora knew good and damn well that she rolled with a bus pass, day in, day out, and all night long. "Whatever, bitch," Allie said to get a rise out of her.

Vlora squinted and talked through clenched teeth. "Okay, you got about one more 'bitch' left. And then I'm going to—"

"Woop! Gotta go. I'll meet up with you all later." Allie cut her off and walked in the direction of a large portly man with a full-length fur coat draped over his shoulders, Gators on his feet, and gleaming and sparkling from bling, it seemed, from every extremity. Light bounced off his gold tooth when he opened his mouth to speak, blinding anyone who dared to look in that direction. All he needed was a golden wine goblet and his outfit would have been complete. Allison walked right up, introduced herself, and handed him a business card. He handed her a card as well, and I imagined what name and business could possibly be on it: "Dollah Bill—Owner/Operator/Head Pimp of Whup Dat Trick Enterprises."

"Okay, now that you've got the business thing going, we're going to have to find a man for your personal life because I know you're feenin' on Russ. And sooner or later, that dam's going to break," Vlora said as she began to scan the room.

"I'm doing just fine, thank you very much."

"Who are you fooling? Working with Russ has got to be pure hell. That man is fine. And got it going on, too. And he's interested in you? Humph! I don't know how you're doing it. Me myself personally? I'd be all over him. That's on you if you don't want to mix business with pleasure, but I damn sure would get me some. He'd have to hit it once for me and get it on out of the way."

"Speaking of which," I said. "Why are you always trying to hook me up with someone and you don't have a man yourself?"

"Because I'd be done killed one of these little men running around here. I don't have time for all this BS that's going around these days."

Vlora didn't play when it came to letting someone in her life. If, and that was an extremely big if, they passed the interrogation, then they had to play by the rules. Some of which were no public displays of affection. No staying over beyond eight in the morning after a night of passion unless you were invited to, and don't even think about asking to stay at her place alone if she had to leave. No extra clothes or personal items were allowed at her home. All items were to be brought with you when you came, and taken with you when you left. If not, they would be immediately discarded. And going out more than two consecutive nights or more than four times a week was a definite no-no. Vlora liked her space.

Sometimes it was hard to tell when she was interested in a man. She took "unemotional" to another level. She kept a straight face when she spoke to men; you couldn't get a vibe for what she was feeling. Ever since she lived with and had her home cleaned out by a prescription-drug abuser three years ago, Vlora seemed to morph into this straight-to-the-chase, no-nonsense personality when it came to men. She analyzed them, chewed them up, and spit them out if she felt even an ounce of deceit.

"Don't you get lonely sometimes?"

"I love my life. There are too many gifts on this earth to have room for loneliness."

"What about love and companionship?"

"I got love. I love my family, and they love me. I love my friends."

"Okay, I see you're going to make me say it. What about sex?"

"Sex and love are two different things. I can have sex anytime I want."

"I know, but meaningful sex. Passion, intimacy. Don't you want it?"

She looked at me and wrinkled her forehead. "What makes you think I don't have that?"

I had never seen Vlora with a man since David, the substance abuser. That had been a very traumatic experience for her, so it would be understandable for her to want to keep her distance until she really got to know a person. I just hoped she hadn't sworn off men forever just because of one bad experience. Some women tended to do that, and that would be a big mistake for her.

"You never talk about a special man in your life. Haven't really talked about anyone since David."

"I don't have to be in a serious relationship with just one man to have passion, intimacy, and meaningful sex," she said rather bluntly. "And if I haven't told you about them, that means they weren't significant enough to mention. They're doing the job I brought them in to do and I let them go when I'm done or ready to move on to someone else. Simple as that."

I stood corrected as Vlora and I sipped on our complimentary cognac, and Russ walked up to us. As soon as I saw him coming my way, I had to stop the smile that crept up to my face and replace it with a more professional greeting. He seemed to glide with each step he took, and he possessed the sexiest charm. Just that quickly, I had imagined his greeting me with a sensuous hug and a wet-lipped kiss to the cheek. Feeling his breath on my temple as he pulled away and ran his thumb lightly across my bottom lip. For some reason, I began to feel weak in the knees, a tingling sensation ran through my thighs, and my crotch became hot.

"Hello, Naja," Russ said, snapping me out of yet another trance.

I looked upward and found his eyes. "Hey there, Russ."

Okay, will someone please tell me that I wasn't just staring at the man's privates as he walked toward us? What in the hell was I doing? How was I going to be able to work like this for years to come?

"Okay, you want to get your face out from between the man's legs?" Vlora leaned into me and whispered.

Damn! I *was* staring at the man's dick.

Russ exchanged pleasantries with Vlora before saying, "I met a couple a little while ago that I want you to meet. I told them all about us, our business, and what we're doing."

Russ caught the attention of an older couple and waved them over. They were both dressed in business attire, and looked like they could be on their way to an awards banquet where they were the honorees.

"Gloria and Jeffrey Hughes, this is my business partner I was telling you about, Naja Rodgers. And this is her friend, Vlora Dern. She has an insurance business."

We all shook hands and exchanged cards. "This is good, you know," Jeffrey said. "Gloria and I were actually talking about finding someone to evaluate our insurance policies for us. The whole gamut. Life, car, house, business. We're concerned about our current policies, whether we have accurate coverage and whether or not we're paying too much."

"Oh, I can definitely help you out with that. Give me a call at my office tomorrow and we can set up a time to go over everything," Vlora said.

"Sounds great," Jeffrey said. He looked at his wife and smiled. Then he focused on me and Russ.

Gloria and Jeffrey were independent computer instructors, and they offered classes for corporations. Russ thought it might be a great opportunity if we could also offer computer training at our Internet café and allow the Hugheses to provide instruction. They were quite excited by the nature of our business, and especially by its location.

"It's just great to see businesses like yours in Mill Creek Valley," Gloria said. "Something that people can use."

We all nodded in agreement. Russ and I caught each other's eyes and smiled. It felt so comfortable. So right. Then he wrapped an arm around my shoulder and pulled me in for a tight squeeze.

We talked about the possibility of working together, and

Russ took the lead in the conversation, although he looked to me for agreement. We had worked out a plan before Jeffrey and Russ headed to the bar to refresh our drinks.

"So, are you two involved?" Gloria asked when they left.

I almost choked. I was taken aback, because that was the last question I'd expected. Gloria picked up on my surprise. "I mean, you look so close and so at ease with each other. Plus, you look like a cute couple."

"We're just in business together," I said.

"For now. But she's on the verge of caving," Vlora added, just to start something.

"Vlora," I said loudly.

"For now," she stated again, looking at Gloria.

Gloria chuckled and followed it up with a mild hum. "Just take your time and go slow, honey. It'll all work itself out in due time."

"Really. Just business," I asserted.

"Well, that's what she says," Vlora said. "But they're attracted to each other. Ms. Business here has a thing about mixing business and personal relationships."

I tried to take Vlora's glass, which only had a drop of alcohol left, but she pulled it back.

"Oh, honey," Gloria said. "If I had that attitude, I wouldn't be as happy as I am now. Jeffrey and I became involved after we became partners."

"Really?" Vlora asked. She nudged me. "Do tell."

"Well," Gloria began. She seemed thrilled that Vlora asked so that she could tell the story. Her eyes lit up as she shifted her body. "We used to work together in a computer department and were both laid off at the same time. While we were looking for other jobs, Jeffrey came up with this brilliant idea of going into business together as consultants. Well, long story short, we started our business, and ended up spending so much time together that a relationship developed. One thing led to another, and here we are today."

"You don't say! And how long ago was that?" Vlora asked. Irritatingly.

"Let's see. We've been married twelve years, and we started the business three years before that. But it's like we've been married fifteen years, because going into business together is like being married. You share everything anyway."

"Yeah, I've heard that somewhere before," I muttered.

"You work together every day, you share financial information. Then you get to know each other's personalities and if you can get along together, then really, what else is left for a relationship?"

"Sex!" Vlora exclaimed. She held her mouth open for the laugh that wouldn't come out. She slapped me on the back. She was getting a little too spirited.

"I know it obviously worked out for you," I said, "but didn't you have a period when you wondered whether a relationship gone bad would hurt the business?"

Gloria paused and pondered the question, then answered, "No, not really. Because it was natural. We were building a dream together, and we understood everything the other person was going through. We weren't focused on dating or impressing each other, so as a result, we were ourselves from the beginning."

Vlora nudged me again.

"I do know what you mean," Gloria added, "but don't knock him just because you're in business together. I'm going to tell you, I sense a vibe between you. You look like you belong together."

"Hmmm . . . ," I said. Not what I wanted to hear.

Vlora smiled. She'd had her dose of instigation for the day.

Jeffrey and Russ returned with drinks for all of us, right as the main doors to the dance room opened up. "Well, this is our cue to finish this up and get out of here," Jeffrey said. Gloria moved to his side.

"You mean, you're not going to get your groove on on the dance floor?" I asked Gloria. "You look like you can get it crunk."

Gloria simulated jerky moves that were supposed to mimic the epileptic-like dances of the younger crowd. We shared another round of laughter.

"Chile, I might break something out there. But you all have a good time."

They headed toward an empty table across the room. Gloria looked at Russ, then at me, and winked as she left.

"What was that all about?" Russ asked.

"Nothing," I said, avoiding his eyes.

Allie came bouncing over to us, clapping her hands and jerking. "They're playing my shit!" she shouted. Seemed like every other song was her shit.

Allie grabbed Russ by the arm and pulled him to the dance floor. I took his drink out of his hand so I could let my little sister have her way with . . . my business partner.

TEN

"I'M SO PROUD OF THEM," I SAID TO CHANEY AS WE admired Jarvis and Manny from the counter. They sat across from each other with hungry faces buried in the entertainment section of the newspaper. I was rounding up sodas and French fries for them, and had asked them to read and discuss articles from the *St. Louis American*.

We'd been tutoring the boys for three months now, and we were starting to see some initial success in both their reading and attitudes. Jarvis and Manny were very distant at first, trying hard to maintain a tough exterior. But along with tutoring came the constant talks of self-awareness and pride from Chaney, and Jarvis was slowly responding. In the first days, he'd charge through the doors, loaded down with resentment, overflowing with anger. He went from rolling his eyes to whistling and freestyling during the sessions, appearing to participate under duress. But now that he was seeing signs of improvement and starting to believe in himself, he put in more effort. He even started asking questions that Chaney and I almost fought over to answer. Manny followed behind whatever position Jarvis took, so it was clear that getting through to Jarvis would set the tone for both of them.

"Yeah, they're getting better, but they've got a long way to go. They're both still reading at only a sixth grade level," Chaney said with his arms spread across the counter.

"Yeah, but that's up a level, thanks to you," I said. I reached across the counter and patted Chaney's forearm.

A crooked smile slowly crept up his face to his eyes as he watched my hand. "Thanks to you, too," he said. "You know, we really work well together."

I paused to think. "Yeah, we do," I said with a reflective smile.

"Speaking of working well together, how are you and Russ doing?" Chaney tapped a cigarette out of a pack and lit it. I hated the feeling of secondhand smoke creeping down my throat, invading my lungs and taking them hostage. I coughed. He was conscious of my reaction, and blew his next puff of smoke behind him.

I squinted and cleared my throat. "Everything's going great. We're having a grand opening in a couple of weeks, Memorial Day weekend. I hope you can make it."

"I'd love to be there to see you open your business. You know that." He looked over my shoulder at the customers. "But I have to make sure I have good reliable coverage for the store . . ."

"Sure."

He sucked and puffed. "So I take it the partnership is working out?"

"It's working out great. I couldn't have asked for a better business partner."

"Oh yeah?" Chaney asked rather dismally.

"Well, other than you," I flirted.

"I wasn't fishing," Chaney said through a bashful smile.

"Look, Chaney, I know you're very protective of me and Vlora," I said, "but Russ really is a great partner. I honestly don't think I would be at the point of opening the store this month if it wasn't for him. He has a lot of knowledge in areas that I don't. I owe him a lot."

"Just make sure that you don't turn all your control over to him. Make sure you learn what he knows and you don't. Make sure everything's balanced."

"You don't believe the partnership is going to work out, do you?" I coughed, and Chaney moved his cigarette to waist level.

"I don't know, I can't explain it, Naj. But I just get a bad vibe from him."

"You've seen him only a few times. What has he done to make you feel negative vibes?"

"Nothing," Chaney said. "It's not what anyone does, just the energy they give off. I care about you. Just watch out, okay?"

"I will."

"The two of you must be getting closer on a personal level," Chaney stamped out his cigarette in an ashtray while focusing on me.

"No, we're not. I'm focusing all my energy on the business. That's it."

"That's a good thing," Chaney said with exasperation in his voice. He looked out the front window and across the street at Mooncents. The coffee shop was buzzing with activity.

"Is Mooncents affecting the business?"

Chaney nodded. "Starting to see a decline in my cash flow."

"They're a new business. A novelty right now. Everybody's just checking it out, but they'll be back over here. You've been a part of the community for years, and very supportive. Not just taking, but you give back, too. Look at what you're doing with Jarvis and Manny. You think the people over at Mooncents would do something like this?"

"They've got advertising, Naja. Big signs. Trendy, upscale appearance. People like to feel they're buying into something special. Something exclusive. You feel me?"

"Higher prices for the same coffee drinks," I added. "That's going to get old after a while."

"Same reason people live beyond their means. Their higher prices make people feel valuable. It's a sign of class and status." He blew a hard breath. "I've lowered my prices, run specials, offered giveaways. But nothing's working. I'm steadily losing business to them."

"Your customers will be back," I tried to reassure Chaney, but I wasn't sure myself. Mooncents did have some damn good triple caramel lattes; Allie had brought one to work the other day and I'd tasted it. I was starting to salivate just thinking about it, but I didn't need to add pounds of cellulite to my ass. A surge of guilt ran through me, and I hung my head.

Chaney gathered up the French fries and I grabbed the sodas and we went back over to the boys, who were now in discussion about the article they were reading on a hip-hop summit that had just taken place.

Russ blasted through the doors like a great gust of midwestern wind fresh off the banks of the Mississippi. In he strutted in a pair of baggy jeans and a Sixers throwback jersey. He headed toward us and the boys, tailed closely by a woman holding a microphone and a guy holding a camera that displayed "City 10" on the side.

He introduced us to the city cable station TV crew, and let us know that this was an impromptu TV interview. Russ had used his real estate connections to get us a spot for publicity for our grand opening, and consequentially, a full profile of himself had come out of it. He had already conducted a sit-down interview about his continued successes in property investments in Atlanta, his new joint business venture, and the grand opening of Exodusters 1879—complete with a tour of the café. Now he was to show his life as a role model and leader in the community through tutoring the youth.

Chaney shook his head in disgust and lit another cigarette. I was torn. We needed publicity, and this would definitely alert the community to our grand opening. But uneasiness settled in my mind. Russ had tutored the boys only once, for twenty minutes. I had long since wondered why he had volunteered in the first place.

"What's up, Black?" Russ said to Jarvis and Manny. He extended his hand to Jarvis. Manny caught on and followed suit when Russ extended his hand to him.

"What we got here?" Russ directed his question to the boys, but spoke to the camera with a broad grin. He pulled up a chair and placed it between Jarvis and Manny. The bright light from the camera hit their faces, and the boys instantly went into homeboy mode. They changed from normal to hard in two seconds flat, while their near-perfect postures turned into well-practiced sweet gangsta leans. They gave two pounds to the chest, then kissed their fingertips before flashing peace signs for the camera as they were introduced. They were styling and profiling for the audience.

Chaney fumed as the reporter, Laci Mays, began asking questions about Russ's history and commitment to community service, and praising him for molding today's youth for the future. Russ was lapping it all up like it was hot syrup on a buttered pancake with a side of ego, super-sized.

After fifteen minutes, the TV crew wrapped up. Laci said they had to get to a location clear across town, where the city's top official had been intoxicated and caught inhaling on his pregnant mistress's balcony—naked. They needed to hurry so they could make it the lead story for the ten o'clock news.

Russ escorted them to their van, then came back in with a dozen yellow roses and handed them to me. His grin was a mile long and deep.

"What's this for?"

"Just to celebrate," he said, holding up his hands. "Nothing more. This is going to be great publicity for us and for the opening."

Giddiness seeped in as I took the roses. He was a sweet guy. So thoughtful. I saw Chaney gasping behind Russ's shoulder. He was at the cash register, and he slammed the drawer shut and snatched the receipt from the register, but handed it to the customer with a smile.

"You know, Russ, your interview might be a little deceptive," I said.

"Deceptive? How so?" He looked perplexed.

"You really haven't spent much time tutoring Jarvis and Manny. It's been me and Chaney."

"I've been here," he flatly stated.

I tipped my head to the side as I spoke. "Yeah, you've been here, but all of your tutoring time added up is less than a couple of hours."

He knitted his brows as he adjusted his stance. "That's only because I've been taking care of business. Our business. Every time I'm here, I get a call and I have to leave. Look at where we are. Did you think that we would be opening up the store so fast? We got custom-built computers and leather chairs and couches. And now, we got free citywide publicity. Are you complaining?"

Two girls seated at a booth nearby quickly turned their attention to the agitation in Russ's voice. I retreated. "No, no, no. I'm not complaining. I just want to make sure that we're not trying to get publicity by pulling the wool over people's eyes, or that we're portraying ourselves to be something that we're not."

"I'm not doing that," Russ said intensely. "I'd love to spend more time tutoring the boys, as I promised. But I can't do both. As soon as we get the business running, I will be able to spend more time with them."

My response was stalled. "Okay," I said slowly.

"You know what I see?" The intensity in his voice was replaced by excitement. "I see us doing free tutoring for kids at the Internet café. Yeah. Free tutoring for low-income family kids. We do that, and we can get the attention of news crews, local radio and TV stations, and magazines, and . . ."

"See, that's it. I do stuff like this because it's in my heart, because I want to do it. Not because I can benefit from it, get publicity, and draw attention to myself or my business."

"Baby, we all volunteer for those reasons."

Did he just call me baby? I'm feeling like butta.

He continued, "But there's nothing wrong in letting others put the spotlight on you. Just accept it and shine."

Russ fidgeted as if he wanted to leave, but now, in light of what I had said, he didn't want to appear to rush away from the boys. Jarvis and Manny had been slapping high fives. They had been on their cell phones ever since the TV crew left, calling family and "dawgs" to tell them they were going to be on TV tonight, and to get the video recorders in place and set the TiVo (and that if they didn't have one, they knew where they could get one, but they didn't hear it from them). They were now local celebrities fully intent on extracting one hundred percent of their fifteen minutes of fame.

"I have to make a phone call to follow up on one of my properties in Atlanta, but I can do that later. I had an important meeting with Harold Angstrom. He's coming to the shop to install a security system. We got all that equipment in there, and we need top-of-the-line security. But if you want me to stay here and help you tutor the boys, I can do that. I'll just call Harold and see if I can meet with him another time." He pulled out his cell phone, flipped it open, and began to scroll through his directory, which was alphabetized by last name. "Whew, I just hope we can meet soon, because it took me damn near a month to finally get him out today. And it would be nice if we had security before the grand opening." He was still scrolling.

"Go meet with Harold."

"You sure?" he asked as he quickly flipped his cell phone closed and slid it into his pocket, before I could even give him an answer. "Because I don't have to go."

"We need security."

"All right. Since you said that then, I'll go ahead and meet with him." He slapped me on the shoulder and looked down at the flowers in my arms. He bent over and took a whiff so deep that I'm sure even his momma could smell it. "Mmmmm. Have Chaney fetch you some water for these. Okay?"

I whipped my head around to make sure Chaney didn't hear that comment.

Russ raised a fist to the boys as he left. They nodded and raised fists back at him. He had won them over. He was now "the man" in their world.

MY BED WAS COVERED with five different outfits. I needed to choose one for the grand opening and be there in less than three hours. My legs quivered with anxiety and I felt like they were going to give way at any moment as I absentmindedly walked from the closet to the bathroom and then to the bed-room. Couldn't remember what it was I was planning to do next.

I needed to be successful. I'd been living off my savings com-fortably, but that wouldn't last forever. I needed to start drawing a salary if I didn't want to go back to work for somebody else. I needed the Internet café to be successful, and today would be a good indicator.

My stomach turned as I stopped before the bed and placed one hand on my hip and the other on my neck as I tried to pick out the best outfit. I decided on the beige skirt and loosely fitting black blouse and called it a day. My hands trembled as I put on my clothes and my makeup. I had two hours before I was to meet Russ at the café.

"NAJA, I'D LIKE YOU to meet Wayland Bentley. Wayland, this is my sister, Naja Rodgers. She's the owner of this place, along with her partner over there, Russom King." Allie pointed out Russ and waved at him. He was in the corner of the café, talking to yet another one of his groupies. Since we'd started working together, various women had called Russ and tried to latch on to him. Several of them had come to the opening, and it was a spectacle to watch them compete for his attention.

"Pleased to meet you. This is a very unique business you have here. Very upscale. Exquisite," said the six-foot-tall, strikingly handsome man with the gentlest hands that I'd ever shaken. My sister stood next to him, glowing like a radioactive rock.

"Why, thank you very much, Wayland. I hope you'll come back even after this grand opening and patronize us."

"Most certainly," he said.

"I met Wayland a couple of weeks ago at First Fridays, and

we've been inseparable ever since," Allie giggled. "We've been to see a play at the Muny, a concert at the Roberts Orpheum Theatre, dinners, lunches, and a whole bunch of other stuff. Man! I feel like a tourist in my own town." She laughed a laugh that I had never heard before. In all the years I've known her, I'd never heard from her the kind of staccato, harmonic laugh that she just threw out. I stared at the spot where I knew an Adam's apple would have been and wondered. "Wayland owns two clubs, an upscale barber shop, and beauty salon," Allie added.

"Sounds nice," I said.

"Wayland, baby? Would you mind if I talked to my sister in private? I need to ask her about a personal matter."

"No problem. That'll give me a chance to look around and meet Russ." He shook my hand before he dismissed himself. Allie fanned herself and stared goggle-eyed at his backside as he walked away.

"What's up, sis?"

"I was wondering if you could give me an advance on next month's salary? We've been going out almost every night since we've met, and I owe the babysitter like a crap-load of money."

"Damn, Allie!" I fussed. "You really need to learn to manage your finances better. And leaving Andi with a babysitter that much? You're a parent. She's watching everything you do. You need to set a good example for your daughter."

"I do," she shot back. "And when you have kids, you can tell me how to raise mine." Then, like a quick shot of painkiller, she suddenly came to her senses as she stood there watching my blank stare, waiting for an answer to her begging. I said absolutely nothing as I stared a hole into her.

She eased the tightness in her forehead. "You took that the wrong way. What I mean is"—she pulled out the mop for the cleanup job—"Andi's almost in bed by the time we go out, and she's asleep when I get home. She's none the wiser, and what I do doesn't affect her at all."

"Kids are smarter than you think, Allie."

A bookish-looking young woman with black-rimmed glasses walked up to us and asked where the restroom was. I pointed her in the right direction.

"I'll be careful. I promise. Now, can I get an advance?"

"I'll give you an advance, but this is the last time. I mean it. I gave you a job, but it seems like you run out of money more now than when you were trying to stretch your child support. I don't understand why you don't finish your degree. You can double your earning power over what it is now."

"I'm going to finish school."

"You've been saying that for years. When?"

"Finishing school takes time. That's a whole year. Then who knows how long it will take to find a good job after I graduate? I'd have to quit working full-time, and that's a lot of time to go with little to no money. That's why I'm trying to find a man to help me out."

"You don't need a man. You can stand on your own two feet."

"I really don't want to get into this. That feminist stuff is fine for you. But since I have a daughter, I live in a world of reality. If I'm going to find a man, there's absolutely nothing wrong with trying to find Andi a father who is a man of means so we can have a financially secure life. I'm not trying to be superwoman, working myself to the bone to single-handedly provide for her, just to prove to others that I'm a strong baby momma and that I can do it alone."

"That's it, though. You're not doing it alone. You're doing it with me. And this is the last time—"

"Last time. Cool," she said quickly, as if to end my lecture. "I'm going to go catch up with Wayland. Love you." She gave me the usual tight squeeze and kissed me on the cheek while I sighed. I took in a deep breath and blew it out through my nose. Now was not the time to let Allie's actions mix with the anxiety of this night and cause me to stress out. A clammy feeling hit my face, and I excused myself to soak up the oil from my pores.

At some point, I knew Allie was going to ask me for money again. It was going to be time to exercise the tough love that I'd never been able to give her before. But I knew what would happen. She would try to use Andi as the sympathetic bait. I would just have to remember that Andi happened to have a father, who at least had the decency to faithfully pay non–court-ordered child support, even though he didn't see her much. And I had to admit that Andi didn't seem to want for anything. It was Allie who had the priority problem, but she didn't take it out on Andi.

People were starting to flow in. Colored balloons decorated the outside of the building, and signs announced to Mill Creek Valley that we had indeed arrived. The street parking spaces were now filled on the block, and people were still walking in from blocks away. When they did, they were engulfed by an atmosphere of intelligence and luxury.

Plush leather chairs and couches—flanked with flat-screen computer monitors and keyboards on swivel stands—rested on top of rug-covered hardwood floors that ushered them past the doorway. Soothing aromas from fragrant incense floated around the seating area. Today, we had the wall fireplace and the one in the center of the room burning to show how cozy it would be in the wintertime. The bar was open, where customers could order beverages, soups, salads, and sandwiches while they surfed the Internet and viewed it from the custom-built computer screens underneath the glass countertop. Jazz and neo-soul sounds rotated through the stereo system.

Future customers sipped on the complimentary wine and Imo's pizza from next door, while they tested out the couches and browsed through magazines or engaged in conversation. Others experimented with the computers and ordered from the bar to try on the place and get the full effect. Vlora worked the room, talking to people and getting their opinions. She would find my eyes to give me the thumbs-up after talking to very satisfied customers.

Russ came through. He was indeed able to attract the attention of the local media. I spent a lot of time posing for pictures and giving interviews. Jarvis and Manny came in and took advantage of the photo ops, as well. It made me smile.

In my mind, the grand opening was a success, and the cash registers agreed. The only thing that would have made it better was seeing Chaney's face in the place.

"LOOK AT THIS," Russ said. His chest stuck out proudly as he brought a stack of newspapers to the back office of the café and shoved the business section of the *Post-Dispatch* in front of my face. Big as day was a picture of me and Russ at the café's opening. The story was continued in a two-page layout in the center of the section. I opened my mouth and could do nothing but gasp.

I looked up in awe at him holding the remaining stack of local papers. The world's biggest grin was plastered all over his handsome face. His eyes beamed with achievement. "There's more where that came from," he said as he dropped the stack of papers on my desk. "That's right, baby. We're a hit. I did it. I did it." He closed his disfigured hand into a ball and shook it.

An overwhelming sensation of excitement took over me. We had done it! Our opening day attendance tripled our expectations; sales for that weekend were off the charts; and now, we had garnered the front-page attention of every single newspaper in the city.

I leaped out of my chair and vaulted onto Russ, wrapping my legs around his waist, pressing my breasts against his chest, and pushing my lips into the crook of his neck. I felt his strong hands under my butt as my thighs circumferenced him. I pressed harder into him, and we laughed and laughed together. Joyously and harmoniously.

I pulled my head back and held his beautiful face between the palms of my hands, and laughed as he spun me around and around. He planted a kiss on my lips. "Mmmuuuuaaaahhhh!" We twirled in vivacious circles as we continued to whoop and laugh.

I planted another kiss back. Just like he did.

But my lips got stuck.

I lingered on his lips as the energy electrified us. Ran through us. I couldn't back off.

I slid down his front and my arms stayed around his neck, pulling him into me. I kissed him. Tasted his lips. Tasted his tongue. Repeatedly. Urgently. We were entering into a different world. A new world where business mixed with pleasure.

My nerves jolted as I realized what I was doing and I pulled back quickly. I touched my lips with my fingertips as I stared at Russ.

"Don't stop now. Things are going so well." He reached for my waist. I stepped back another step.

"We can't do this."

"We were doing it just fine," he said with a smile. He moved toward me again.

I held out an open palm to his chest. "No, really. I'm sorry. I shouldn't have. We can't do this."

I walked behind my desk, pulled open the bottom drawer, and got my purse. "I'm going to step out for a minute," I said. I was frazzled.

"Naj—"

I cut him off. "I'm sorry. I'll be back later." I held my head down as I brushed past him and walked out of the office.

ELEVEN

"IT'LL JUST BREAK LITTLE ANDI'S HEART IF I HAVE TO pull her out of dance class," Allie said to me with doe-like eyes, her lower lip in her lap. She got up to pass Russ the printed reports he was waiting on. He took them from her and murmured a low "thank you" that he could have kept because she didn't notice it anyway.

We had reached the next step, where she was going to pull this shit on me again. I loved my little niece, bowlegs and all, and I'd do anything to ensure her happiness. Allie took notes on that and, as a last resort, would intentionally use her to get money out of me. Well, little sister was going to be in for a mighty big surprise now, because I wasn't having this. Not this time. She might as well scoop it back up and put it in a jar, because she wasn't about to get one damn dime from me.

"And they have a performance coming up next month. We just got her little outfit. Aw, you should see it, Naja. It is just too cute." She smiled, shaking her head reminiscently as if thinking fondly of the dead.

From the corner of my eye, I saw Russ's pupil ride the rim of his eyelid, as he peeped my reaction to Allie's words. He'd just hung up the phone from making travel arrangements for his periodic trip to Atlanta to address issues with his property investments there. He had witnessed this scene one too many times before. His opinion sat like a lump in his throat whenever I caved in. Ears perked, he went back to balancing the books and paying bills.

My fingers tapped away at my keyboard as I spoke to her at the desk across from me. "You haven't even paid me back from the last loan that I gave you. Plus, I just gave you an advance on your salary last month, and on top of that, you still asked for your salary on payday."

"Yeah, I know. You're right, you're right." She let out a sigh so heavy that I thought she might have deflated herself. The back office was filled with the sound of my fingernails dancing on my keyboard before Allie strategically decided to discuss her thoughts openly with the air. "I got to figure out how to tell her. Dang! And she's been working so hard. Watching music videos and try-ing to dance along. Learning her routine . . ."

Russ cleared his throat loudly as if to signal, "Bullshit!"

I continued typing my letter to a prospective employee, thinking that she'd soon shut up.

She went on. "And she just got that split down, too. Those little chubby legs." She chuckled with a bounce to her shoulders and followed it up with a long soft "Aaahh," placing her hand on her heart. "She's going to miss rehearsals with her friends: Deirdre, Connie, Lee Lee. That little Lee Lee was her best friend, too. Silly girls."

She slapped the top of her desk. "They would play dress up and get all in my makeup. I would try to be all mad, but I couldn't. I just look at them and burst out laughing. They're so cute together." She snatched a tissue out of the box on her desk, and put it up to her nose as she sniffled dry air. She put her right hand over her chest again while holding the tissue to her nose. "Her little heart's going to be crushed." She sniffled again.

"All right, already, damn!" I screamed at her. "I'll give you the damn money."

Russ stared at his computer and groaned.

"But this is it, Allie. I swear, this is really the last time. You've got to learn how to budget your money, prioritize, and make sacrifices." I snatched open the lower drawer to my desk and fished my checkbook from my purse.

I reasoned with myself that I was actually giving the money to Andi, and not Allie, and I was going to make sure of just that. "What's the name of the dance company?"

"Why?" Allie asked. She had already dropped the tissue and her nose was quite clear.

"Because that's who I'm making the check out to."

"You don't have to do that."

"What's the name of the dance company?"

"You don't trust me?"

"For the last time, what's the name of the dance company?"

"I don't know the exact—"

"Fine." I snapped closed my checkbook, threw it in my top drawer, and slammed it shut. The slamming of the drawer must have jogged her memory, because she quickly spit out the full name of the dance company and the amount due down to the penny. I wrote the check and handed it to her without looking at her.

"Thanks, sis. Andi will love you for this. I'll make sure to let her know that her favorite aunt paid for her dance classes."

Favorite aunt? How about only aunt?

Allie retrieved a cinnamon roll and a slice of bologna from a brown paper bag on her desk. She placed the bologna on top of the roll and began attacking it with her mouth.

"That's what we need," Russ said to me. "Lunch."

"You want some of this? I got more," Allie said as she opened the bag and held it out toward Russ.

Russ winced as I held back a laugh. "Noooo, thanks. I'm looking for something a little more . . ."

"Oh, you want more of a meal," Allie stated.

"Well, just something more edible."

She hunched her shoulders, pulled the bag back in, and laid it on the desk with the open end facing her. "Suit yourself. More for me."

Russ picked up his keys and we headed out to lunch. The car ride was quiet after Russ shared his opinion about giving Allie tough love. He said she was playing me like a fiddle. I knew it, but tough love was a lot easier said than done. After our mother died and Allie came to live with me, we had spent so many years in battle with each other. Enduring Armageddon would have been easier than going from a sister-sister relationship to sister-guardian, and we both had the internal scars to prove it. Things got better as we grew up and got closer. With those wounds now closed, I didn't want to risk opening them again. Those were years of sheer unmitigated hell for both of us.

After Russ finished talking, the space got quiet; an uncomfortable, tight kind of quiet.

We hadn't really spoken on a personal level since the kissing episode. I had felt torn as I went home that night, but by sunrise, I had managed to come to my senses. Leaving him there looking as succulent as ever hadn't been the easiest thing to do. But I had, and I was glad that I had because things could have been a whole lot uglier by now. I still didn't want to risk losing my business in the long run. Reminded myself the next morning that when I actually decided to look for a relationship, there were plenty of men in this city to choose from besides Russ.

My finger manically switched radio stations until I had gone through the dial three times. I went into a state of constant fidgeting, adjusting my seat and rolling the window up and down until I found the right height. By the time I was finally comfortable for the ride, we were parked.

"Okay, are you going to clue me in to what's wrong?" Russ asked after we were seated for lunch at Gary's Fine Dining. A small blues band played for the crowd, offering a midday oasis before their return to drudgery.

"I don't want it to seem like I'm leading you on or playing games or anything."

"You're telling me you don't want to take this to a personal level after we were all over each other the other night."

"I'm sorry. I just had a weak moment. I just lost my mind," I said. I threw my hands up and let them fall in my lap.

"Well, gee, thanks."

"I didn't mean it like that. It's not you. I'm very much attracted to you."

"If it matters at all, and somehow I think it doesn't, I think we should give it a try. I'm not going to sit here and lie to you and say everything's going to work out, because I don't know. I can't tell the future. But we're two mature adults, and I think we can handle being involved and working together."

"It's not just working together. If it was just the idea of seeing you all the time, then it would be a no-brainer."

We looked over the menus, and the waitress came and took our orders.

"Actually, a relationship between us would be special," Russ said.

I gazed at Russ with skeptical eyes.

"Really, no lie. Check this. We know each other better than people who've been dating for months."

"I'm listening."

He used his fingers to list his points. "We know each other's favorite music. You like neo-soul."

"And you like old-school jazz," I said playfully.

"Very good," he said and nodded. "We each know what the other is like when we get angry. You're one of those calm angry people. Gotta watch out for your type. You're the kind to keep it all in, then go set your man's house on fire."

We laughed. "Yeah, remember that," I said. "And I can always tell when you're angry. You fold your arms across your chest and your lower jaw twitches." I steadied my lower jaw, then demonstrated.

"I do not!" Russ exclaimed, smiling because he knew he was pegged.

"Yes, you do. Next time you get angry, run and check yourself out in a mirror."

"Moving on. Point three." He held up three fingers while I continued to chuckle. "We know all about each other's finances. We've read each other's credit reports."

"Yeah, I was impressed. The first black man I've met with good credit."

"See, now, there you go. You wrong for that," he said, teasing me with a pointed finger.

I continued to snicker. He was making me feel at ease. I rolled my kinki curls with my fingers. "No, no. I'm just kidding. You're the second."

"All right, Miss Smarty Pants. But what I'm saying is, we're already five steps ahead of other people who date. We already know more about each other's stuff than most people discover in years. If I was the type that would come between you and your business, you would have had an inkling of that by now."

I nodded.

"Hell, I know you were joking, but some people don't find out until after they get married how jacked up their spouse's credit is."

"Or when they decide to buy a house together."

"Exactly," Russ said.

The waitress brought our food. We laid our napkins in our laps and began to eat while Hot Johnny sang about how his woman left him high and dry.

"You're right." I held my fork over my plate and looked up at him. "But what if?" I asked.

"What if what?"

"Like you said, nothing's guaranteed. So what if it didn't work out? Things could be awkward. And"—I looked down at my plate—"I don't think I can run this without you. I wouldn't want to lose you."

Russ's face turned thoughtful. He swiped his mouth with his napkin. "Is that what this is really about? You think you'd lose me as a business partner?"

"That, too. It's possible."

"If it doesn't work out, it doesn't work out. And we go back to being friends and business partners. No hard feelings."

"We go from being lovers to being friends? Come on. Even without a business, do you think that's possible?"

"It may take some time, but yeah, I do think it's possible. With mature adults."

"It takes a lot of time. And with a business, we wouldn't have that time. So what would happen? The business would suffer somehow."

"Look, you seem to be forgetting something. I've got half of my money invested in this business, too. I wouldn't let a failed relationship empty my pockets. You're fine, but you ain't that fine," he said, smiling.

I huffed.

He finished, "If I messed it up, I'd be messing up my own money. I'm in the business of making money, not throwing it away."

I took a deep breath and chewed on his words.

"I'm trying to be a millionaire," he said as he reached across the table and grabbed my hand. "And I want you to be one with me. We could be a power couple."

"Russell Simmons and Kimora Lee?"

"Bigger."

My heart was telling me to go with it. It felt too good to be wrong.

"It makes no sense for two people to have such a strong vibe between them, to be so attracted to each other as we are, and to not pursue it because of fear of failure. Every relationship is a crapshoot. We have only one life to live, and we could be each other's soulmate. The least we can do is give it a chance and find out. Besides, it's typically women who do that revenge type stuff after a breakup because they get all emotional and shit."

Okay, great fucking way to convince me.

I patted his hand before I withdrew mine, and held back my approval with tight lips. I asked how we were looking on profits for the week, and Russ accepted my change of topic back to the business luncheon that it was. But not before telling me with his eyes that it wasn't over. We finished up our lunch and went back to work.

.   .   .

"I THINK I'M ON the same page with you now. You're doing the right thing," Vlora said to me behind dark sunglasses. The St. Louis sun bore down heavily on us as we sat rooftop poolside in the yellow lounge chairs at my downtown Paul Brown loft apartment building. Being miles away from coastal shores, we would periodically get together with Allie and create our own beach in the midwest. We'd take turns being the waitress and running two flights down to bring up fresh tropical drinks for one another.

Vlora picked up her cup of ice. "I understand what he's saying. I mean, yeah, you do know more about each other from the get-go than average couples. But now that I think about it, you're right, you could be fucking with your livelihood if you mess up and get with the wrong person. I see your point. Regular people can just screw each other over lightly and walk away. Call each other a bitch, key each other's cars, or maybe one will stalk the other for a week, and they're done with it. You'd have to try to work with someone who either broke up with you or whom you broke up with. You couldn't even change jobs or get a transfer to avoid him. And God help you if he brings drama to the job."

"Russ thinks it's only women who do that revenge stuff."

She shot me a look that said I must be deranged. "Girl, don't be stupid. Men can be just as vengeful with women when they get rejected and get their little feelings hurt." She uncrossed and recrossed her legs, a thin layer of stubble shading them. "Well, it's your life and your decision. But me myself personally, I wouldn't do it. Not with somebody I really don't know. Just don't say I didn't warn you."

Allie returned from my apartment with a round of Bahama Mamas. "Oh, Naj. I forgot to tell you. I really need the day off Monday." This time she didn't even bother to supply me with a reason.

"Like in hiring your sister," Vlora said.

"What?" asked Allie as she took a sip of her drink. "Mmmm . . . this is good." She smiled and sat back in the chair, forgetting about the comment or the necessity of providing me with an explanation for her absence on Monday.

RUSS AND I wrapped up the board meeting with our team in our conference room at the Internet café. We met with our systems administrator, Candis Cross. Candis was once a very close friend of mine. We grew up on the same block and went to the same grade school and high school together. I began to just keep in touch by phone periodically after she went to Boston for college. She would try to save my soul every time she came home. She had gotten religious on me, and God was speaking to her every chance He got. I got tired of her attempts to convert me, but she could whip the ass off a mainframe. So when we needed someone on the board with experience to man our systems, I knew she was the girl.

Also on the board and joining us were Russ's contacts: William Wilks, our attorney, and Hezekiah Reid, our accountant.

Things were looking good. Business was going great, and financially, we were sitting pretty. We decided to move forward with expanding to a second café. We had the meeting to get everybody on board. We spent hours going over the plan, the schedule, and any concerns that anyone had, which turned out to be numerous. But we got through them all, and some required going back to the drawing board. Russ and I were exhausted by the time everyone left.

"How about a drink before we call it a night?" Russ suggested after coming back from locking the front door.

"I'd really love to, but I'm exhausted."

"Actually, so am I. But I was looking for an excuse to keep you in my sight."

There was a brief knock on the door, and before either of us could answer, the door was slowly opened by a slender woman in a tight blouse and push-up bra and miniskirt, holding a brown paper bag. Her eyes lit up as she eyed Russ and overlooked me. "There you are," she said in a high-pitched squeak. "The lady up front told me I might find you here," she bubbled as her breasts brimmed over her scoop-neck top. She giggled.

"Heeeyyy, Dinky," Russ said as he got up to greet his friend. He hugged her around the waist as I stood there in my greenness. A sour taste developed on my tongue as I looked her up and down, from her long, lustrous snap-on ponytail to her six-inch, red stilettos. She was not his type, I decided.

"What you got good?" Russ asked, alluding to the brown paper bag that was now smelling up the room.

She let out an irritating giggle before she spoke. "You never have time to take me out, and you're always so busy with work, so I thought I'd make a little something and bring it over. A man's gotta eat. A little yummy for the tummy." She slid a Tupperware plate out of the bag and stuck her rear end out as far as it could go as she bent over and placed it on the table.

For some reason, my jaws tightened and my lips pursed in disgust. Women were always calling and looking for Russ for some reason or another, trying to get his attention, but rarely did any stop by. Russ was serious about his work, and hardly paid attention to the women who were practically throwing themselves at him. But that didn't keep them from trying. It just made them try all the harder.

"Lasagna?" He tilted his head and looked at her from the corner of his eyes. "You know that's my favorite." He gave her a cheesy smile. I wanted to throw up.

She giggled and dipped at the knees, "Uh-huh. I know." She giggled again.

If she giggled one more time, I was going to scream.

I cleared my throat for a good five seconds. They both looked at me as if they realized for the first time that I was in the room.

"Oh, Dinky, have you met my business partner, Naja?"

She giggled. I cringed. "No. Howdy-do." She shot a hand with three-inch fire-engine-red nails with diamonds at me. I shook her hand reluctantly.

"Dinky, is it?"

She gave a high-pitched "Uh-huh," and giggled again. My stomach curdled.

"You're one of the ones that calls all the time, looking for Russ?"

Her smile froze in place as her eyes went to Russ. "I guess so," she said slowly. Then she perked back up again.

Russ glared at me.

"And you're the one who works at the pet store?"

Her smile dropped and her giggle faded. "No. I'm in cosmetology school." She turned a questioning face to Russ for an explanation.

Russ shot a cold look at me.

"Oh, sorry. My bad." I bounced the palm of my hand off my forehead. "It's hard to keep track. Say, you don't have enough lasagna for me, do you?"

I went over to the table, where she had taken the lid off the plate. Steam was rising from the lasagna. I picked up the fork she had laid out and dug right in. I smacked as I chewed. "Mmm . . . this is good."

Russ looked bewildered. "We work so much together that we share everything," he explained to Dinky with an unsteady voice.

Dinky didn't seem to be paying attention to me. She wanted an answer to the question of who else was calling him. Apparently, she thought she was the only one. She scratched her head as I continued to eat, staring at Russ.

"Well!" Russ slapped his palms together and rubbed them as if he were trying to get toasty. He grabbed Dinky by the waist and began escorting her to the door. "Tell you what, I'll call you later. As soon as I can. We're finishing up a business meeting here, and, well, I'll get back to you. I promise."

She squeaked, "But who is—"

"I'll call you and we'll have more time to talk."

I took another bite, licked the fork, and broke off a piece of Italian bread as I watched. "See you, Dinky," I said and waved to her back.

She whined, "Are you seeing other—"

"Thanks for dinner. I really appreciate it. I'll call you later." He pushed her through the door and closed it behind him.

He sighed and turned to me. "That was just plain evil."

"Dinky? Yes, that's the perfect name for her. Dinky," I said as I took another mouthful of lasagna.

Russ stood firm and stared at me for a few seconds before he erupted in laughter. "You are so bad!"

I laughed, too. "She is so not your type. She's an airhead. I can't even see it."

He walked toward me and took the fork from my hand.
"Like she said, a man's gotta eat." He ate a forkful of lasagna.
Then he slowly picked up another forkful and fed me while gaz-
ing into my eyes.

"What do you see in Dinky?"

"Food," he said. "Anyway, it seems as if I can't get the one I
really want." He fed me another bite of Dinky's good-ass lasagna.
Dinky might have been ditzy, but she could cook the hell out of
some lasagna.

Holding on was mission impossible; jealousy was making me
crumble, and my guard was falling. He did have just as much to
lose as I did. Other people had relationships while sharing a
business, and it worked out. Maybe I was being too shortsighted.
Focusing on the negative. Maybe I just needed to loosen up a little and let go. Let things happen.

"If we did get personal, we'd have to have ground rules," I said.

"What exactly are you saying?" he asked slowly. His lips attempted a smile, but failed.

"I'm saying that if we were to date each other while being
business partners, we'd have to establish some ground rules, like
no bringing personal disagreements that have nothing to do with
the business to work."

He dabbed the corners of my mouth with Dinky's napkin,
moved closer to me, and thoughtfully nodded his head. "Uh-
huh, okay. That's good. And how about this: No hanky-panky in
the office?" He took little steps toward me, as if he were sneaking
up on a prowler.

"That would work." I pushed back the plate of lasagna. "And
we'd have to keep our relationship out of the mouths of our
board members and employees."

I stood up. Russ moved closer still. "You mean you would

want to keep us a secret?" His mouth went from neutral to smile in slow motion.

"Not a secret, but if we were to do this, we shouldn't wear our relationship on our sleeves. Like calling each other 'baby' at work or affectionately touching each other."

He was on me now. "Wouldn't that fall under the 'no hanky-panky' rule?" He brought his face close to mine.

"It could, but not really. It's a more subtle form of hanky-panky."

"So, what else couldn't we do?" he asked me. His breath grazed my lips. The tip of his nose touched mine.

"This," I said as I kissed his lips. Russ slid his hand around my waist and pulled me tighter. He hungrily went back at me. I sucked his lip. He explored mine.

I whispered, "You know, Vlora agrees with me that I shouldn't do this."

"What does she know?" he murmured, kissing my neck. "I think you need to watch out for her anyway. Success can make friends jealous. You might want to back away from her."

I pulled back. "Why would Vlora be jealous of me? She has her own successful business."

He grabbed me tighter and resumed working my neck. "Unh-unh. The last thing we're going to do is talk about that darn Ms. Dern." He ran his tongue over my collarbone.

"That's quite all right by me." I tilted my head back to allow him better access.

"It doesn't bother you that we're breaking rules one, two, and three right now?" he asked between kisses as I untied his tie.

"I'm going to review the list of things not to do for you, so you'll have a clear picture." I unbuttoned his shirt. He unzipped my skirt and it fell to the floor. I fiddled with his belt buckle and slid my hand inside his pants. I found him and began to stroke, while his tongue danced circles on my neck.

We gingerly lowered our naked selves to the soft rug, and Russ went over every bit of me with his hot tongue. My body quivered underneath his. I gasped as he entered me and settled in my mind, took over my heart, and took charge of my every inch. He coursed through my veins, delivering himself to every part of me. He rolled like thunder between my thighs, sending rhythmic vibrations through my body that curled my toes and arched my back as we climaxed together.

Sweat layering our bodies, we slowly came back down, hand in hand. Lips to lips and tongue to tongue. Sharing our breaths.

"Okay, none of the previous will be allowed," I finally said as I lay exhausted on the floor.

Russ hovered over me. Kissed my eyes, then my lips. He stroked my cheeks with the backs of his fingers. "What's that? Can you show me again?"

TWELVE

SINCE GETTING TOGETHER WITH RUSS, HIS ACTS OF kindness became more romantic. The day spa passes became personal oiled massages, sometimes with fruit, sweet sauces, and whipped cream. Lunches and dinners turned into romantic and spontaneous park or living room picnics, or spur-of-the-moment barbecues on his patio. He'd even taken me on one of his business trips back home to Atlanta and set aside enough time to make a romantic mini-vacation out of it for us.

And so came the frequent delivery of cards and flowers, and hidden wrapped jewelry boxes in spots where he knew I would find them. Outfits that I had casually talked about getting would magically appear on my side of his closet, or would be delivered to my home with a card with no name attached. He got me to the point where my heart would beat in rapid excitement at the sight of a FedEx or UPS truck. He always kept me guessing. I loved that about him.

THE ROSEBUD CAFÉ was unusually empty, except for a couple of people on the bar side and kids playing video games. Around this time, Black Hole Incident usually performed and there would be a gregarious after-work crowd, whooping it up, drinking, and socializing on the bar side. Instead, the last song had just played on the jukebox and a short, portly woman with golden hair waddled over to select additional songs to keep a spirit floating in the room.

Chaney leaned his broad back on his chair and peered out the window, watching the fervent crowd at Mooncents. Umbrellaed café tables and chairs lined the front of the store, and the patio area was nearly full with tank-top-wearing customers sporting summer shades, sipping on drinks, and snacking on desserts.

"Things not going well?" I asked Chaney as I walked toward him. I took a seat at the table and his eyes remained glued on Mooncents.

"Bad. Pretty bad," he said, worriedly. "This keeps up, they're going to run me out of business." His shoulders slumped. He pulled out a half-empty pack of cigarettes and started to tap out one, but decided against it and put the pack back in his pocket.

"Well, all the kids still come here," I said, trying to find a bright spot.

"The kids don't keep the store open though. They're school kids. They don't have any money. I give more away free to them than they pay for."

I was at a loss for words to comfort Chaney and keep him from feeling dismal. Business was booming for Mooncents and here Chaney was, a pillar of the community, starting to drown in his own kindness.

He rotated his head away from the window, faced me, and banged his hands on the table. "But enough about Mooncents already. How's the business working out with you and whassisname?"

I smirked at Chaney. "You know his name."

He bent his neck from side to side to pop it, then laced his fingers together and stretched his arms before him. "You know who I'm talking about," he said. "So how are things going?"

"The business is going really well. We're looking into expanding," I said. A sudden stroke of guilt came upon me, and I stopped my words short.

Chaney sensed my hesitation to share my good fortune. "You don't have to hold back on your success. I'm glad to hear it. I don't have that crab-in-a-barrel mentality. If you're starting to make your way out, you'd best believe I'm going to be under you pushing you up. Feel me?"

"Thanks, Chaney."

"So you don't need for me to straighten your partner out for you? I can jack him up if you ever need me to, now."

I chuckled at his swift uppercut move. "Things are great."

"All jokes aside, I hope you'll let me know if things ever start to get out of hand. I just don't feel all good about that character. Especially after the TV self-promotion thing with the kids and frontin' for the camera. I've seen his type before, and—"

"Chaney, we're . . . um . . . we're kinda dating now." I don't know why it was hard for me to tell him that, but for some reason, it felt uneasy as hell.

Chaney's entire body froze. It looked like he'd just been told that his wife had died all over again.

This was more than a friend being upset. It wasn't even upset. I sensed his compassion for me. It leaped from his soul, and a helpless gaze settled in his pupils. Like I had just condemned myself to hell, and there was nothing he could do to get his friend on the right path to heaven. My reflection in his eyes revealed a dead woman walking.

"It's not the end of the world, Chaney. Really," I said. His reaction was freaking me out.

He shook his head as if to shake himself out of the trance he was in, and to put his best face forward. "I feel you, Naj. I mean, if that's what you want. That's good," he said unconvincingly.

"You still look like you've got something to say."

"No," he said. "If that's your man, that's your man. And I'm not going to say anything bad about him, unless I got proof." He paused, and I could see that he was grinding his teeth in his mouth. "You happy?" he asked me.

"I'm very happy. We connect, you know? I fought it for the longest. But I had to admit to myself that I could be passing up a good thing just because of this rule I've created for myself. We could be soul mates."

"I'm happy for you. Really I am." He moved his chair around next to me and planted a kiss on my forehead before hugging me. "But if you ever need someone to give him the one-two punch, you know where I am."

"Chaney!"

"I'm just saying."

RUSS AND I put in more long hours to line up our potential investors and a presentation to woo them over. We both attended First Fridays, and any other networking event that we could find to exchange services and ideas with others and to make connections. Russ was a genius at it. He took the lead in this, and soon, in other areas that were his strength.

Gradually, Russ became the spokesperson for Exodusters 1879 and, at the time, I thought nothing of it. I focused my energies on other parts of the company, to balance everything out. I immersed myself in researching geographic and economic demographics of various neighborhoods so we could determine the best location for the next store. Used my expertise to put together powerful presentations that would knock the socks off our potential investors and have them begging us to take their money. The truth was, Russ wasn't very thorough at fact-finding and presentations, so together, we became the entire package. We became a force to be reckoned with.

"Come on in," Russ said as he took my hand and guided me into his spacious candlelit dining room. It was Saturday evening, and we had plans to "do something spontaneous," he'd said. Which with Russ could mean anything under the sun.

The dining room table was elegantly set for two with fine tableware. A bottle of champagne chilled on ice, while soft jazz bounced off the walls of the room. The windows were open, and a soft summer breeze blew across the sheer white drapes and caused them to perform an easy ballet.

My eyes danced. "To what do I owe all this?"

"We are celebrating tonight," he said as he guided me with a gentle hand to the table. He pulled the chair out for me and allowed me to sit down, then helped me to move closer to the table. He took the cloth napkin off the table and snapped it open before laying it across my lap. I giggled with delight as he took his seat across the table and stared at me with his chin propped up on his knuckles.

We sat before empty plates and waited. Exchanging smiles while listening to the music, aromas from the kitchen seeped through the doorway and made my stomach grumble.

Russ didn't make a move to get the food, so I wondered if he was expecting me to. "Okay," I finally said when nothing was happening. "Who's going to serve us?"

"Serve us?" Russ faked a dumbfounded look. He nearly crossed his eyes and looked playfully disoriented. "Oh! Serve us." He clapped his hands twice and a thin, lanky gentleman dressed in a black suit with a white cloth draped over his right arm came from the kitchen bearing salads.

I laughed. "You are too much, Mr. King."

The server placed the greens before us, then filled our glasses with champagne before retiring to the kitchen.

"Again, exactly what is it that we are celebrating?"

Russ grabbed his champagne glass and beckoned me to do the same. "Here's to the grand opening of Exodusters 1879 II." He clinked my glass and took a sip.

I took a small sip, then licked the confusion off my lips. "What do you mean, grand opening? We're still working on investors. Right? We haven't even made the presentation."

"Well, babe, that's it," he started. Enthusiasm spread through him as he gestured. "I got three investors to sign on, and everything's a go. We signed papers yesterday. You need to sign as well." Pride twinkled in his eyes as he took another sip.

"But I still have the presentations. What information did you give them?"

My temperature was starting to rise. I had been all over town to bookstores and libraries, and had spent long hours scouring the Internet for information for our presentation, which took several weeks to put together. I'd even spent numerous hours buying materials and creating letterhead to make professional-looking folders so that they could take the information with them to go over later. I had wanted us to look as authentic as possible. And now he was telling me that they discussed God knows what and worked things out on a napkin in a bar?

"Baby, these are either men that I know directly or through somebody, so we didn't need that formal presentation routine. We just get together over a beer or golf and hash things out. Men don't need those colorful presentations and cute little folders to cut deals." He chuckled at something that he thought was funny, but there wasn't a damn thing funny to me.

The space between my shoulder blades filled with tightness. My face tingled with heat that rose to my scalp and caused my hair follicles to singe. I put my glass down. "What do you mean? When did this happen? Why was I not a part of this meeting?"

"Calm down, baby, calm down. Like I said, these were spur-of-the-moment meetings that just came about. You know, getting together with the guys at the sports bar, and at, uh, other places."

"What other places?"

He'd stopped abruptly, which meant that he didn't want to say where else they'd met—which could only mean one thing.

"As in"—I made air quotations—"'women not allowed' places? As in gentlemen's clubs other places?"

"Babe, relax. You're getting all worked up over nothing. That's how a lot of deals are done these days. Nobody makes deals in conference rooms anymore. They're done over a beer and nuts."

"And dollars and G-strings? Tits and ass?"

"Don't get bent out of shape." He put his glass down and dragged his hand down his face. "It's a man's type of thing. Don't worry. You and I can now find the location, and you can do all the interior stuff. Get some plants, put some trinkets here and there."

I couldn't believe how straight a face he was keeping, as if he weren't saying anything wrong, and as if it was a shame if I was going to have to fuck him up.

"I can *decorate*?"

He caught my drift. "Babe. You're looking at this all wrong."

I leaned forward, looked him sternly in the eye, and bounced my index finger into the table with each word. "Look, fifty percent of this business is mine. I expect to be at any and all meetings we have with potential investors, board members, contractors, employees, or whatever. We should present a united front. I expect us to make agreements together. I should know about all business dealings *before* they are final."

"Everybody's aware that this business is a partnership and that you're the other partner, Naj."

"It's not enough for them to be aware, I need to be present. People need to respect me as much as they respect you."

Russ hesitated as if to proceed with caution, as he damn well should. He clucked his tongue and looked off to the side. "As partners, we play off each other. You're strong in some areas, I'm strong in others. You're weak in some areas, I'm weak in others. Our skills complement each other."

"Are you saying that I'm weak in proving a case or persuading investors?"

"No, that's not what I'm saying."

"So what are you saying, Russ?" I folded my arms over my breasts and crossed my legs.

He swiped his face again.

"Spit it out," I said.

"All right. What I'm saying is that I think it's better for men to negotiate the deals, especially with other men. I think you should let me do the negotiating as the man, and you should be the silent partner. In these instances."

I couldn't believe what I was hearing. I was sure that my mother was rolling over in her grave, but not before telling me to insert a foot up his ass.

"What are you thinking?" Russ asked. Minutes had passed, and I had said not a word.

"I'm thinking you're out of your fucking mind." I picked my napkin up off my lap and flopped it on the table. "I can't believe that you just sat there and said that to my face. What kind of

1950s, June Cleaver, backward-ass shit is that? I'm more than capable of negotiating with men and handling myself."

He rolled his eyes and sighed. "Naj, I'm not speaking of this in a sexist kind of way. I'm talking reality." He submerged deep in his thoughts, then resurfaced. "Look at it this way. You're capable of walking into any car dealership and buying a car, right? And negotiating on the price. Fine. But since I'm a man, no matter what, my chances of negotiating a better deal are statistically greater. I'm not saying it's fair, I'm not saying I agree with it, I'm just saying that's just the way things are. I don't make the rules."

In a quick second, my mind flashed back to my early days. Days when my mother would tuck me in and sit by my bedside and read me bedtime stories. But instead of Goldilocks or Cinderella or Little Red Riding Hood, she would read from her favorite books, one of which was *The Female Eunuch*. Russ's sexist words evoked a sudden clashing in my gut that twisted, sloshed, and turned within.

"So I should be the silent partner?"

He grimaced. "You're making this personal when it's not."

"It *is* personal."

Russ searched the air for a valid point and gambled on the next play. "There are decisions you've made in the business that I disagree with, but I don't take it personally. Never even said anything about it. Just went along with the program."

"Like what, for example?" I put my hands on my hips as I continued to sit. Our waiter peeped through the door to see if we were finished with the salads that we hadn't yet begun. He popped his head back in the kitchen after being slapped in the face with tension.

"Remember, you started this," he warned me with a wagging finger. He cleared his throat. "For example, the administrative assistant position that your sister is filling. For us, for our type of business, that position isn't really needed. We both can do what she does ourselves. You created the job without consulting me. You hired her without consulting me. Half of her salary comes out of my pocket."

"My sister needs a job."

"Cool. Then let her go find one."

"Are you suggesting that I fire my sister?"

"I'm not suggesting anything. I'm just proving my point. Which was that there are some things you do in our business that I disagree with, but that I don't whine about. We're a startup. We could use every dime we have toward the business, especially since we're expanding so soon. We could use that thirty thousand a year—which, by the way, is extremely generous for what she does—for the new café. We've agreed on every employee and contractor we work with, except your sister and that position.

"I'm not going to discuss eliminating that unneeded position, but I'm not going to lie about how I feel, either. I like Allie, but I do think you should make her get a real job instead of continuing to bankroll her."

I folded my arms across my chest and tapped my fingers on my arms. My foot tapped against the carpet as hot breath lifted and collapsed my chest.

Russ's eyes drooped. "This was supposed to be a celebration." His cheeks dipped a mile long off his face.

"I don't know how you expected me to be happy about you telling me to be seen and not heard, stay in my womanly place, and to fire my sister. Yiiipppppeeee!" I twirled a finger in the air before dropping my phony smile. "I'm not firing my sister."

"I'm not asking you to. Again, you're missing the point."

Our words hung high in the dry air.

"Okay, this has gotten out of hand," he said, standing.

"You think?"

Russ conceded as he positioned himself by my side. "Even though I don't mean it that way, I can see how it looks like a sexist move. But baby, I'm just trying to do what's best for our business. Really, I am."

I stood up to face him. "I know you are. But this is *our* business, we're equal partners, and I expect to know everything that's going on, be aware of every detail, meeting, and agreement," I scolded.

Russ nodded. "I understand how you feel."

"And you know what?" I asked. "There may be times when either one of us may say, 'Hey, you should handle that,'" but we decide that together. Can you do that?"

He encircled me with his arms. "Yeah. I think I can do that."

We hugged and made up. He caressed my back and I caressed his.

Russ drew back and asked, "Have I been a good business partner? In making decisions and growing the business? Do you trust my decisions?"

"Yes, I do. The reason we're where we are today is because of you. I know that, and I'm not complaining about that. I just expect to be treated like an equal partner."

"That's what I like to hear. How about a new toast then?" Russ said and grabbed our glasses off the table. "Here's to an *equal* partnership. From now on, we'll make all decisions together." He flashed a toothy smile.

I slowly turned my angry look into a smile. I couldn't be mad with Russ because I really did know that he meant well. Nobody's perfect.

I clinked his glass and took a sip of champagne. Russ grabbed me for a dance and we kept drinking. By the second glass of champagne, we had completely made up. Even so, I couldn't help but feel that a small seed had been planted. We danced, but all of me didn't flow. Still, we managed to share laughs through dinner, and made love for dessert.

VLORA CAUGHT THE tutoring spirit and joined us for a session with the boys. After about fifteen minutes, she felt at ease with Jarvis and Manny. She said that being around them reminded her of her childhood. She was the only girl in her family and had three brothers, who had first planted a chip on her shoulder. She had been a tomboy and had spent very little time around girls, until our friendship in college.

Russ was busy in a meeting without me, to which I had given my blessing because we had agreed on the details and there was no need for both of us to be there. Chaney was outside the shop giving out flyers of café coupons to passersby.

The tutoring session with the boys ended for the day, and Vlora and I decided to hang around a bit for a drink. We went to the bar and practically had our choice of any seat in the room. The bartender looked extremely happy to see us.

I told Vlora about Russ's surprise dinner and how the whole thing went down. She was unusually quiet through my entire spiel. She gave only an occasional nod as she looked down into her drink, as if she'd lost her courage and was desperately trying to find it.

"What's wrong?" I stirred my drink with the tiny straw.

"What makes you think something is wrong?"

"I don't know. Maybe because you're not responding?"

"Don't want to overstep my bounds."

Vlora saying she didn't want to overstep her bounds meant that she was really about to let me have it, and that I wasn't going to like whatever it was she had to say.

She proceeded without caution. "I think you're giving him too much control. You're not you anymore. You used to be a take-charge, no-nonsense type of person, and it's like you're taking a backseat to him. In the business, and in your personal life."

I grappled with her words. It wasn't what I expected to hear.

"I didn't know you felt that way." I went into my mind and tried to prove her words right. Or wrong.

"I wasn't going to say anything. But then I thought, I'm your friend. And that's what friends are supposed to do."

"What? Rain on your parade?" I asked sarcastically.

"Never mind. Forget I said anything."

"Maybe you haven't said enough because I don't quite understand you. The business is going great. Our relationship is great."

"I know it is. I just think you're losing yourself in Russ and your success."

"How so?"

"Where's Russ right now? You said he's handling a meeting with investors. It's your business, too. Why aren't you there?"

"I told him to proceed without me."

"Yeah. You do that a lot. He makes all the power moves while you stand in his shadow."

"I know you said you were against me getting into a relationship with him . . ."

"And so were you at first. As a matter of fact, I came around to *your* way of thinking. So don't try to make me the heavy on that one."

"Yeah, I admit that. But I'm just trying to figure out where all this is coming from all of a sudden. You never said any of this before."

Bile filled my stomach. What I needed right now was the comfort and assurance of a friend. A shoulder to cry on. A girl-friend to listen to me bitch and moan. Not fault and blame. My resentment turned upon Vlora.

"I was holding back," she said.

"Why are you letting it all out now? Are you jealous?"

Vlora looked like she had stopped breathing. She set her drink down firmly on the counter. "No. You. Didn't. Just go there."

"No, *you* did," I snapped. "You know, Russ said that about you. At first, I thought he was off the mark, but now I'm not so sure."

We were silent and Vlora's nostrils flared. Guilt was already creeping up on me, but pride kept me from correcting myself.

"I've been your best friend for years. I've encouraged—no, pushed—you to start your own business. I initially supported Russ as your partner. I helped you in any way I could. I'm *here*. I'm helping you tutor Jarvis and Manny. Why would I be jealous?"

I was unmoved, but in the back of my mind, I realized that I didn't know why I was arguing with Vlora. Yet for some reason, I couldn't stop the nonsense. My ego kept it going. "Momma al-ways said that a lot of times your enemy will be smiling in your face while they're stabbing you in the back." I looked deep into her eyes. My momma never said it, but I was sure that somebody else's momma probably did.

Vlora shook her head as she fumed. "I don't believe this." She snatched up her purse and stormed out without a backward glance.

I'd succeeded. But why I was glad about that, I didn't know.

I didn't understand. In an instant, a storm had come over me. Made my heart heavy and drenched my soul. Something had taken over me—something ugly.

I paid the drink tab and passed Chaney as I headed to the door to leave.

"You storming out, too? What happened in there? Vlora just blew by me in a rage. Muttering something about someone being knocked the fuck stupid by love. I didn't get it. Did somebody try to hit on her or something?"

"Never mind her. The woman's got issues" was all I said as I left. I was still being stubborn.

I headed over to the office to see if I could catch the last of the meeting with Russ and our investor.

THIRTEEN

RUSS FINALLY FOUND THE TIME TO HELP OUT WITH
tutoring Jarvis and Manny like he had promised five
months ago. True, as Chaney pointed out, Russ came
after the major overhaul had been done. But my thought
was that at least he kept his word and came. Better late
than never, as they say.

The boys were actually enjoying their tutoring sessions at the café. It was now the middle of summer, and
they still wanted to come. Over time, they began to chill
out and formed a liking for Chaney, and for the fact that
he believed in them and didn't put them down or talk
down to them. Chaney tried to get them to value themselves. To see who they were inside, and to realize that
they had the power within themselves to do anything they
wanted to do. Only he never made his lectures seem like
lectures. He broke it down for them in that hip-hop lingo
and brought it out as good lookin' out from one dawg to
another. It always ended in a brotherly handshake.

So now with tutoring added in, Russ and I were in
each other's faces almost twenty-four hours a day. Since
our blowup about decisions, Russ had bent over backward
to make sure that I was aware of every minute detail, and
he included me in all business meetings and discussions.
In other words, he did what his ass should have been doing in the first place.

Russ had turned on the charm full blast. But as much

as Russ tried, nothing could prevent me from becoming stressed out. He seemed to thrive in the midst of pressure. It wore me down, and as we trudged through the fire, I leaned on him more. And he was always there for me.

Four board members and three full-time and four part-time employees later, Russ and I were working our butts off even more. Seemed like we were forever in meetings for status updates, to determine and execute the next steps toward opening the second café; employee concerns and issues; contract negotiations; and agreements with contractors and our attorneys. It went on and on, nonstop. My previous guaranteed eight hours a day in corporate America on somebody else's time had turned into ten-, twelve-, and even sixteen-hour days, working for myself.

I thanked my lucky stars that I had Russ there with me to get through it all. My mind was overloaded and exhausted, but he knew exactly how each muscle and bone in my body felt and how to make it feel better. He took time to make sure that I was loved and treasured. Long stressful days at the café would end in soothing nights in his strong arms at his house. Even though I had my own place, I was practically living at his by the end of summer. And by summer's end, I had leaned on him so much that I was totally and blissfully in love.

RUSS AND I continued to go to the First Fridays events to network. We weren't going to open the next Internet café until April of next year. Despite how well things were going, we decided to wait a year from the first opening so that we could make sure our first location was stable. But in the meantime, we wanted to continue to network and get to know other entrepreneurs.

It was the First Fridays event to end the summer, the beginning of the Labor Day weekend. Allie had gotten a babysitter and was going roller-skating instead with an Ira that I'd never met before. She picked him up after Wayland filed for bankruptcy and lost his clubs. And this would be my first First Fridays without Vlora, whom I hadn't talked to since her little fault-finding stint. So I knew the night wouldn't be the same as in the past. Not without my girls.

I hadn't called Vlora in over two months, and she hadn't called me either. It was hard for me to admit that I missed her. Pride kept me from being the one to go groveling to her and apologizing. But I was a big person. Because if she would just call me, I wouldn't even bring up the past. I'd forget about everything and let bygones be bygones. But I couldn't do that, because she hadn't called me yet.

Russ thought I did the right thing after I told him what happened between me and Vlora and what she said. He liked Vlora, he said, but he didn't like how deceptive she was to me, especially with her being my supposed best friend and all.

Russ's brick house in Clayton had "interior decorator" written all over it and not a stitch out of place. He displayed art by artists he didn't know and whose names he couldn't pronounce, but whose pictures gave the illusion of status, power, and class. His office, bedroom, and dining room were embossed with an assortment of trophies, employee awards, and every certificate imaginable from completion of a computer class to CPR certification to degrees. It took a while for me to feel comfortable there. His place gave me the feeling of being in the waiting room of a new and unfamiliar OB/GYN and awaiting a thorough probe job. The air seemed thick, stuffy, and hard to breathe, and it just seemed like the world would come crashing down should

I accidentally bump into something or move something out of place by two centimeters or more. It took a couple of months before I eventually got comfortable.

"Are you wearing that?" Russ asked with a scrunched-up face as his eyes were glued on my outfit.

"What, you don't like this?" I looked down to observe any wrinkles in my dress, or perhaps a dropped hem.

"No, no. It's not that I don't like it." He paused and looked me up and down thoughtfully. He paced in front of me while studying my body, like he was about to design a divine creation, which I knew was not the case because Russ just didn't possess a talent like that. "I think you should wear that black suit. You know, the one with the broad lapels. And wear your white shirt under it."

"That's so stuffy-looking," I said, instantly thinking of Vlora. She liked that suit as well, for work but not for First Fridays.

"It's more professional-looking. I find that so sexy." He added that last line as an afterthought. Like it was going to sweeten the deal and make me go for it.

I paused as if I were considering it, but I really wasn't. "Thanks, baby. Maybe next time. I think I'll just keep on what I have on tonight." I turned my face to the mirror to add moisturizer to my hair.

Russ's next words were stifled. He just stood in the doorway with a blank face as I worked moisturizer into my dark kinki curls. He backed out of the room and walked away, and I could hear scuffling and hangers being dragged across the bar in the closet in the other room. I assumed he was getting ready himself. Yet five minutes later, he came back with said black suit and white blouse in hand, with an extra layer of determination over him.

"I really think this would be better. Why don't you wear this tonight? Please?" He had an overly exaggerated puppy-dog expression in his eyes.

I chuckled at his cuteness as he gave a few quick blinks. "What difference does it make? Why are you so concerned about what I wear?"

"I just think you should look more professional. More business-like."

"This is not really a work-related function, and there's nothing unprofessional about what I'm wearing now. This would be considered business casual. It's perfect for First Fridays because I can look professional and still be loose enough to party later. Besides, it's too hot for that suit. It's bad enough that I have to blot my face almost every hour as it is."

"You can take the jacket off when you get inside," he persisted as he twirled the suit by the hanger.

He was starting to irritate me.

"Really, I'm capable of picking out what I want to wear. Been doing it for years."

He came closer and put an arm around my waist and placed quick soft kisses on my lips. "You trust my judgment, don't you?"

"Of course I do. This has nothing to do with your judgment."

"Didn't I get the investors that we needed to expand?"

"Yes." I pulled away from him and went back to the mirror to put on my face.

He stood next to me and looked at my eyes in the mirror. "Don't I do a great job at negotiating and getting us what we need? At a price we can afford?"

"Yes and yes. You do a wonderful job. We wouldn't be where we are today if it weren't for you." A mild pain began to settle behind my eyes.

"Then trust my judgment now. I want you to wear this instead of what you have on now. It would be better for you. For us."

I sighed heavily and swallowed the lump in my throat. "Russ, baby, with all due respect, I just don't want to wear that outfit tonight. I'm wearing what I have on, and that's that."

Russ's hand lowered as he held the suit. He looked as if he were quickly trying to figure out what angle to try next. "Babe, you look so beautiful in this suit. I like the way it fits you. The way it hits your curves. So sexy."

"I'll wear it another time. I've already got this dress on," I said without even absorbing his words. I lowered my head and pinched the bridge of my nose to try to ward off the growing pain. I widened my eyes and shook my head out.

"Yeah, but—"

"All right already!" I snapped. My face throbbed. I snatched the suit out of his hand and snarled, "I'll wear the damn suit!"

Russ wasn't at all bothered by my agitation, but rather, it seemed like he wanted to pump the air twice and do a victory dance. "Thanks, babe. You're gorgeous, you know that?" He grabbed my head and kissed me on the forehead before he whisked off into the other room to get ready.

I stroked my cheek and reasoned that wearing the suit wouldn't be so bad. I could take off the jacket once I got in. This would be just a small sacrifice to make, even though I didn't know why I was making it. But as I changed outfits, my mind went to how far we'd come, and I had to admit that Russ always acted only in our best interests. He had always been concerned about image and presentation, so naturally, he would be more concerned with how we appeared together than style or comfort. He worked hard for us, and it had been paying off, so this was the least I could do.

·   ·   ·

ON THE RIDE OVER, I wondered if Vlora would be there. I didn't know what I would do or how I would react if she was, but deep down, I wanted to see her again. I dreamed that we could magically repair our relationship. I felt lost without her, and I missed her.

We could barely get to the place without a constant reminder from Russ about how good I looked. It didn't matter how much he flattered me, I was hot as hell and starting to feel itchy and bitchy already. I repeated in my mind over and over that I was doing this for the best interests of our store.

This First Fridays was a bust, and the worst time I'd ever had. I loved Russ, but hanging with him at First Fridays was no joy. He was about as much fun as getting an enema with Louisiana hot sauce. It wasn't like being out with Vlora and Allie. Russ didn't know how to loosen up and have a good time while networking. With the girls, we'd attend the seminars and presentations, mingle, talk about the people we'd met, look at what others were wearing, share laughs, then go get our groove on. With Russ, everything was about figuring people out and strategy. On the one hand, I could see why we were so successful so fast. On the other hand, I had been so stressed lately and needed to let loose, relax, and have a good time.

"Stay by my side," Russ instructed. He tugged my arm just as I was about to divide up and go mingle as normal.

This month's First Fridays event featured a cigar bar. A table was set up by the bar and the vendor had a huge assortment of cigars: hand-rolled, machine-rolled, Cuban, Brazilian, Cusano 18, Sancho Panza, CAO Brazilia. They supplied all your needs to guarantee the ultimate choke-fest for the evening.

Russ extracted his purchased stogie from his jacket pocket and lit it. He puffed several times while keeping a stoic expression on his face. He ordered a cognac and I got an apple martini, and together we mixed and mingled.

Russ had a way of sizing people up to determine if they were legitimate, or if they would be a total waste of time to talk to. He would look at people, the way they dressed, their speech, and every distinctive little mannerism, and make a call on what they did for a living and how much education they had. A good seven times out of ten, he was wrong, but that was good enough for him to certify himself as a genius. And in his mind, he wasn't really totally off-base, because he always had an excuse for his misguided assessments. He had the uncanny ability to somehow draw a connection from the wrong answer he'd concocted, to show that he was still right.

He charmed his way around the room with me on his arm. I got to see firsthand how he swooned listeners in the midst of cigar smoke with intrigue and double-talk, and make them feel like they would miss out riding the tail of a rising billionaire if they did not latch on to his coattail now. And they did.

"Why Mill Creek Valley?" Alfreda Williamson asked as she puffed with the men in the cigar huddle that I somehow found myself in. Alfreda was CEO of Lohr Distributing Company, a local distributor of Anheuser-Busch products. She was dressed in a designer suit with shoulder pads that helped her to achieve that linebacker look. She wore expensive pumps and held an equally pricey handbag. Her ears, neck, wrists, and fingers dripped diamonds, and her flawless face could have been done only by a makeup artist.

"I know a lot of people dismiss Mill Creek Valley, but it's actually a very promising area." After I coughed, I explained to Alfreda about the low cost, community interest, and the fact that there was a lot less bureaucratic nonsense to deal with. I choked, cleared my throat, and sniffed. I retrieved a tissue from my purse to dab the tears that formed in the corners of my eyes.

Alfreda stared at me blankly, then looked to Russ and cocked her head to the side. She shifted her eyes to me, then back to Russ.

"Oh, this is my business partner, Naja Rodgers," he clarified for Alfreda.

I smiled at her. Her condescending eyes burrowed down on me and wrote me off. She blew a generous puff of smoke above our circle, eyed my apple martini, and said, "Mmm-hmm." She erased me from her line of sight and looked at Russ, directly this time, and asked, "So, why did you choose Mill Creek Valley?"

It was just like Russ to either not comprehend that I'd just been dissed, or to just roll right over it because this top executive was the cream of the crop. They continued to talk about the plans for my Internet café without me.

I had grown tired of the networking and was ready to unwind. The tension between my shoulder blades had started to send a mild ache through my body that could be relieved only by shaking it loose on the dance floor—even in this stiff suit. Finally the time came for everyone to unmask and shake their asses, only Russ didn't want to stay when the velvet rope was unclasped. So that's how the night ended. Two hours of flying bullshit, and it was all over.

I missed Vlora and Allie.

We stepped inside the door of Russ's house and I immediately went to the bedroom to take off my shoes and remove my suit. I took two aspirin as Russ put on music, turned it down low, and ran a warm bubble bath for me. He eased into the bedroom, removed my bra and panties, lifted me off the bed and gently lowered me into the bathtub. He tenderly lathered up a wash-cloth and slowly bathed me by candlelight without saying a word. He lifted me out of the water and softly toweled me dry.

He swept me off my feet and carried me to the bedroom. "Thank you, baby, for wearing the suit for me," he said as he laid me on the bed and began kissing me sweetly. "That's why we work together so well. Why we're successful in business as well as our personal relationship." He stroked my hair and spoke quickly. "You're perfect. You're beautiful. Submissive. Strong. Smart. All rolled up in one. See, I told you this would work." He breathed heavily over my mouth, kissed my lips, and cut off any response to be formed on the tip of my tongue.

My body devoured every bit of him while my mind stag-gered, unsure of whether I had actually heard him say I was sub-missive. It tensed so I could retrace and address his words, but it slowly relaxed and gave up as Russ continued to ease the tension that he built up. I decided to let go. To ride the waves in hopes of ebbing on a tranquil shore.

My fingers curled against his chest as he touched his soft wet lips to my eyelids, my temples, my neck, then my collarbone. Russ's strokes to my midsection were long, deep, and heavy, and sent a warm pulsation through my hips, my thighs. I continued to release and my mind drifted to serenity with each fondling lick of his tongue across my broad and aroused nipples. My body felt like it was suspended in midair as his warm hands caressed me. My fingers traced the neglected muscles of his back and shoulders as he melted into me, slowly becoming one with me. I hungrily kissed his cool pecs and tried to catch my breath as he kneaded and stroked my inner thighs, getting closer and closer until he finally reached the crux of me. I opened up, giving him more and more of me.

My lower back arched as my body took him in and swallowed him up whole. My legs wrapped around his waist and my arms went limp as he sent intense pulses of love through me, reaching every limb, every vein.

I was ready. Ready to reach the maximum. I wanted to guide him to take me there. I pulled his face down to my neck for the hot strong kisses that I knew would drive me into a frenzy. My legs moved at a rapid pace as he got closer to the spot inside me that I knew would unleash my orgasm and throw me over the top. I needed that right now, and I was almost there.

He moved away from my neck and kissed my lips and my face, subsiding the building fire within me.

I moved his hand to my protruding nipples to build it back up.

He moved away. He ran his fiery tongue over me and caused me to sizzle, but not send me over the edge.

"Work my nipples," I told him as he thrust into me long and hard. I pulled his hands over my nipples and guided his strokes. He pulled away when I let go.

"I got this," he said to me.

My insides were enduring a pleasing burn against his slow, rhythmic grind, but I needed so much more. I was on the edge and ready to explode. On the edge and wanting to go over.

"Faster, baby. Give me more. Faster."

"Let me work this" was all he said to me.

He rocked my body slowly. Danced with it. Some type of foreign waltz. He was lulling it to sleep.

"Give me you, baby. Come on. Give it to me."

My heart pounded in my chest as I grabbed his ample ass. Tried to pull him into me at a faster pace. My body was hungry for him. I needed more. Harder. Faster. Now. I needed him to bang me to the moon.

He reached back and grabbed each hand. One by one. He pulled my hands above my head. Locked me down by the wrists and continued to move at his slow, now monotonous pace. "I know what you want," he said, basking in his own confidence.

Russ continued his slow-motion grind until my body had lost its fizzle. And when it did, he gave a low throaty moan, slightly increased his pace, stiffened, and let out a loud agonizing strain while my body continued to ache with longing beneath him.

He huffed as he rolled off me and gave a satisfied groan as he rubbed me in the middle.

"You don't have to worry, baby girl. See, you got a sensitive man. I know what you want. I read *Essence*."

Proud of himself, Russ breathed heavily with satisfaction.

Unsatisfied, I drifted off into much-needed sleep.

"YOU NEED TO CALL HER and apologize. That was just foul," Allie said at the Jazz at the Bistro when I told her exactly what had happened between me and Vlora. "Real foul, Naja."

"I don't know what happened. I just got so pissed when she started telling me . . . about my weakness and how I'd changed. I wanted her to talk about Russ. Not me. I wanted to have a gripe session, but instead, it felt like she was attacking me." I looked down and sighed with my head in my hand. "I screwed up."

"She's up front with you all the time. You never seemed to have a problem with that before in all the years that you've known her. Not until you met Russ."

I felt defeated. "Right."

"And you let Russ come between you and your best friend?" She laughed low. "He's from Atlanta. You need to watch out. You know brothers from Atlanta are on the down low."

"Russ's not on the down low. And to say that he could be because he's from Atlanta is stereotyping."

She shifted. "You know," she pointed and shook her finger as her face displayed heavy thoughts. "He could be like those married men who cheat. They get all scary and nervous about their wives and start accusing her of cheating if she's one minute late. And why is he doing this? Because he knows that when he's one minute late, he's out cheating."

I twisted my nose up at her.

"Don't you get it? He accuses you of what he's familiar with and does himself. He figures if he does it, then why not his woman? That's why he wanted to cut you off from everybody."

I laughed. "It's not that deep. Russ's just not as good a judge of character as he thinks he is. You should have seen him at First Fridays trying to sum people up based on their appearances. He was almost always wrong."

"You know that, and you still listen to him anyway? And in the same breath, you won't entertain any possibility that he could be on the down low? Hmmm . . . what's wrong with this picture?" Allie shifted again. "And then you bring *me* here to listen to this jazz crap? I thought we were going to a concert concert."

The jazz band played a sultry song while Allie sighed. I could tell she wanted some booty-dropping music, and this just wasn't cutting it for her.

Vlora loved coming here with me.

"You're going to have to call Vlora and call her soon and tell her you made a mistake. Cuz I don't think I can take any more of this crap." She shook her leg restlessly.

"I really wish I could. It's not that simple."

"I'm going to the bar. I need liquid sedation to go along with the mental sedation I'm getting." She got up and left me alone with my guilt.

THIS TIME, I took a seat at the counter. Sitting alone at my usual table would only allow sadness to pull up the chair across from me and sit where Vlora usually sat. Well, sadness or guilt.

Chaney gave me the usual smile he gave anyone who entered his shop. He didn't even ask about why I was at the counter as he put a cup of coffee in front of me.

"You look like you could use a friend," he said.

"Have you seen her?"

"Mmm-hmmm" was all he said. He knew I wanted to know more, but he obviously wasn't going to tell me without my prodding him for information. He wanted me to beg for it, but I said nothing.

"Maybe you should give her a call," Chaney finally offered. He picked up his watering can and began watering the plants.

I mumbled something inaudible.

"Sooooo, how's everything going otherwise?" he asked, after seeing that we were going nowhere with this.

"Business is going great," I said glumly.

"Oh yeah? I can't tell," he said with raised eyebrows.

"It's just a lot of work. I might be starting to stretch myself too thin."

"Yeah, running a business is a lot of work, even if you have a partner. You work way more than you do if you got a regular nine-to-five working for somebody else."

"And fewer benefits."

"More satisfaction, though. Right?" He finished up and put the watering can underneath the counter.

"No doubt about that. Regardless of how I feel, it's mine. My own little slice of the American dream."

"I feel you." He patted me on the back with his free hand.

I threw my elbows on the counter. "But how do you not get stressed out? Tell me what the secret is."

Chaney smiled. "You gotta have balance."

"What do you mean?"

"Well, what do you do besides work?"

"I don't have time for anything else right now." While Russ still did little things for me, we were going out less and less, and we both were working more and more.

"There's your problem, little lady," he said as he lightly touched the tip of his finger to my nose. "You gotta lead a balanced life. You gotta exercise, have a social life, eat right, work on spiritual development."

"Okay, and who mans the business while I do all of this? Russ can't do it all on his own."

"Please, let's not bring him into this conversation," Chaney said. "We need positive energy, not negative."

"Chaney!"

"Oops. Sorry," Chaney said unapologetically.

"Do you do all of that? Where do you find the time?"

"You have to make the time. And it doesn't require as much as you think. Thirty minutes of exercise, three times a week. Maybe meditate five minutes every morning to get your day started, and again in the middle of the day. You'd be surprised how much of a difference that'll make in relieving some of your stress."

"You meditate?" I asked. I had a hard time picturing Chaney in his hip-hop gear in the lotus position.

"Don't let the baggy pants fool you," he said, tugging on his jeans. "You should try it sometime."

"I don't know how to meditate."

"You don't know how to meditate? Sure you do."

"No, I don't." I sipped my coffee.

"Have you prayed before?"

"I'm really not a religious person, so only a couple of times. Like when I was more than three days late for my cycle. Come to think of it, I did pray a lot in college. Usually on the weekends in the bathroom about four A.M. A lot of us prayed then. On a weekly basis."

"Very funny," Chaney said. "Give me your hands." He held his hands out, palms up.

"Here?" I looked around. There was an old couple sitting at a booth playing cards and drinking coffee.

"Yeah, I'd say now is as good a time as any."

I placed an open hand on each of his.

"Now close your eyes. Focus on your breath as you breathe in and out."

I breathed in and out slowly, and Chaney matched his rhythm to mine. Instead of relaxing, though, I felt jittery. My hands began to shake over his as chills ran up my arms.

"This is hard," I said, drawing my hands back. "My mind is going a mile a minute. I can't relax. I'm thinking of everything I need to do and . . . This just isn't working."

"No, no," he said as he pulled my hands back over his. "Give it a minute. Just focus on your breath. Imagine that you can see each stream of air as you breathe it in and out. Come on, do it with me."

He closed his eyes again and I followed suit. Chaney took the lead and took a loud breath in through his nose and blew it out through his mouth. His breaths became lighter with each one that followed until I couldn't hear him breathing at all.

My mind began to empty as I focused on each breath.

Slowly, the tension in my neck dissipated and my shoulders fell. I blew a long, slow breath through my nose. My heartbeat slowed. I started to feel relaxed.

Chaney removed his hands from underneath mine and I slowly opened my eyes.

"See, five minutes," he said with a smile.

I shook my head in disbelief as I stared at Chaney. "Wow. I need to learn more about this," I said as I rolled my neck.

"Well, if you're interested, I can teach you a little more. I have some books, and I can show you my setup at home."

"I'm game."

"Cool. Let me get my calendar and we can plan a day for you to come by my place." Chaney grabbed his calendar and we agreed on a day and time.

Russ walked into the café and spotted me at the counter. He smiled as he came to me, gave me a kiss on the cheek, and sat on the stool next to me. "Hey, baby. I knew I'd find you here."

He looked up at Chaney, who still stood before me. The silence in the air brought tension to the forefront, and Russ seemed to feel it, too.

"Cup of coffee, bruh," Russ said to Chaney, more as an order than a request.

Chaney gave a hardened unrelenting glare. "No problem, Black." He grabbed the pot and poured Russ a cup before walking off.

"I missed you, babe," Russ said. He squeezed my hand and the tension returned to my jaw, shoulders, and head.

"I've missed you, too," I said as I leaned over to kiss him. Then I pinched the sudden pain in the bridge of my nose and squinted.

FOURTEEN

"BOTH OF YOU ALL ARE ACTING LIKE LITTLE KIDS. I can't believe I'm the one to have to tell you this," Allie said to me as we drank complimentary drinks from the bar. "You let the holidays go by and New Year's, and you still haven't spoken to Vlora?" Allie shook her head and sipped. "That's a damn shame."

"I'm too old to be begging someone to be my friend. If somebody doesn't want to talk to me, then don't." I worked my neck from side to side, thinking how it's funny that even though I knew I was wrong, my pride kept me from calling and apologizing. Mainly because I knew Vlora and she wouldn't accept my apology before running off at the mouth and making me grovel. I wasn't about to go through that.

Allie pulled out her cell phone and held it out to me. "You need to call her up now so you all can get past this. This is ridiculous." She looked at me with scornful eyes.

"Yeah, well, it *be's* that way sometimes." I wrapped my left arm around my waist while holding my drink in my right hand. I softly tapped the floor with my foot in double time.

Allie said, "Look, you can either agree with me, or you can be wrong." She continued to hold the cell phone out to me.

My heartbeat quickened and my chest began to rise and fall much more rapidly. I actually wanted to make the call because I missed having my best friend here. I missed not hearing her voice, not hanging out with her. Not having her pick out every ugly man in the room for me. I'd do anything to have all of that back. My heart was willing, but my ego wouldn't allow me to do it. I stared at the phone like it was steak and I was in the midst of a forty-day fast.

Allie could see that I was on the edge. She stood upright and prepared herself to give her best Vlora impression. "See, me myself personally, I would do it. But I know you're not me. That's all I'm saying."

I busted out in laughter and tears. She mocked Vlora to a tee. So much so that it made me miss her even more.

"Okay, okay. I'll call her," I said as I took her phone from her. I dialed Vlora's cell phone number because we always caught up with each other by cell phone. So much so, that I didn't even know her home number off the top of my head. It rang several times before it went to voice mail.

I flipped the phone closed. "Voice mail."

"Leave a message," Allie demanded.

"I'll call back later. Promise."

Allie said nothing, but ripped the phone from my hand and put it back in her purse. Her cheeks popped out as she drew her lips together in a pinch. I put on a stubborn pout and we stood side by side, silently people-watching and drinking for about five minutes before Allie said she was going to go mingle. She sauntered off without looking at me. After coming and going several times to see if my funk had faded, Allie got fed up and announced that she was going to leave early and call it a night. Apparently, my bad mood was ruining even her night.

"It's not the same. It's not fun," she said. She looked at me with a twisted face like she wanted me to do something about it.

"Damn, I miss that bitch," she said before she headed to the coat check. She didn't bother to come back to say bye before she left.

CHANEY ASKED THE BOYS to do something special in the next week to commemorate Dr. Martin Luther King's birthday. We were a month away from their one-year tutoring anniversary, and Jarvis and Manny were continually improving. Their reading level, comprehension, and writing had increased significantly, and, just as important, their confidence was skyrocketing.

They both kept their hip-hop looks, but they removed the silver and gold grills from their mouths. Manny had done away with the spiked piercings on his lower lip and eyebrow, and both boys enunciated better, except when they were around other kids. But just the knowledge that they could use good En-glish and knew when to use it was enough to make Chaney feel proud.

There were only a handful of people in the café when Jarvis and Manny expressed themselves. Jarvis performed a poem that he had written himself to commemorate the life of Dr. Martin Luther King, while Manny tapped out a beat on bongos. They had worked hard. They had practiced long. They wanted to show Chaney how he had affected them. How he had changed their lives. Manny beat out every ounce of effort they had put in, while Jarvis closed his eyes and spewed out his soul as he brought his words to life. At the end of their piece, the sparse crowd whistled and gave them a standing ovation. In just one year, we had come a long way from the truant thug wannabes who first stepped foot in the Rosebud Café.

You would have thought Chaney was their father. He stood at attention with the bill of his cap pulled low, shadowing his eyes as everyone clapped, but it was all he could do to keep his composure. Tears welled up and he tried to mask them by pulling his baseball cap even lower.

"Go on, let it flow, man!" came a voice from the audience, followed by welcoming laughter.

"That's right, Big C," Jarvis said.

He and Manny took turns speaking and telling the customers of that day almost a year ago when Chaney cared enough to take responsibility for them and to tutor them. Their voices trembled as they painted pictures of two scared and lost souls who donned gristly exteriors to buy them the neighborhood's respect they thought they had—but didn't. They told of their revelation and how they evolved as stewards of their own ships, thanks to Chaney.

"And we got something else for you," Manny said to Chaney. Chaney didn't look like he could take more good news. He was overwhelmed.

Jarvis grabbed Chaney by the arm and led him to the picture that hung on the wall that he had stood before almost a year ago. He put a hand on Chaney's shoulder and read the caption under James Baldwin's picture: "Know whence you came. If you know whence you came, there is really no limit to where you can go. *The Fire Next Time.*"

As cool as Chaney tried to be, it wasn't long before he lost it. Jarvis read it as clearly, smoothly, and loudly as he had ever read anything else. In his determined tone, he let us know that he appreciated us investing our time in him, our not giving up on him, not allowing him to be the thug that he was pretending to be.

We all hugged each other. I wiped one tear of joy from Chaney's face, but let the other one fall commemoratively.

.　　.　　.

"I DON'T THINK I'm going to be able to hold out much longer," Chaney said.

It had been ten months since Mooncents opened across the street, and Chaney's business hadn't been the same since. He had done all he could. Hell, he was already offering more than when the store first opened up. But apparently aesthetics were worth the high costs that they demanded. Chaney had even started closing earlier, and on Sundays he tried to manage the drop-in customers alone, but it was getting the best of him.

"Give it until spring," I offered emptily. "When it warms up, that's sure to bring more people in. They'll be back," I said, doubting my own words.

"I'd have to update. Doesn't matter how low my prices are or how much I have to offer." He took in the view of the café. "I just don't have the extra money to put into this place to compete."

Despair put a sag in his body and I felt an aching sensation in my chest. I really felt for him. I pulled his hand close to me and stroked it. Tried to rub the worry away, but I knew it would be no use.

Russ came in the door and focused on us immediately as he slowly removed his hat. He took off his scarf and shook it out before unbuttoning his coat, not taking his eyes off us as he came toward the counter. I patted the top of Chaney's hand that now rested on the countertop.

"What's going on?" Russ asked. His skeptical eyes went from my face to Chaney's and back.

"Chaney just told me some disturbing news," I said.

Russ looked at Chaney and tried to at least display concern. "Oh, yeah? What's so disturbing, bruh?"

Chaney retrieved a cigarette and lighter and lit up. "Not your concern, bruh." He gave Russ a look of dismissal before turning to walk away.

Russ turned to me. Angry. "What's up with your boy?"

"He's just got a lot of things on his mind. That's all." Since Chaney didn't care for Russ, I didn't want to tell him about his business problems if he didn't want me to.

"That's fine and all that. But he doesn't have to disrespect me. I don't let anybody disrespect me." He spoke loud enough for Chaney to hear.

I patted calmness into Russ's thigh as he sat on the stool next to me. "Baby, he's just got some heavy things on his mind. Nobody's disrespecting you."

Russ was getting to me with this disrespect thing. I hadn't noticed till a few months ago how much he focused on being constantly disrespected by other men. Most of the time, I never saw it. I knew that it was some type of testosterone, territory type of thing, but whatever it was, Russ had an extra dose, and it was getting on my last nerve. We could hardly be around another male who wasn't his friend without his finding some way that he had just been disrespected. It was wearing thin.

"I've never liked that guy. He's got too much attitude. Way too much attitude." His lips twitched as if he had some type of nervous tic.

"Chaney?" I asked in disbelief. "Chaney doesn't have attitude. He's just not one to tolerate a lot of bullshit."

"Is that a comment about me? I'm bullshit now? You're going to disrespect me, too?"

I waved my hands at him. "Baby, calm down. I'm not calling

you anything. Okay? And Chaney's not in a good mood right now. That's all."

"Humph! Well, bruh better not take that shit out on me. I'm not going to stand by and let any man challenge my manhood. If he disrespects me again, he's going to find a foot up his ass." Again, he spoke loud enough for Chaney to hear, but Chaney ignored him, which ticked Russ off all the more, just like Chaney knew it would.

I wanted to laugh. Chaney had Russ by at least four inches in height and thirty to forty pounds. My mind flashed an image of Russ putting his foot up Chaney's ass, and Chaney swinging around, and wiping up the floor with Russ, then going back to business as usual, unfazed.

"Yeah, okay," I said with my head turned away from him. "Coffee?" I asked.

"Let's go," Russ demanded.

I patted his thigh again. "But you just got here and it's freezing outside. Why don't you have just one cup and then we can go."

"I'm ready to go now," he said, his voice low and forceful.

I didn't like his tone, and it was a record being played more frequently in our relationship. Unless I said something about it, Russ would continue on in that manner and get even worse. I would have to say something, I knew. But for now, I didn't want to make a scene, so I got up to leave.

I didn't see Chaney after we put on our coats. Since Russ was in such a hurry, I left without saying good-bye.

"I DON'T WANT you to see him anymore," Russ said while we lay in his bed.

I had taken two aspirin and was waiting for them to kick in.

"Who?"

"Chaney."

I turned a shocked face to him. "First of all, I'm not *seeing* Chaney."

He lay with his hands folded over his chest and his eyes pointed to the ceiling. "It's obvious that the man is feenin' for you. I don't want you to go over there anymore."

"Russ, if women stopped hanging out because certain men were feenin' for them, they'd never step outside the house," I tried to joke.

"I'm not joking."

"Then I think you're insane. Besides that, you never read people right anyway. You're more than wrong half the time."

"You're my woman. I don't want some other man drooling over my woman. Period. End of story."

"Even if I wanted to, we're tutoring the boys together. I'm not going to flake out on a commitment to those boys just because you have a jealousy problem."

"You've been tutoring them for a year now. They've improved enough. You can see the change in them. Besides, Chaney's doing more work on their self-esteem than tutoring. Those boys will be all right."

"Okay, you're being ridiculous right now. Chaney's my friend. We've been friends for years. I can't believe you're going to suddenly get jealous, or just mad, and tell me to dump my friend. For nothing."

"Don't make me out to be the hardass here. You're my lady, and I'm asking you not to hang around Chaney's place. He's got a thing for you. Going around his place is only leading him on." He paused and tried to turn the tables. "Unless that's what you want." He opened his hands to the air and gazed at me.

"Of course not!"

He turned away with easy eyes. "Well, then. I guess you know what you gotta do." And with that, he reached over to turn off the light on his side of the bed, pulled the covers up to his neck, turned his back to me, and went to sleep.

FIFTEEN

MY BODY ACHED IN THE WORST WAY. SINCE RUSS'S ultimatum, I felt like I was going to explode from the pressure that was building up and banging on the walls of my brain. I needed to step back and assess, but more than anything I needed to relax and drain my body of the stress. It was causing me not to think clearly. The tension in my back and neck had given me a headache that was not responding to the aspirin I'd been taking all day. I took another two as I defiantly pulled up to Chaney's place.

Chaney had an old-looking house on Josephine Baker Street that was shrouded with snow-dusted bushes and flowerbeds that I'm sure attempted to give it life in the springtime. Even the new paint of last summer could hardly conceal its wrinkles and sagging features. The steps groaned loudly, and I could feel them give with each step I took. I could only imagine what the inside looked like, but it didn't matter. Chaney was my friend. It was just like Chaney to live in Mill Creek Valley since he had his business there. He believed in supporting the community that supported him, to the point of living there even if he could afford something better.

The screen door creaked loudly as I opened it, only to be outdone by bamboo wind chimes on the front door as Chaney opened it after I knocked. The inside of his house caught me completely off guard.

"Not what you were expecting, huh?"

"I'm sorry," I said as I brought myself out of a trance. "I didn't mean to gawk."

"No harm done. Doesn't matter how things look on the outside. It's the inside that counts." Somehow I got the feeling that he was talking about more than his house.

Chaney's place was exquisite. The house was garnished with enough greenery to constitute a forest. His furnishings were sparse; he seemed to have only what was necessary, and that was placed on highly glossed hardwood floors. Pictures of nature, waterfalls, and heavenly scenes decorated the walls, and fragrant incense filled the air.

He directed me to a small room that had a futon directly across from a zafu and zabuton set, on top of a tatami rug on the floor. An African carved altar with an incense burner and candles sat in front of it, against a mahogany shoji screen. More lit candles filled the room on ledges and in holders and floor stands. He had enough candles to completely light the room.

When Chaney told me to have a seat, I dropped like an anchor to the futon under the weight of all the tension I was carrying. I was in so much pain that I actually wanted to cry, but I didn't want to make Chaney aware of the ultimatum Russ had given. He could see that I was burdened by something tremendous. He looked at me like I had an open wound.

"What's going on?" He sat next to me and put a hand on my shoulder.

"I'm just tired, that's all."

"This is more than a little tired."

"Pressure. It's just the stress and pressure of . . . everything. I just need some relief. If learning how to meditate can do what those five minutes did for me, I'll be in good shape."

Chaney looked at me as if he knew there was more to my stress than the business, and wanted to ask, but didn't. Instead, he slid my shoes off and pulled my legs around to allow me to lie on the couch, and began telling me about different forms of meditation, sitting positions, and breathing methods as he sat on the floor in front of me.

In an instant and without warning, the dam of my tension overcame me and broke, and I burst into tears. My shoulders heaved as water rained from my eyes, down the sides of my face, and into my ears. Chaney got on his knees, pulled me close to him, and cradled my head in his arms. He didn't ask what was wrong or the reason for the sudden outburst. Instead, he rocked me from side to side and told me to "let it all out."

And I did. The stress and strain of Russ was getting to me; it tore out of me, clearing the pathway for a clearer vision. I now felt confinement where I had once felt freedom. I now felt his growing power over my mind and actions, where I once used to think and act for myself. I now felt a buttoning of my lips, where I once had the freedom of speech. And it was all coming to a head.

I felt loved by Russ, but that love was coupled with pain, and love is just not supposed to bring that along for the ride. I didn't want to let go of the love, but I wanted to get rid of all the bad feelings that came with it.

All of these emotions poured out of me and onto Chaney's shoulder. I tried to speak, but he *shhh*-ed me with a soft press of his finger to my lips.

"I want you to relax," he said.

I tried. My vision was blurred from the tears and I was trembling. Chaney sat on the edge of the couch and folded my arms across my middle. He then dabbed the tears from the corners of my eyes and where they had streamed down my face. He pressed comforting lips to my forehead before he got up and put a CD in the player.

Chaney came back and began rubbing my feet. His fingers skirted under my arches and began to massage my heels. He kneaded, pressed, and caressed my feet from the heels to the tips of the toes. I began to relax, from my toes to my ankles. The feeling from his warm hands on my feet slowly eased up to my calves and my thighs. Reverberated under my rib cage. Made calming waves in my shoulders and temples.

My soul began to take in the music. The soft beats filled me, lifted me. Comforted me. Erykah Badu stuttered, "I want you," and her words crept into the crevices of my mind.

Heat began to rise in my body. My insides warmed with each stroke of Chaney's hands. He bent over and blew hot breath on the tops of my feet, then soothed them, then blew a cool stream of air across my toes. He lit me up; I was on fire. A throbbing feeling replaced the soothing feeling that ran from my soles to the crown of my head. And Erykah was asking, What we gon' do?

My body was struggling over an answer. I knew what *I* wanted to do.

While my mind fought my actions, my hand reached up and grabbed Chaney's forearm. His eyes followed mine and our gazes became locked. He was reading my thoughts. Feeling them. I told him with my eyes everything I wanted and needed, and that I wanted it now.

Chaney's hands stopped moving, and he seemed to be searching for the answer of what to do now. He was motionless. Until he moved.

Chaney got up and left the room.

Embarrassment filled me now. Here I had a friend who saw I

was hurt, and he had gone to every length possible to try to comfort me. To make me feel better. And what do I do? I hit on him. I make a play for him. Without speaking, I ask my friend for sex. I had sunk to an all-time low.

The best thing to do here would be to pick my face up off the floor, put my shoes back on, and sneak out. I was about to get up to make an excuse to leave, when Chaney came back.

"Chaney, I'm sor—"

He wouldn't let me finish. Chaney put my legs back on the couch and *sshhh*-ed me again. I lay back as the scent of fresh incense that tailed Chaney began to circle the air. "Just relax," Chaney said.

He took my feet in his hands again and resumed his massage. He stroked, caressed, alternated hot and cold breaths, and drove me crazy. I began to get hot all over again as the pounding beat settled in the curve of my spine.

Then he did it to me. Chaney kissed my feet. The wet softness of his lips sent a quiver through my body. A weakness developed in my knees, and I began to sizzle between my thighs. Chaney was working my feet, but I was feeling it all over. I moved my hands from my middle to my thighs to point out the fire that raged there. I couldn't take any more.

"You feelin' me?" he asked.

"I feel you," I whispered. I moaned.

Chaney ran his tongue over the tops of my toes and hit a spot somewhere in me that made me shoot up to a seated position. This boy was good. He paused, only to push me back down by the shoulders, and resumed working me over. He kissed, licked, then sucked each and every toe while using stroking motions to send me into a frenzy.

The pressure built up and exceeded the maximum. Chaney

gave my toes one more good suck and I felt it channel through my whole body. Pressure ran up my thighs and between my legs. My heart pounded hard in my chest, and I couldn't breathe. My back arched intensely as I looked at Chaney, and he looked intently back at me.

And I screamed as it came. I screamed, and my body quaked as he continued to rub, to stroke, to suck my toes. Passionately. It rushed, rushed, rushed and I couldn't hold it any longer.

And it all came down.

I screamed. I began to shiver all over as it came charging out of me. My breath was hard, fast, and fierce. My body jerked hard with each pulse.

He moved from my feet to my ankles and up to my calves. Slower. Longer strokes. To cool me down. My teeth chattered.

"Now relax," he said with a smile of satisfaction.

Chaney got a blanket from somewhere and covered me with it. He turned the music down, and sat next to me. He stroked my hair. Stroked it until I relaxed and fell asleep.

All the tension and feelings I had when I first came to Chaney's house? Well, all those were now gone. I couldn't remember what they had been.

MY LEGS HESITATED and my stride was stiff as I entered the Rosebud Café. It had taken me days to realize that Russ was right, and that I was leading Chaney on. There was a strong chemistry between us that I denied. And if I didn't know it before, I knew it after I left his place. I had to stop coming around him. I was going to have to let the tutoring go and distance myself from Chaney and the Rosebud Café.

After the positive feeling wore off from Chaney's orgasmic

foot massage, chagrin set in. I shouldn't have allowed it to happen. When I got up to leave, I felt the urge to apologize, but Chaney wouldn't allow it.

"There's nothing to apologize for. You had a need, and I as a friend was able to fulfill that need without taking advantage of you," he said. Plain and simple.

But like Russ said, I was leading him on. There was obviously a strong vibe between us. A stronger vibe than just friends. But I was with Russ. I was in love with Russ. Granted, the ultimatum didn't sit well in my mind. But I couldn't deny that continuing to be around Chaney, in the midst of this vibe, was wrong. It invited trouble.

Chaney greeted me with his usual charming crooked smile as I walked in. He poured me a cup of coffee as I took off my coat and headed to the counter.

"You're looking less stressed," he said. His smile grew deeper.

Blood rushed to my cheeks and I blushed. Then Chaney blushed. I felt a flutter in my stomach, and I knew I had to do something.

"Chaney, I feel a strong vibe between us."

His eyes went from my face to the floor.

I, too, looked down. Began to search my lap for the strength I needed to pull the words from my gut and release them. "And I really think it would be best if we sort of let things die down a bit. I think I should stop coming around for a while. The boys are doing a lot better. I'm going to tell them that I need to take a break from tutoring. And—"

"No," he said with fright in his eyes. He shook his head. "No," he said again, slowly. "Don't do that. Look, you did nothing wrong. *We* did nothing wrong. You don't have to do this," he pleaded.

"This isn't right. What happened the other day, that shouldn't have happened. But I encouraged it to happen. And I shouldn't have. I'm with Russ."

"That was just a moment. We both got caught up in the moment." He stalled. "You didn't cheat. We didn't sleep together."

"But it was still wrong. And it's bound to happen again, sooner or later." I twiddled my thumbs on the counter.

"Okay, I can see if you want to distance yourself from me, even though I really don't want you to. But don't take it out on the kids. They need you."

I took a deep breath into my lungs, then slowly exhaled. I tilted my head to the side and spoke softly. "The boys are doing fine now. Besides, I think you can handle it on your own. You're doing a fine job." I pushed a smile onto my face.

Chaney continued to disagree, but stopped after he could see that my mind was made up.

My heart ached as I walked across the black-and-white-checkered floor and out the door. I felt as if I were cutting the line with my best friend.

As I walked out the door, it hit me that I was having to sacrifice a lot just to be with Russ.

SIXTEEN

IT WAS PRETTY FUCKING RUDE THAT VLORA HADN'T called me back. Even though I didn't leave a message, I knew my number showed up in her "missed call" list on her cell phone. So for her not to call me back could only mean that she didn't want to talk to me. *Well, fuck her then*.

Vlora wasn't the world, and I decided I was going to create a new crew. Vlora? Hmph, Vlora my ass. I called up a couple of friends I hadn't talked to in years, to hang out with me at the next First Fridays.

Jayna. Back in the day, Jayna was suffering from MJ syndrome. Michael Jackson. She slathered her initially chestnut brown skin with bleaching cream three times daily, and had developed her own brown-paper-bag test. She wouldn't date anyone who was less than two shades lighter than her current skin tone, whatever that might be at the time. One year, she had even dumped a guy because he had fallen within the two shades zone after her skin color became a hair lighter from the hydroquinone. Other than that minor issue, which I had previously de-friended her for, she was cool. But everybody's got their own little issues, so who am I to judge?

Heidi. I have to admit that I thought that Heidi could have been a misguided borderline modern-day Black Panther. In the past, after studying the civil rights era, Heidi had sported a permed Afro, worn dashikis, and referred to every fabricated injustice as being a conspiracy of "the man." The fact that she would have been considered a counter-part of "the man" or that she was the spitting image of Gwen Stefani didn't seem to bother her as much as it bothered other people. But, hey, that was back in the day. First Fridays would be her type of crowd and she would feel more than comfortable, as she preferred beats from descendants of the motherland over Top 40 any day.

Allie opted out when she heard whom I was going with. She had known them well from my past and wouldn't be caught in the dark with either. First Fridays was at Seven again. We all met up there, and I immediately felt sorry upon arrival.

Jayna would make sure there was a barrier between her and any dark-skinned person. She kept wiping her hands on the front of her dress while drawing up her face like a raisin. She scanned the room with a scrunched face and a bad attitude. I don't think she caught a happy feeling all night.

Heidi constantly complained that everyone there would be better off if they unmasked themselves and stopped trying to blend in with capitalist pigs of this so-called free society just to make a grip.

Between the two, I got nauseous and drank myself to near drunkenness.

I thought things would be okay once we all hit the dance floor. But Jayna couldn't stand to be that close to *them* for fear she might catch a case of melanin from them. And Heidi no longer wanted to hang out with these bourgeois blacks who didn't "know themselves." After being unsuccessful at getting malt liquor from the bar, she wanted to ditch this scene to hang out in the hood, where they "keep it real."

I decided to call it a night and go home. I just made peace with the fact that my run at First Fridays was over. I could come alone, but it just wouldn't be the same without Vlora and Allie. As they say, all good things must come to an end.

PEACE WAS A HARD THING to come by nowadays, but I was determined. Russ was still at the café, and I had a few moments alone before he came home. I took a hot shower, slipped into a short silk nightgown, and snatched my favorite Dove almond chocolate ice cream bar from the freezer. I had sunk into the sitting room couch and settled on reruns of *Girlfriends* when Russ came bustling in. He pulled off his coat and hung it in the front closet before he came back to the bedroom.

His nose turned upward as he shot out a breath of disgust, which had become a frequent reaction. More times than not, he was starting to be unhappy about things that I said or did.

"Do you really think you should be eating that? Especially this late?" He propped up a forearm on the doorpost.

"Yep," I answered, keeping my eye on the television.

He balanced himself and used the heel of each foot to slip out of his shoes. "I'm not trying to be mean, but you *could* work on your shape a little bit."

I instantly got pissed. He had barely closed the door behind him, and my blood pressure was starting to rise already.

I added an extra dose of attitude to my tone. "What's wrong with my shape? What's so different about it than when we first met?" I took an extra-large bite of the ice cream bar.

No, I wasn't in tip-top shape. But I knew I hadn't gained weight since I'd met Russ, either. I had thought about putting a workout plan together and going to the gym or something. I hadn't yet done anything about it, but that didn't give him the right to say anything about my body.

"I can't say anything's different from when we first met."

Damn right.

"But that's no excuse. You could work on your body a little bit. Lose some of that gut."

My hand immediately went to my middle. "My stomach has been the same since you met me."

"I know. And that's the problem. Baby, you could make an effort to improve yourself a little bit." He stood directly in front of me and spoke with extended arms, as if this were an intervention and he was pleading for me to just say no to drugs.

A burning sensation ran through my body and up my spine.

"Honestly, I've been giving this a whole lot of thought lately."

"You've been thinking about me getting in shape?"

"Yeah. You're not a bad-looking woman."

Gee, thanks.

"Only thing wrong with you is your gut. I was thinking that you should get liposuction. Suck that fat right out of you." He grabbed his own spare tire to show what should be sucked out. "I'm willing to pay for it."

My appetite took a flying leap. I don't think anything can hurt as much as your man telling you that you're so big, you should have surgery to lop off some of the fat. *And* that he's willing to foot the bill. Because you're just that disgusting. The pain of his words darted straight to my core.

I wanted to cry, but I refused to.

Then my eyes moved like a magnet to his midsection, which looked like he was at least three months' with child. It was starting to lap over his belt. I just stared at his stomach.

He caught my gaze and sensed my thoughts. He patted his stomach and said, "Oh, before you say anything, I know I have a gut, too. But I'm a man. Once I get back to the gym, all I got to do is run for a week and this will fall right off." He grabbed it with both hands and jiggled it up and down.

"So why haven't you?"

"I will. It won't take me but a minute to lose this here." He paused. "Hold on."

Russ left the room and returned with a large white envelope and handed it to me. It was from a Dr. Westcomb in Richmond Heights. I pulled out a series of pamphlets on tummy tucks and liposuctions, the procedures and aftercare.

Damn! Not only had he been thinking about it, he'd been running around town telling doctors that his girlfriend was a fat heifer and asking them what could they do about it.

I was outdone. Hurt, and outdone. My eyes got wet, but I refused to cry and let him see that he had gotten the best of me. I put the rest of the ice cream bar back in the wrapper and set it down on the side table. Russ picked it up and discarded it. My mouth still had a layer of chocolate that I no longer had the gumption to swallow.

"That's a start," he said. He actually thought I was on the same page as he was. He thought we were in sync. That's how out of sync we were becoming.

Russ left to shower, while I cracked and crumbled on the inside. Step by step, Russ was slowly breaking me and destroying me. My mother would not be proud of me right about now.

I ran my hand back and forth over my middle as I thought. For a lifetime, I had felt self-conscious about it. No matter what I did, it never went away. In college, I had been fifteen pounds lighter than I currently was. I was almost skinny, but I always had the pooch. I would cleverly disguise it with the right style of clothing or clever body slimmers. But I had never thought about going under the knife to cut if off. Never even considered it.

Until now.

I stood before the bedroom mirror while Russ showered. I turned sideways and pulled my stomach in. Then I let go and sucked in air. Russ was right, and I hated the thought of that. If there was a way to cut off my gut, then why shouldn't I do it? I would look slimmer, much nicer than I did now.

Russ wasn't tactful, but he did look out for my best interests, I knew. At the same time, I felt like shit inside. Like I had lost myself somehow. Like I was trapped, and I couldn't escape.

I tapped two aspirin out of the bottle off the nightstand and gulped them down with a glass of water. I lay down on the bed and was in another world before Russ finished his shower.

AFTER RUSS LEFT for the café the next morning, I lay back down. My entire head was throbbing, and I sat back up to take two more aspirin. I picked up the near-empty bottle that I had just bought last week, and stared at it.

Thoughts ran through my mind. Since getting with Russ, aspirin had become a part of my daily diet. I realized that I was having it for breakfast, lunch, dinner, and in-between snacks. And in each case that I needed it, Russ was at the root.

I paced the bedroom as it occurred to me. Somewhere along the way, I had lost myself. In the name of love and for entrepreneurial success, I had given Naja away. I had lowered my self-esteem and handed all of my power over to Russ, for him to do with what he willed. Everything my mother had taught me not to do.

I paced and thought.

My eyes roamed the bedroom that shouted "Russ." Was this what I traded my best friend in for? And Chaney? A good friend who cared about me dearly? And was I actually considering mutilating my body, not because I wanted to do so myself, but because Russ said I needed to? I knew I needed to work on my body, but not do it by way of surgery. And from a man who always looked three months' pregnant himself!

I paced and thought.

I loved myself more than that. It was time to regain control of my life. It was time to take my power back.

I stopped pacing and charged to the bedroom bureau.

My tears were held back by the dam I created as I packed up every stitch of clothing I had at Russ's place. I didn't have a suitcase, so I threw it all in garbage bags from the kitchen, scurried across the February snow, and packed it in my car. I removed all of me from his apartment. Then I got myself ready, and left for work.

Russ always made good on his promise not to bring our personal issues to work, but for some reason, I was unhappy about that. It bothered me that, somehow, he was able to talk to others and have meetings like he didn't have any other cares in the world. Like we hadn't just had an argument. Like I was an insignificant little thing in his life that didn't affect his day, or worse, that I didn't matter at all.

I didn't tell Russ until after work that I wanted to "take a break for a while." I called him from my place.

"In other words, break up," he stated over the phone that evening, more in the form of a statement than a question.

"Not permanently," I said. But I really did mean permanently. "I feel like I need to take back control of my life."

"Take back control? You think I'm trying to control you?"

I hesitated, then swallowed. "You can be controlling, yes."

"Baby, I told you in the beginning that I'm just a hard, down-to-business type of person. I'm aggressive. That's why I'm successful."

"Business is one thing, but you're trying to control my personal life as well," I said. I told him how he constantly criticized, caused me to dump two of my closest friends, and had me considering plastic surgery when it was an option I wouldn't have considered on my own. How he tried to control what I wore and what I ate. The more I talked to him, the more it all came to the forefront. I began to realize just exactly how much control I had given up. It made me see that I should have done this a long time ago.

"I wasn't trying to control you. I only suggested things to better you. To better us as a couple." There was a ruffling sound like he was switching ears. "But I see now that you're ungrateful."

"*Ungrateful?* Who made you God? And what makes you think that you're so perfect that you can stand back and criticize me all day and that you know what's best for me?"

"I'm a man. Men are the head of the household. They lead their family. They're the leader in their relationships. Since we're in business together and we're in a relationship, it's my responsibility to lead us."

"So what's my responsibility? To stand behind you and do whatever you say?"

"Well, I wouldn't have worded it like that. But yeah, a good woman submits to the man. That's what the Good Book says."

"Negro, you ain't even religious. Probably never even read the Bible, so how are you going to all of a sudden get holy and quote it? I mean, misquote it?"

He skipped past that and softened his tone. "Naja, I love

you. I don't want to break up, but I agree we need to work on some things. You're not submissive enough. And you're selfish. I might have some problems too, but if things stay the way they are, we're going to continue to have problems." His voice was cool and unwavering. He believed the letter of every word he had spoken.

"Hel-lo!" I sang. "You want to join me in the new millennium here?"

His tone stiffened up now. "I'm sorry, but I don't buy into that feminist fairy tale your mother taught you. I'm a realist. I didn't make the rules. Like it or not, it's a man's world. Deal with it," he spat into the phone.

I pulled the earpiece away and stared in disbelief. "I'm glad we're having this conversation. Because you are the most egotistical, self-righteous, condescending man I've ever met."

He paused. He spoke with a slight tremble in his voice, and if I didn't know better, I'd think he had tears in his eyes. "You're right. It *is* good we're talking about this because on second thought, I don't think you're the woman that I thought you were. You're not right for me. You're unappreciative and you don't respect me or my opinions. I'm not going to be constantly challenged by a woman. I'm not going to have a woman who disrespects me. Nobody disrespects me."

"You really need to get off that challenging you and disrespecting tip. You act like you've got little man's syndrome."

A realization formed in my mind. The loss of his finger. How he constantly repeated that he would never be a whole man.

Russ's end of the line got quiet and I began to feel sorry for him. But, at the same time, I saw that it was not my battle.

We ended the conversation and our relationship for good.

My only question now was how it would affect my business.

SEVENTEEN

I COULDN'T BRING MYSELF TO ANSWER CHANEY'S calls, so I'd let them go to voice mail. He still called to check on me, and had even sent me flowers and friendship cards. Which, of course, made me feel like an even bigger heel because I hadn't even extended the courtesy of a thank-you. And each morning that I meditated, I thought about Chaney. Not only because he taught me how to meditate, but I sat on the zafu and zabuton he sent over as a gift. Somehow I would have to summon the courage to apologize to him, so I added him to the list. Right after Vlora. But at the moment, that would lead to me talking about Russ and how right they both were in what they thought about him, and I didn't want to talk about that right now.

Russ went on with business as usual in the office, as he had always said would be the case, and that made me nervous as hell. No one seemed to know that we had just broken up, or that we were personally on the outs with each other. Russ talked about business with me at work as if the breakup had never happened. Like everything was normal, and we would see each other at his place after work.

I was on edge. Things were going too smoothly, and it's never that way when you break up with someone. You have to go through drama somewhere, at some point, before things get better again. Those are the rules. Without a blowup, I just felt like the other shoe was going to drop, and I wanted to be alert when it did.

"I'm really glad to see that we're able to continue to work together," I finally said to Russ a week later as he sat going over a new contract.

"What? Did you expect me to bring our personal life to work? I told you I didn't do that. Business is business, personal is personal. Two separate things. Remember?" His eyes looked up at me while his face was still pointed toward the contract.

"Sometimes people say one thing when a relationship is new, fresh, and perfect, but then if there's a breakup, it's a different story."

"You're not as significant as you think you are, Naja. You need to get over yourself," Russ said in an emotionless tone without looking at me.

I suppressed a rising surge of irritation. I was not going to let him get a rise out of me. "I'm not going to take this to a different level, so I'm going to stop while we're ahead. Just wanted to make sure everything was cool."

"Why wouldn't it be?" he asked.

"Good. I'm glad," I said. I held out my hand for a handshake and a smile. He got up and brushed past my hand without saying a word.

JUST WHEN I got comfortable with our new way of relating to each other, Russ's controlling ways began to resurface with a vengeance. The first thing he did was give Allie a two-week notice, which left Allie furious and mad as hell at me.

"You could have said something to me if you didn't want me working there," Allie said to me over the phone, in tears.

I was forced to let Allie in on the situation that had gone down between me and Russ. "Bubble-eyed bastard!" she called him.

I assured her that her job was intact, and that she should return to work as normal. I even granted her the day off that she requested because she said that Russ's actions had "messed her up inside" and that she needed a day to regroup.

Next, Russ went back to holding meetings with our contractors, investors, bankers, and even employees without my knowledge. He was doing nothing to hurt the company, and continued to work his ass off to make us successful. He just didn't include me in any of his business interactions.

I decided to let things go for a little bit and to let things die down. Let him get it all out of his system. It was apparent that Russ was running on emotion, and I thought it best to let it run its course, then have a discussion with him. Besides, as long as he wasn't hurting our business, all was good. Right?

"I WANT OUT of the business," Russ said to me in our conference room before our board meeting. It had been a few weeks since our breakup and his antics had finally died down, until now. His tone was flat. His face was blank. "You can either buy me out or I have someone that I'm going to sell my half of the business to," he said matter-of-factly.

"I thought you separated business from personal," I said to him.

"I do. Have I ever brought our personal issues to work? No." He answered his question to me before I could even think about it.

"What about what you're doing right now? This is about me."

His body bobbed up and down from his laughter. "You really need to check your ego at the door, little girl. Everything doesn't revolve around Naja Rodgers. Now," he said as he sorted through papers on his desk, "if you *must* know, I've gone over my business involvements and investments and decided that I'm in too deep." He lowered the papers, leaned back, then looked up at me. "I've spread myself too thin. I've decided to sell off all of my interests except my real estate investments. And move back to Atlanta."

"What about the café?"

He shook his head with indifference and hunched his shoulders. "Not my problem. That's between you and your new partner, if you get one, and your board members."

"You fucking bastard!" I yelled. I clenched my fist and burned a hole through him with my eyes.

He turned toward me and spoke in a mellow tone. "Look, I'm sorry I couldn't work out something that would make you just as happy. Working with you has been great. It really has. I couldn't have asked for a better partner. But now," he shrugged his shoulders, "it's time for me to move on." His words were laced with sweet venom.

"You're a sorry-ass motherfucker!" My cheeks puffed with hot air as my lips puckered. My body rocked with anger.

Russ said calmly, "Do you need some time alone to gather your emotions? We can get together and talk about the particulars later when you've regrouped." He pulled a tissue from a box that he had conveniently by his side and extended it to me. I ignored it.

"The only thing I'm going to regroup is my foot up your ass."

"Whoa. Easy now, little girl. You're going to hurt yourself or break something."

"You are *not* going to fuck up my business, Russom King! You hear me? I will cut your bitch-ass down before you do."

He cleared his throat. "You all are going to have to excuse

her," he said to someone over my shoulder. "I think Ms. Rodgers is going through something in her personal life that's making her emotional. Might be PMS. Not quite sure."

I looked behind me to see two board members who had entered the conference room with manila folders in their hands.

Russ focused back on me. "Are you okay to sit in on this meeting, or do you need time?"

"This isn't over, Russ." I headed to the exit. I was too pissed and embarrassed to stay.

"Okay, get over that little thing you got going on, then get back to me. We have a lot of things to wrap up. I'm about to go over it with everyone else right now."

I brushed passed everyone, stood behind them, and gave him my middle finger.

"Oh, and Naja? Get a grip, will ya? It's a business decision. Nothing personal."

IT WAS TWO WEEKS after Russ's departure when I got word that most of our investors were pulling out. The reasons varied:

"We've decided that the current business is no longer in our best interests. We wish you well."

"We are currently seeking more aggressive business opportunities. We wish you well."

"Your business no longer falls within our core directives. We wish you well."

It was clear. Russ was leaving, and he was taking all of his contacts with him. It was two months before we were set to open the second store.

"Excuse me. Ms. Rodgers?" came a voice from the doorway. I

turned around to see Rikayah Mays, one of my part-timers. She was a business student at the University of Missouri, St. Louis, and was working her way through school.

"Come on in, Rikayah. Have a seat. What can I do you for?" I asked, trying my best to sound upbeat.

Rikayah fidgeted and rolled her hands in her lap. She adjusted herself in her chair several times while starting and stopping her sentence.

"I had to ask," she finally got out. "There've been rumors floating around that, well, that we're going to close. I was just wondering if there was any truth to that because I'm working my way through college, and I'm kinda depending on money from this job. So, if we're going to close, I was wondering if you could tell me that now so I can look for something else?"

"Where'd you hear that?"

Her hand encircled the air in front of her. "It's just around the whole shop. Everybody's been talking about it. Then, I overheard Russ talking to some people in a meeting before he left."

"Meeting? What meeting?"

"Few weeks ago. He was in a meeting with one of the men that came here before." She gave me a description and I guessed it to be one of our major investors. "He was telling the guy that he was leaving the company and he could no longer vouch for its continuing success under the current management."

"I see," I said as I tapped a pen on my desk.

"So, are we going out of business?"

I assured Rikayah that we were not going out of business before she left.

In no way was I going to lose this battle against Russ. He was trying to push me to failure, and I wasn't having it. I had to work out a plan.

• • •

I DECIDED TO GO see Chaney. It had been weeks since I had last talked to him. I was finally able to bring myself to talk to him again. I have to admit that I felt I had no one else to turn to. Russ was gone, and I still hadn't been able to bring myself to call Vlora yet. My world was falling apart, along with my business.

I pulled down my hat over my head as I turned off the car. I braced myself for the wind and cold as I got out of the car and walked down the street to the Rosebud Café. I tried to pull the door open and almost fell backward as I let go and the wind took me, and my momentum kept me in motion as the door remained fixed. That's when I looked up and noticed that the shop was empty and the lights were off. I cupped my hands over my eyes as I put my face up to the window to peer in. Was Chaney closed for the day? Was there a busted pipe? No heat? I knocked on the glass to see if Chaney was in the back room. No answer.

As I stepped back, I noticed a sign in the window: OUT OF BUSI-NESS. THANK YOU MILL CREEK VALLEY FOR YOUR YEARS OF PATRONAGE.

My heart sank to my stomach. The sharp, cold air cut me to the bone.

I looked up across the street and saw a lively Mooncents crowded with customers. I briefly contemplated a caramel latte, but couldn't bring myself to do it. I somberly walked to my car and drove home. I called Chaney and left a message on his voice mail when I got no answer.

EIGHTEEN

I TRIED TO REACH CHANEY BY PHONE, BUT COULDN'T get an answer or a return call.

I didn't have time to cry, and if I had, I wouldn't have allowed myself to do that anyway. I'd be damned if I let Russ try to destroy me, try though he might. I would show him. I didn't need him to continue to be successful and I would show him how dispensable he was to Exodusters 1879.

For three days, I worked on a plan to continue to move forward with the opening of the second store in Pine Lawn. I would proceed on a much smaller scale, but move along nonetheless. I'd cut back on part-timers, and I'd ask the managers to take a pay cut. It wouldn't be the best thing for them right now, but I'd be able to save everyone's jobs. And I would still need to get at least one investor in order to pull this off so I could buy Russ out. All in all, it could be done. Without Russ. He wasn't the shit that he thought he was.

I called a meeting with board members, contractors, management, and Allie. After distributing my well-put-together folders, I led the group through a PowerPoint presentation that laid out and explained my plan. Thirty minutes later, I turned up the lights.

"Now, I know there are going to be tons of questions. I know there are lots of concerns, and that's okay. Let's get it all out. Let's put it on the table for discussion. Any questions?"

The room was still. Only the sound of the projector filled the room. I got up to turn it off. Some cleared their throats. There was a sniffle, followed by the drop of a pen on the floor.

"Come on," I said sternly. "I know there must be questions or concerns."

Candis Cross was the first to speak. She cleared her throat twice, pushed her glasses up on her nose, then spoke slowly. "First and foremost, let me say that it has been a pleasure working for Exodusters 1879 and Russom King. Oh, and, um, you, too, Naja."

Okay, not a good sign.

"But in light of recent activities, I took it upon myself to explore other opportunities. And, well, in considering things, I decided to go into business for myself and open up my own software business. It's something I've always wanted to do anyway, and I thought that the crumbling of this business was a sign from God for me to go ahead and do just that. God is good!" She pumped her palms in the air twice and raised the roof. "But, Naja, I wish you well . . ."

There goes that "wish you well" crap again.

". . . and I will certainly give you my all in the remaining two weeks. But I'll be moving on after that." She handed me her letter of resignation, then pushed her glasses up on her nose again.

"I wish you the best," I said as I flashed a fake smile that made my cheeks hurt.

The party was kept alive by my store manager, who was quitting to be a stay-at-home mom and who had also been signaled by God. To be followed by our attorney, William Wilks, who was just offered a position in a law firm. My accountant, Hezekiah

Reid, who had decided to start a reggae band, was the only one to admit that his divine inspiration came straight from hemp.

One by one, my team handed me their resignation letters. Everyone but Allie.

"That was a kick-ass presentation, though. You go, girl!" Candis said as she patted my back when they all left the conference room.

He has won. I'll be damned. Russ has won.

Allie sat quiet in her chair for the longest. She finally came over, sat next to me, and drew me in for a comforting hug. "I know this is the worst timing ever," Allie said as she backed off.

"Don't tell me you finally got a job elsewhere?" I asked. I could do nothing but laugh. After all this time, now she gets a job? It was the perfect way to end the day.

"Don't be silly," she said and slapped me on the arm. "I would never abandon my sister. How insensitive do you think I am?"

I blew a short laugh through my nose. "Sorry. What is it? Go ahead and tell me. It can't get any worse than this."

"CompuTex is not renewing our lease on the computers. No reason as to why."

I threw my arms up in the air. "Aaaahhhh!" I slid my legs from under me and slumped in my chair. "But then again, I'm not surprised. They were contacts of Russ's, buddies or people he met through his buddies."

Allie hugged me again. She put her head up against mine and held me tight for several minutes. I patted her on the arm and dotted the corners of my eyes. "You know this means this is it, right? There's no way I'm going to be able to go on," I said.

I was silent for a good minute while I searched my mind for a miracle solution. None came.

"I'm going to have to close the business. I'll figure out what I'm going to do after that."

Again, we were silent. Allie put her arms around me and leaned her head on my shoulder.

"Naja?" she asked.

"Yeah?"

"Does this mean I'll get severance pay?"

NINETEEN

I DIDN'T HAVE ANYWHERE TO GET UP AND GO TO, but I could no longer bear to sit at home. There'd been too much time to think. Too much time to think about my initial reservations about dating a business partner, and the fact that it could lead me to the very position I was in now. I knew much better than that, yet I had done it anyway, and I didn't have anyone to blame but myself.

Seeing Andi always made me feel good. Her little smile could make a bear forget about honey. As I drove to Allie's place, I kept bringing my mind to thoughts of her chubby face to keep myself from thinking about the mess my life had become.

"Oh, cool!" Allie said after I told her I wanted to take Andi off her hands for the day. The best way to save myself from a complete meltdown was to stay busy, to keep moving, and to keep talking. And Andi was the perfect little person to spend the day with to do that. She was full of energy, and she was at that age where she asked questions all day long, her favorite being, "Why?"

"She's in her bedroom. Probably up watching cartoons," Allie said, forcing the front door closed quickly behind us.

"I know it's kind of early. So if she's still sleeping—"

"Nonsense," Allie said as she flew out of the living room and made a mad dash to Andi's room. "She would kill me if I made her miss a Saturday of hanging with her favorite aunt."

Only aunt.

"She hasn't hung out with you since you quit your nine-to-five. She'll be thrilled."

She'll be thrilled? More like, *her mother* will be thrilled.

I heard the violent squeaking of a bed, as if Allie was trying to shake life into the child. "Andi. Andi. Wake up. Auntie Naja wants to take you out for the whole day. The *whole* day!"

Andi's soft voice mumbled and whined before it came alive as she finally caught the meaning of her mommy's words.

"We got to get you ready. Yeah," I heard Allie say as I heard the sounds of closet doors and dresser drawers being thrown open and slammed shut. "We gotta find you something to wear real quick. And you need a bath."

"Really, take your time, sis. I'm not going to change my mind." I laughed to myself. "I'm going to get something to drink, okay?"

"You go right ahead. And nonsense. I'll have Andi ready in a flash."

I made my way to the kitchen while Allie got Andi ready in record time. I got a glass from the cupboard and went to the refrigerator for the overly sweetened grape Kool-Aid that I knew she had. The freezer door was spattered with business cards, some with pictures taped next to them. All of them were men. I pulled a few of them up and flipped them over where she had notes written. All of the cards were from people she had met at First Fridays events over the past year.

"Are you still searching for a rich business man at First Fridays?" I asked.

"You must be looking at the cards on the fridge, huh?" she asked as I heard the sudden blast of bathwater hitting the ceramic tub.

"Yeah."

She sauntered into the kitchen for a brief moment. "Don't knock it. It's working." She started pointing out cards, tapping her fingernails against them. "This one's legit. So is this one, and this one . . ."

"So, are any of them matches?"

She pointed to the same cards again. "Well, this one's happily married. And this one's unhappily married, but about to get a divorce. Any day now, he says. He's just waiting for the right time to tell her. And this one's engaged, but not sure she's the right one. . . ."

"And you say this is working?"

"Yeah. I'm getting closer. Before, I was just meeting a bunch of shysters. It's only a matter of time before I either find one that's unattached, or one of these will become unattached. That's why I'm holding on to their cards. To see what happens."

"Mommy!"

"Let me go finish her up. She'll be ready in a jiffy." Allie zoomed out of the kitchen faster than a bolt of lightning, the loose strands of her weave swishing behind her.

"Seriously, Allie. Don't bust a gut. Really."

"Nonsense!"

Fifteen minutes later, Andi was dressed in a pretty spring Baby Phat jumpsuit and Nike shoes, ready to go.

"Where we going, Auntie Naj?"

I didn't know. I turned to Allie as I grabbed Andi's hand. "I'm not sure where we're going, but it's safe to say that we might be out for a long time. It might be pretty late when we get back."

"Not a problem at all. Keep her overnight if you like. You want to stay overnight with Auntie Naj?"

"Yeaaaahhhh!" Andi said as she jumped up and down excitedly, her barretted ponytails bobbing and slapping her ears and neck.

We spent the day keeping my mind saturated with thoughts other than my failed business and Russ. Andi enjoyed the Eugene Field House and St. Louis Toy Museum and having her hair stand on end at the Magic House. After lunch and games at Dave & Buster's, she dished out her fill of questions, and there were a lot of them, at the Science Center. Her questions started slowing down midway through the zoo, and her head nearly fell into her plate of pizza by the time we made it to Chuck E. Cheese's for a late dinner. She was worn out, and didn't want to play games by then.

In the silence of the car, I thought about Vlora. I still hadn't called her back, and hadn't heard from her since. I was ready. And at the end of my thoughts, I found myself parked outside her house.

I pulled a staggering Andi behind me as we walked to Vlora's doorstep and rang the bell. I rolled on my ankle, then bounced on my knee, as I waited for her to answer the door. I didn't know what to expect from her when she saw me.

Vlora answered the door clutching the middle of her bathrobe over her frame and crunching on something in her mouth.

"Naja!" she said. Her eyes were wide as she opened the screen door. I walked in. Andi stumbled in behind me and immediately slumped to the floor and was out like a light in a second.

Vlora hugged me tight and rocked me from side to side. She moved back, looked at my tear-filled eyes, and touched her lips to my cheek.

Andi rolled over on the floor beside me and drew Vlora's

attention. "My goodness, is the child drunk?" she asked jokingly as she kneeled down to examine her. "Or dead?" She collected Andi from the hardwood floor and gingerly placed her on the couch and covered her with a purple throw.

"We kinda had a long day. I had a lot on my mind," I said, then told her where we had been and all that we had done.

"All that in one day?"

For the first time, I burst into tears. It was something I hadn't done in a long time. Something I hadn't allowed myself to do, until now.

Vlora pulled me to her and pressed my head to her shoulder. "I guess this means that I'll have to wait a few minutes before I curse you out, huh?" I felt the cool tip of her nose on my forehead.

"Vlora, I'm so sorry," I blubbered. "You know I never would have ended our friendship on my own. I got so wrapped up in Russ. Everything you said was true. I should have listened to you."

She asked me if all this meant that Russ and I were no longer together, and that made me cry even harder because I realized I would have to go through the whole story. But I did. After she took Andi to her guest bedroom, I told her every little sordid detail.

"No 'I told you so'?" I asked when she was silent.

"No," Vlora said. She pulled herself back from me and stared at me with pity in her eyes. Then, she popped me in the head.

"Ow!" I said. I rubbed the back of my head and looked at her with wide eyes. "Uh, remember me? I'm the one in pain here," I said sarcastically.

"That's for not taking my advice. The opinion of a fellow-minded entrepreneur like *moi*, who's stuck by you through thick and thin for years!" She pressed her fanned-out fingers against her chest.

A stream began to trickle from my right nostril. Vlora reached over to the side table and retrieved a tissue for me.

I took in a deep breath and shook my head. "I don't know how I could let somebody influence my thinking like that and have me turning on my own best friend."

"It's the power of the dick, baby. Does it every time."

"I'm sorry."

We sat next to each other on the couch and Vlora examined her nails. "I'm not going to lie. I was hurt that day at Rosebud's. And then, I suddenly had an empty void in my life. A void that needed to be filled. I—"

Down the stairs thundered a shirtless well-muscled body: chestnut brown, hazel eyes, with a delectable cleft in his chin.

"My bad. Excuse me, baby." His tone bore the peacefulness of a wave of an ocean deep. "I didn't know you had company. I was just going to get a snack." He pointed to the kitchen.

My mouth dropped. I gave Vlora a swift sharp elbow to the ribs.

"Ow!" she shrieked and rubbed her side. "Honey, this is my best friend, Naja Rodgers."

I stood up to shake his hand.

"Naja, this is my man, Mel."

"Your man?" I turned and mouthed to her. "Nice to meet you," I said aloud, turning back to him.

"Best friend? I haven't seen you in the months that I've known Vlora."

"You are so goofy," Vlora said to me as I intentionally stared dreamily at Mel. She then directed herself to Mel. "You remember, honey," she said sweetly. "This is the one with the Internet café. She never came by before because she was swamped trying to run it."

"Oh yeah," he said. "How's business going?"

I placed one hand on my hip and used the other to rub my neck back and forth as I reluctantly tried to think of an answer that wouldn't get me to crying again.

"Bad question. I'll explain it all to you later, babe," Vlora said.

"My bad, again. Well, it's a pleasure to meet you. If you ladies will excuse me . . ." He made a gesture toward Vlora's kitchen and went that way. We watched his tight, rounded ass as it floated off.

"Sure," I said. "I hope to see more of you, ahem, I mean, see you again soon."

Vlora laughed, and we both became giggling idiots.

"Ooohh, girl!" I said. I shook out my hand like it was on fire and I was trying to put it out.

"Pretty good, eh?"

I kept laughing until a thought hit me. "Wait a minute! So you started talking to him right after we stopped talking? So that's why I haven't heard from you in months. What happened to that void that I left? That void that needed to be filled."

She shrugged. "He filled it," she said nonchalantly. Her eyes danced as she giggled.

"Okay, you know what? I ain't even mad."

"And now that that buster-ass Russ is out of your life, we need to get you somebody. I still think you and Chaney look cute together."

"Ah, see, there you go. Although—" I told Vlora about the orgasmic foot massage I had received from him.

"Damn. How'd you get your back blown out from a foot massage?" She shut one eye and looked cock-eyed at me through the other.

"I'm still trying to figure that out myself. I still get aftershocks when I think about it." I faked a couple of jerks to represent my orgasmic convulsions.

"You so crazy."

We shared laughs together like old times until our chuckles faded. We topped it off with an airy sigh at the end.

"You know what would be cool?" Vlora asked as she stared off into space. "If me, you, and Allie got together and went to the next First Fridays again. The first week of May. The weather will be nice."

"That'll be music to Allie's ears. She missed you, you know."

Vlora looked at me with skeptical eyes. "In her words, that bitch missed me? Now I know you're lying to me."

"No, seriously," I tried to convince her. "She even walked out on me at a First Fridays because she said it wasn't the same without you."

"Lawd, the child does have a little sense after all. Now, if you can just get her back in school, she'll be straight."

"She's still trying to find a rich man at these events to take care of her and Andi. She even has a method to the madness."

Vlora rolled her eyes to the ceiling and dismissed the thought. "Okay, so what's next for *you?*"

"I told you. I don't want to date right now. After all I just went through, that's the last thing on my mind."

"I'm not talking about that. How are you going to get back on your feet? What are you going to do next?" That was just like Vlora. State the problem, and get right to planning a solution.

"Tell you the truth, Vlora, I hadn't even thought about that yet."

"I can see that. Too busy trying not to think, and taking it all out on Andi. Poor child." She tilted her head downward and her eyes looked upward at me.

"She's usually hyper and talkative. She just gave out at the end."

"With all the stuff you had her doing in one day? I'm quite sure you've violated child labor laws or something."

I laughed as I thought about all we did. "I guess I did take her through a lot."

"Naja, the girl is barely breathing."

I lightly slapped my hands against my thighs. "Okay, well, next week, I'm going to work on my résumé and prepare to interview for a position somewhere. I guess."

She blew through her tightly pressed lips and threw both hands up in the air. "So, it's over just like that? You're going to let a man stomp on your dream like that? Me myself personally—"

"He did more than stomp on it. He killed it."

She grabbed me by the chin and steadied my head. "Honey, can't nobody kill your dreams but you."

I pulled away. "That looks great on the back of a postcard, but this is life."

As usual, Vlora was right, in theory. But resurrecting Exodusters 1879, even the one store, wouldn't be easy. I didn't think I had the energy to start a new company right now. Then there was still the issue of a partner. I wasn't down on partners, and still actually preferred one. A one-woman operation was tough, I didn't care who the woman was.

"I hear you though," I offered as I lifted my head.

"Okay, well, we'll talk about that another time. But how about we choose a different city to go to for First Fridays?"

"That's a great idea. We can make a mini-vacation out of it." I perked up at the possibility.

"It's settled then." She slapped me on the thigh. "We'll get together with Allie and decide which city."

"Sounds good."

I went to get Andi, who was still drunk with fatigue.

"I know you had fun today," Vlora said to Andi. "You looking forward to hanging out with your Aunt Naja again real soon?"

Andi rubbed her tired eyes. "Noooo," she whined. She yawned as I picked her up and carried her to the car.

TWENTY

AFTER CONSIDERING CLEVELAND, HOUSTON, INDIAN-apolis, Philly, San Diego, and other cities, we decided on First Fridays at the Chromium Niteclub in Chicago. We planned a road trip and hit the highway. We fantasized about having a bonding experience, and agreed to go a few days early to have time for shopping, sightseeing, touring, and just basking in our rekindled sisterhood.

We rented a roomy SUV for the three of us and took turns driving. We shared laughs and one another's music, talked about men, our bodies, food, and sex. Anything but work and business.

We all gasped simultaneously as we pulled up to the House of Blues Hotel. The SUV achieved total silence for the first time since we had hit the road eight hours before. The handsome valet took our car, and the gorgeous bell-boy handled our bags as we stood together in the lobby and gawked.

From the vibe of the hotel, we could tell that we were about to embark upon the weekend of a lifetime. The House of Blues Hotel thrived along the river and in the midst of Marina City. The exotic architecture and decor, coupled with the onslaught of attractive and sexy men—both hotel workers and guests—we saw in the hotel lobby was enough to flood us with all kinds of ungodly urges. I hadn't done anything, yet I felt the sudden need to repent.

Vlora and I must have been thinking the same thing. "Um, you know, I'm thinking that the suite we're all sharing might be too small for us." Her eyes scanned the lobby and went from scrumptious body to scrumptious body as she spoke. The place was littered with them.

I licked my lips and swallowed lust. "I think you might be right. Maybe we should get separate rooms?" I offered, but it was more like a demand.

"Wait. I can't afford my own room for four nights," Allie stated.

Vlora and I were working things out in our minds.

"Look, I'm willing to go half on your room, if your sister will go the other half." Vlora nodded her head toward me and raised both her eyebrows three times to signal me.

"Sounds doable," I said and returned the signal.

"Are you both serious? Sweet!" Allie exclaimed. We giggled like sex-starved housewives as we headed to the registration counter.

Since I had hooked back up with Vlora, I had noticed she seemed like a new person: alive and full of life and adventure. She didn't seem as uptight as she had been before, and I was thinking that it was all due to her new man.

"What about Mel?" I asked while she stared down man after man like she was trying to figure out which one to talk to.

Vlora looked at me, confused. "What about him?"

"You all are still together, right?"

"Yeah, and . . . ?"

"Well, you wouldn't do anything, right? I mean, not that it's any of my business. I'm just saying."

She rolled her neck. "I paid for my *own* trip." Vlora then lifted her left hand to the ceiling and spread her fingers. "Besides. I don't see no ring on this finger," she said.

"Well, in that case, what happens in Chicago—" I started.

"Stays in Chicago," we all said in unison.

ONLY DURING SLOW TIMES did I find myself wallowing in sorrow about my failed business and Russ, so, as I did with Andi, I tried to keep busy to avoid the thoughts.

The next morning, we started the day in the hotel spa with massages and facials, then ambushed the city over the next few days. We lunched daily at different outside cafés we found as we headed out shopping or sightseeing. Hours of our time daily were spent shopping on the Magnificent Mile, going from Bloomingdale's to Saks Fifth Avenue to Tiffany to Nordstrom. We hung out at the Navy Pier, went to museums, stopped by the Sears Tower and the John Hancock Center. In the daytime, Chicago made it easy to not think about me. At night, it was easy to find people to occupy our time, and the problem became choosing. For me, after the second or third glass of wine and conversation, I was at a point where I could safely go to my room alone, too tired to sit up and think. Which was exactly what I wanted.

"Damn! Check this shit out," Vlora said as we stepped inside Chromium Niteclub for First Fridays. Chromium was unlike any club in St. Louis, and it was easy to see that this was going to be a different First Fridays experience for us. We toured the club before getting our complimentary drink from this month's sponsor: anything mixed with Bacardi.

The main room had a lustrous chrome metallic motif. The ceiling seemed nonexistent and a large, rectangular dance floor, complete with a suspended disco ball, was flanked by bars on either side of the room. The DJ spun tunes from the Plexiglas spaceship over the dance floor.

The second level offered plush red leather couches and industrial steel go-go cages over the dance floor. Music videos were running on the two fifteen-foot screens on either side of the room.

We came upon the Remy Room, but couldn't gain access. Two heavy-set men stood at attention in front of the entrance with their arms folded across their chests.

After scoping out the place, we went back to the main room, picked up our drinks, and helped ourselves to appetizers as we participated in the professional presentations that were given. A couple of hours into the evening, Lakeside came to the stage to perform.

"How come we don't have First Fridays like this in St. Louis?" Vlora asked as she danced to "Fantastic Voyage."

I shrugged as I danced in place right along beside her.

"You know what we should do? Every month, we should travel to a First Fridays in a different city. To check them all out," said a penniless Allie.

"You ain't said nothing but a word. Next month will be your treat," Vlora joked.

Allie realized how ridiculous her statement was, coming from her. "Whatever, bitch," she shot at Vlora and rolled her eyes.

Vlora followed up Allie's statement with her usual threat and motioned like she was going to choke Allie.

"Well, it's been lovely, ladies, but I need to work out my mission," Allie said as she opened her purse and fished out her business cards. "I got work to do. Fresh meat," she said with a sinister smile. With a twist of her head, she was off on her search.

"That's really not a bad idea," Vlora said. "We need to find you a man here. Looks like there's a better selection here than at home."

I sighed. "Don't start. You know how I feel about that."

"Yeah, I do. This would be the ideal situation for you. A long-distance relationship. That way, you wouldn't have somebody up under you all the time. You can work on your business again. Then, when you need a break, you can fly in your boy toy or go visit him. Now how cool would that be?"

"When I start my business again. Who said I was doing that?"

"Glad you brought that up, because I've wanted to talk to you about that."

"Here it comes." I twisted my lips to the side.

"You're not the kind to work for someone else, and you know it. You go back to having a boss, and you know you're going to be unhappy," Vlora added.

"You're probably right. But I feel so drained from everything right now. I don't think I can go through that whole process again." I tapped my glass with my nails.

"You fail, you get up and do it again," Vlora coached. "You dust yourself off and you go charging back in the ring with your soul on fire." Vlora turned me to face the room. "Now, go." She gave me a small push forward.

She added, "And, if you need me, I'll be at the bar talking to that hottie over there." She waved me off and headed to the bar.

I worked the room, meeting and greeting others, sometimes exchanging business cards with people that I wanted to follow up with for one reason or another. I was in the middle of tucking one business card into my purse when a woman approached me and introduced herself. I was expecting her to either tell me that my SUV had its lights on, or there was tissue attached to the heel of my shoe. After my experience at First Fridays at home, I didn't expect to be approached by another female in a noncompetitive way.

We cordially chatted, then we got into business, and all the while I was waiting for something, I didn't know what. But as she talked, for some reason, I felt comfortable with her. In previous situations, I'd found women the hardest to network with. But I didn't feel this with Charlene. She seemed genuinely interested in meeting another sister and trying to figure out how we could come together to help each other succeed. I didn't know what to do. It was a brand-new experience for me.

Perhaps that's why I felt compelled to open up to her. We had moved to the mezzanine level and sat at a table that over-looked the crowded dance floor below. After a few rum and Cokes, I told her about the business, Russ, and our relationship, and she repeated the things that Vlora had said.

"That's messed up," she said. "But you can't let it end there. I know it's going to be hard, but you got to pick up and start all over."

"You sound like my friend Vlora. She and my sister, Allie, are here with me."

"Sounds like she knows what she's talking about." Charlene reached into her purse and pulled out two cards as the beat vi-brated the tables and chairs we sat in. "This is my card. You can contact me anytime."

I read the card that told me Charlene was a motivational speaker with her own company, UGoGurrl Productions.

"I also have an association, and it would be nice if you joined. It is a local group of women who support one another and encourage one another to succeed. We share leadership, professional, and developmental skills, and hold seminars monthly. Now, I know you're not in the area, but we also have a Web site with tips, articles written by members, a directory of members and services they offer, and a lot more. Then we have an online group that you would be able to participate in. We have more than three hundred women locally, and another hundred or so who are members at large. With that, we have a variety of women with different backgrounds, so there's bound to be an expert for whatever needs you may have."

I was blown away. I squinted my eyes in confusion as I looked at her. "What does it cost?"

She laughed. "It doesn't cost anything."

"I'm sorry. I'm just shocked. Where I come from, women don't . . . it's hard to . . . I mean, it's difficult . . ."

"I know exactly what you want to say. We sisters can be our own worst enemies." She laughed as she crossed her legs under the table. "Actually, that's why I started this organization. To show how powerful we can be if we help one another and put our resources together. And that for one of us to succeed doesn't mean that the rest of us have to fail."

I was speechless.

"I know, it's hard to believe," she laughed. "But it's possible."

I stared at her card before I put it in my purse.

"Hey, and don't knock that business-slash-personal relationship. Just like in anything, you have to find the right person."

Charlene put her hand in the air and waved the rock on her finger. She told me that she and her husband had started off as business partners and developed a relationship afterward, having now been married seven years.

I laughed. "Doesn't work for everyone."

"From what you told me, your man had control issues and low self-esteem."

"Maybe. But still."

She leaned into me as if to make sure I heard her point over the thud of the speakers. "Don't take it out on the scenario.

Sometimes people get so messed up from a bad situation that they start generalizing and making rules and end up passing up a good man."

I nodded.

Charlene pointed down to the dance floor. "Hey, there are some of the ladies from the group." She named two attorneys, a podiatrist, and an engineer. They had formed a circle in the midst of a full dance floor and were getting their boogie on with one another, having a good time.

"Looks like we're up here missing out on all the fun," I said.

Just then, the podiatrist looked up and spotted Charlene and waved both of us down to the dance floor. "You game?" Charlene asked me.

"Of course, my sister," I said. We headed to the dance floor.

I felt rejuvenated and invigorated, and I let it all out on the dance floor. One of the attorneys was letting loose and getting it crunk. The podiatrist joined her for a little friendly dance-off. I had fun with my new sisters as we danced to song after song. As I lost myself in the beat, I vowed to end the sulking now and to pick myself up off my butt and start all over again. How I would do it, I'd figure out later.

"Where are your girls?" Charlene asked. "Have you seen them at all?"

I was having so much fun that I had forgotten that I hadn't seen Vlora and Allie in a while. My sight couldn't penetrate the floor, and I shrugged. I was about to say that I hadn't seen them when I looked up.

"No they not!" I shouted.

"What?" Charlene asked.

I looked up and pointed. "Up there. Those are my girls!"

Vlora and Allie were dancing side by side in the steel cage

above. Vlora had let her hair down. Either that, or it came down from all the wild flinging and bucking she was doing. They were shaking hard, twurking to the beat.

"That's where the party is," Charlene said.

"Nothing but a word," the engineer said. We all headed up to the steel cage.

Vlora and Allie smiled hard when we got there. They didn't even wait for introductions. They pulled me by the hand and the rest of them followed behind me.

"What's up, bitch?" Vlora said to me. She laughed and started breaking it all the way down.

Allie rolled her eyes and smothered a smile.

"What's the matter?" I asked Allie. "I thought that's what you wanted from Vlora. For her to loosen up."

"It's no fun if she's cool with it." She faked a pissed-off look.

"Whatever, bitch," Vlora said to Allie.

Allie smirked and rolled her eyes again. She turned her back to Vlora and kept twurking it while she smiled.

TWENTY-ONE

BACK IN ST. LOUIS, I SPENT THE NEXT FEW WEEKS clearing my head every morning by meditating amid incense first thing in the morning. Then I'd start working on the plan I needed to present to investors and bankers to reopen Exodusters 1879 on a much smaller scale. I spent hours every week in the library and in bookstores, doing research to gain the knowledge I lacked. Minutes turned to hours on the phone, and conversations turned to lunch with the contacts I had made through networking. I even joined a local Toastmasters group to work on my presentation skills, even though they were one of my strong points.

And to wind down each night, I saturated my mind with Germaine Greer, bell hooks, and Angela Davis again. I was coming back bigger, better, and stronger this time.

"ARE YOU SURE you don't want to go to First Fridays with me tonight?" I asked Allie. I had just come from the library, where I had been doing research, and stopped by Allie's place on the way home.

Andi sat down after jumping up to greet me with a hug. She went back to reading a book she had open on her lap. She wore the same no-name jean shorts and red T-shirt as her mother.

"Not this time. I'm going to stay here and hang out with Andi tonight."

Stay home? On a Friday? Something wasn't right.

"Are you having a mother-daughter moment, or something?" I asked with a sugary smile.

She dismissed Andi to her room before she answered.

She hovered close to me, as if she were speaking in confidence. "Last Friday, I went to a house-warming for one of my friends and got home pretty early. I was planning to go out later that night. But when I got home, I found that the babysitter had allowed Andi to play dress-up."

"So." I shrugged. "You've seen her do that with her friends several times before."

"Yeah, but this time they were watching videos. Rap videos. I just couldn't believe my eyes . . ." She stared at the carpet.

"What?" I asked anxiously. "Lewd video girls?"

She looked up at me. "Yeah, but that's not all. Andi had picked out some of my, uh, clubbin' clothes. She found a short miniskirt and a tube top that she rolled up to show more of her midsection." Allie held a hand right below her breasts to demonstrate how high. "And there she was. In the middle of my living room floor. Rockin' my stilettos. Dropping it like it was hot. Right along with the video hos on TV."

"Oh, my." I lifted my eyebrows over my wide eyes as I covered my open mouth with my hand. I could see the tragedy etched all over her face.

"And you should have seen the way she was moving her little hips, rolling her body, bending over, shaking, and making it clap." She reflected. "She was me. The way I dance, but . . . she's a little girl."

I shook my head.

"And the babysitter was smiling. But she's fifteen, and doesn't know any better. She thinks it's cute. I asked Andi what she was doing, and she started laughing and jumping up and down. She told me that this is what she wanted to do. That she wanted to grow up and be a video ho, just like that. And she pointed to the TV. I was so embarrassed."

"Where did she get 'video ho'?"

"Probably from me. I might have used that term a time or two," she said, as she took a big swallow of guilt.

She leaned back on the sofa with suspended thoughts. "It's like it hit me all at once. I don't think I'm a bad mother."

"Of course you're not," I assured her.

"I make sure Andi has everything she needs. She's a good kid. But right then and there, it made me realize what I was charged with." She looked in my eyes. "I'm responsible for her life. For the adult that she becomes."

I nodded my head. I had been telling her this for years, but I guess she had to hear it from within.

"It's like she's absorbing everything. *Every little thing.* She's watching everything I do, even though I try to close the door on some things. But she sees."

"I hear kids are like that."

Allie continued to sigh and shake her head.

"But it looks like you're taking a step in the right direction," I added.

"I couldn't sleep that night. And the next morning as soon as the stores opened, I yanked her butt out of bed and took her to the store. We went and got some books with her daddy's money. Some positive books for her to read. We came home and I turned off the TV, and I read books to her. Like Mom used to do for us. Only I wasn't reading her any feminist stuff, but real stories. We've been reading ever since." She laughed. "And you know what? She doesn't even miss the TV. She loves reading. And I never even knew that." She stared at her hands as she pondered the thought.

I joked. "I'm glad something brought it all home for your butt. I couldn't tell you anything, remember? Because I didn't have any kids of my own?" I mocked the statement that she had made to me all too many times.

"I'm sorry, Naj. I had no right to say that. You had a hand in raising me even if I was a teenager already."

"Don't worry about it. So, you're staying home to read with Andi?"

"That too. But there's more." She smiled at me with her eyes. "I've decided to finish up my last year of school."

I was elated. "Well, all right!" I all but shouted.

"Andi's watching me, and I need to be a good example. I need to be her role model. I'm going to take a summer class. Open registration is tomorrow morning."

I moved over and hugged her. "Well, good for you." I ruffled her hair. "Good for *you*."

I left Allie's and went back home to change before heading to First Fridays. With Vlora gone to the Lake of the Ozarks with Mel for the weekend, I would have to go it alone tonight, which was not a problem. By now, I had come to know a few First Fridays regulars, and there were sure to be others there that I knew.

I made my rounds again, running into old familiars, getting progress reports, and meeting the newbies. I locked glances with George Wilson. George was a top executive in one of the financial institutions that Russ secured one of our loans from. He and Russ spent a lot of time together at the bar after work and on the golf course on the weekends.

Queasiness came over me as George spotted me and came my way. "Naja Rodgers. How nice to see you." His smile was inviting, and he embraced me.

"It's great to see you again, too, George," I said. I felt edgy. After all, he was Russ's good friend, not mine.

"I was really sorry to hear about the closing of the Internet café. That was really a unique business, and I thought you guys were doing well."

"We were. Until things changed and . . . Well, I couldn't continue as planned. But I'm starting over, on a much smaller scale now."

"Tough situation. I understand."

I nodded and looked around the room.

He bent his tall frame at the knees. "You doing okay?"

"I'm doing fine," I said. I bobbed my head up and down. "Yeah, fine."

"I'm glad to hear that," he said. He paused. "This might sound out of line, but I'm happy to see that you got out from underneath Russ. Don't get me wrong, he's a great entrepreneur. He knows what he wants, and he goes after it. He's good at what he does. Work-wise. But I don't think he's comfortable with women in the workforce."

I raised my eyebrows. "What do you mean?"

"He's a bit of an old soul. After I got to know you a little, I was surprised that you were with him. He usually doesn't like women who even appear to be smarter than he is. He's got to be head honcho. Wear the pants, if you know what I mean."

"Yeah, I do."

"You seemed like an intelligent woman, and I got the impression from the way Russ talked that he was intimidated by you."

"Do you still keep in touch with him?"

"Yes, I do. From time to time. He even invited me to Atlanta for a golf outing. His treat." He took a swig of his drink.

I hesitated. I didn't want to ask, but I had to know. "How's he doing?"

"He's doing fine."

I was let down.

"He's only doing property investments now. He, uh . . . has a new woman. She's the total opposite of you. I think she's just what he's been looking for. She's like his mother. Caters to him."

"Better her than me."

"So . . . are you seeing anyone?"

I hesitated. "No, I'm really focusing on business right now. Especially after what I just went through."

"I can understand that. I'm doing the same thing. I think it would be unfair to a woman to get into a committed relationship, because I know I wouldn't be able to give her the time and attention she needs. Relationships take work, and I spend so much time at work, I wouldn't have anything left to give at the moment."

"That's very thoughtful of you."

"Yeah, thoughtful. But it can get lonely sometimes."

"It's a trade-off, I guess. You've never been married?"

"No. Hoping to one day. When I get around to dating, that is."

George gave a long pause. I could tell there was something on the tip of his tongue that he wanted to get off.

"Listen," he said. "I don't live far from here, and you're welcome to, um . . . join me for a drink. At my place." His long deep gaze transferred the exact meaning of his words.

I felt uneasy. "I don't think that would be a good idea. I uh—" I tried to think up a quick excuse.

"Don't worry about it," he said quickly. "I didn't mean to put you on the spot. To be honest, I was just trying to see if you were, you know, down."

"You're not even close to anyone? I mean, seeing anyone?"

"No steady companion. It's difficult. Building a career, I'm not available a lot of times. Women like it when you're successful, but a lot of them can't deal with what it takes to get there."

"So, in the meantime, you—"

"In the meantime, I get with people who are in the same position I am. No strings attached. Don't mean to sound crass, but we get together, fulfill a need, and move on. Might keep each other's number just in case we have time to hook up again."

"Well, to each his own, I guess."

He looked around the room. "There are a lot of people running around here like that."

I looked down at the floor. "Well, I'm sorry, but that's just not me."

"No need to apologize. Just trying to see where you were. Everything's cool." He displayed a smile. He reached into his coat pocket and retrieved a card. "Let me know if you need an investor. I liked your business before, and you did well. Give me a call if you need me," he said with a deep smile. "Don't worry. No strings attached."

"Thank you," I said, smiling on the inside. "You'll definitely hear from me."

Another man caught George's attention with a wave and at the same time, I spotted Chaney.

"Naja, would you excuse me?" George gestured in the direction of his acquaintance.

"No problem at all," I said. I was happy for the excuse to go talk to Chaney.

I walked so as not to allow Chaney to see me coming and tapped him on the shoulder. "Hey there," I said as I displayed an open grin.

He turned and his crooked smile spread across his face from ear to ear.

"Naja! Hey!" Chaney took me in his arms and gave me a tight squeeze after I placed my drink on the table beside him. I returned the hug, and I was surprised that neither of our lungs collapsed in the embrace. I had never before associated any particular cologne to Chaney, but today, the scent of his body brought back memories in my mind. Fond memories that made me stir on the inside. "Long time, no see. How've you been?" He stepped back and scanned me from head to toe.

"Doing good, but what happened to you?" I shoved him in the arm. "You closed up shop. I got no answer whenever I called, and I haven't heard from you since."

He tucked his hands in his pockets. He had on blue jeans with a jacket, and it was the first time I'd seen him without a baseball cap. Anybody else would have looked underdressed, but Chaney fit right in with anything he wore and always looked comfortable. "Rosebud was my life. I had to get out of town for a while after I closed it. Went to L.A. to visit my sister. One week turned into two weeks turned into a month, and, well . . . I had to get my head together."

"Don't you ever do that again without calling me. You hear me?"

"Promise," he said. "What about you?"

I rolled my eyes, then chuckled before I told him the whole story.

"Sorry to hear about the business. But I don't think it's any secret that I never liked the guy, so excuse me if I don't get all choked up about that part."

"He never liked you either. Said you 'disrepected him,'" I mocked Russ.

Chaney laughed. "What, are we gang members now? Were we going to get to throwin' bows?" He gave a hearty laugh from his middle. "But I wouldn't even have been worried about that. He didn't look like he could scrap a lick."

"His buddy over there"—I pointed out George—"thought he had an inferiority complex."

"That's what I thought all along. I would too if I were three-foot-fo'." We shared a laugh at Russ's expense. "But he was your man, so I wasn't going to say a thing."

"Thanks. You've always been a good friend to me."

We both took a sip of our drinks at the same time and I felt warm. Didn't know if it was from the drink or from Chaney.

Chaney reached around and cupped the back of my neck with his hand. "You know I care about you."

I looked at him. "You're one of my best friends. It really did hurt me when you left."

He gazed straight ahead. "I didn't think you wanted me to bother you anymore." His shoulders rose and fell. "I thought I'd give you the time you needed. But, remember, I called to check on you. Sent you meditation cushions, things to make you smile and let you know that I was thinking about you. But after weeks went by, and I hadn't heard a peep out of you, I thought you didn't want to have anything to do with me ever."

"I can't believe that I allowed Russ to get to me like that. To make me drop my friends." I talked to him about Russ being at the crux of the breakup of my friendship with Vlora.

"There's no way to say it other than I felt like an idiot. I felt suckered."

"Won't happen again," he said.

"Promise? No matter how stupid I become?" I stared deep into his pupils.

"You're never stupid. You just have a trusting heart. And I promise." Chaney smiled.

The low buzz of other conversations came between us and filled our gap.

"You still meditating?" Chaney asked.

I lit up. "I am. And it's worked wonders for me. I'm so focused on what I'm doing."

"Which is?" he asked.

"I've decided to reopen Exodusters."

"Cool. Going it alone?"

"I will if I have to, but I still prefer a partner. Sole proprietorship is hard work, plus the total liability . . ."

"You don't have to tell me. I know."

"What about you? What are you doing now?"

"Since I showed my face again in Mill Creek Valley, a lot of people have been putting a bug in my ear about reopening. I resisted for a while. But now, I think I may give it a try. Mooncents increased their prices and reduced their sizes. Pissed a lot of people off. I think they're feeling what they've been missing in Rosebud now."

"Of course they are. See, didn't I tell you that would happen?"

"Yeah. A closed shop and a broken heart later."

"I think you should go for it. They're going to flock like flies to your shop."

"I'm on the same tip as you, though. When I did have the shop and I was doing it by myself, it pretty much took up all my time. With that, I eked out time to be active in the community, and that was it. I had no social life. No time to relax. That's what I wanted right after Melinda died. But now that I've been out here enjoying life for a few months, I don't know if I want to go back to that kind of schedule again."

"So get a partner."

"You make it sound easy. You, of all people, should know better."

He picked up his glass off the table. After taking a sip of his drink, Chaney's eyes widened. "Why don't we go into business together?" A slow smile crept up on his face as the idea settled on him. "Yeah. We should go into business together. We could combine your business with mine. It would be perfect. You feel me?"

I rubbed my neck. "I don't know, Chaney."

"It's like the perfect answer. You bring in the computers, the furniture, the magazines. I got us covered on the café side, and we'd be able to serve more than just drinks and little snacks."

I mulled it over in my mind.

"What's wrong? You don't know about the location, if it would work, or me as a partner?" Chaney asked.

"No offense, but I was really thinking of a female partner this time around."

He twitched his jaw. "You mean you'd choose some strange female over somebody you know?" He nudged my arm. "Have you thought about that? You know how you women are. All y'all want to be the boss. You thought Russ was bad. Think about all the potential catfights." He smiled. I laughed.

I tugged on my earlobe. "You know, you do have a point there. Because the women here have been fierce. It's been tough trying to step into their world."

"Most of you all got that competition thing going on. Don't know why. Y'all don't know it, but it's a woman's world."

"Speak, my brother," I said as I raised one fist in the air, dipped at the knees, then hopped. "Speak!"

We chuckled together.

I ran my tongue over my teeth in thought. "You know what? You do raise a good point. Tell you what. I'll at least think about it, if that's okay with you."

"Might I add that I'm house-trained," Chaney added with puppy-dog eyes. He rested his chin on my shoulder.

"You're silly."

"Okay. Think it over. I'll be patient."

"Thanks."

"Put it there, partner," Chaney said as he extended his hand to me.

"Chaney! I said let me think about it!"

"I know," he grinned. "I was just thinking positive." He grabbed my hand and gave it an exaggerated shake.

TWENTY-TWO

I WAS A COUPLE OF WEEKS INTO THINKING IT OVER and Chaney hadn't bugged me once about a decision. We both proceeded with planning our own businesses, but we helped each other out as we went along. I let Chaney in on the people I knew with whatever expertise he needed, and he did the same for me.

I confessed to him that I needed some help with my new business structure. Chaney agreed to meet at his place to go over it with me and give me his input.

"I'm in the area, and I was wondering if we could just meet at your place instead of mine?" Chaney asked me over the phone.

I gulped. "M-m-my place?"

"If that's cool. I just left from having lunch with a friend at the Bread Company, and I'm just a little ways from where you are. I can hold off a little and give you time to get dressed if you need it."

"N-no problem. I'm dressed. Come on by."

"Great. I'll see you in just a few minutes."

"Sure," I said before hanging up.

I was frantic. Other than Vlora and Allie, I hadn't had anyone over in quite some time and my place was a mess. I was already bad at organizing my files. I left papers out while I worked and they were scattered everywhere. I tried to straighten up as much as I could in the ten minutes it took Chaney to get there. I opened the door when he knocked.

"Uh, come on in," I said timidly.

Chaney held a St. Louis Bread Company box in his hand as he stepped through the door. "Fresh cinnamon crunch bagels, your favorite."

I took the box from Chaney's hands as he stepped in. "Have a seat at the table."

I moved stacks of paper over and made space for me, Chaney, and the bagels.

"Before we get started, I was wondering if you could show me your business structure from before."

"Umm . . . yeah . . ." I eyed the stack of files and papers on the table, and started to go through them. "No, wait," I said. "I think it's over there."

I got up and went through a stack of files on the counter. "Ah, yes, here it is." I handed it to Chaney.

"Do you always work like this? With stuff spread out?"

"When I work at home, I work all over the place. I actually know where everything is. I'm slightly disorganized, I know. One day, I gotta take the time to really organize this place."

"You mean it's been like this for a while?"

"Pretty much. I'm just short on time. Organizing is on the bottom of the list right now. But I know exactly where everything is."

Chaney looked amazed. "That's all good, but why don't you organize it better so it won't be . . . clutter?"

"This works for me right now."

"How about we do it now? I can help you."

"You don't have to do that."

Chaney scanned the room once more. "You got a CD player?"

"Just this." I pointed to my Bose portable 3-CD changer.

"That'll be fine. I'll be back."

Chaney headed out the door and came back minutes later with a CD case in his hand. He pulled out a CD and dropped it into the player.

"We'll make this fun."

Out came sounds from the sixties. The first was "Heatwave" by Martha and the Vandellas. Chaney started doing old-time dances, and I began to giggle. "Come on, join me. Don't act like you don't know."

I let loose and joined him. We ate bagels, labeled folders, sorted my papers and filed them away in my empty file cabinet, while periodically stopping to dance to Frankie Lymon and the Teenagers, Smokey Robinson and the Miracles, Diana Ross and the Supremes, and more. It was the best time I had ever had organizing.

When we finished hours later, we were worn out. We decided that the day's work was done, and we would begin with planning for the business the next day.

At the end of the day, I had come to the conclusion that I knew Chaney well enough and that we'd be a great team. I was ready to take that chance again. We rewarded ourselves for a job well done by going to dinner. At dinner, I asked him to be my business partner and we celebrated with champagne. After he accepted, I made a promise to myself that I definitely would never get involved with Chaney, as long as we shared the business.

THINGS WERE MOVING along for us. We had spent a couple of months working side by side. We hashed out an agreement and planned to open in September, which was now a month away. George Wilson had helped me out with a loan, and we were in the midst of having the Rosebud Café redecorated and equipment installed.

I called Allie. "I wanted to see if you wanted to work here at the café. We're opening next month and doing the hiring now, so we can train."

"Thanks, sis. But that's okay."

"No? You're not looking for a handout? I mean, a hand?"

She laughed at the Freudian slip. "No. I actually got a job on campus. It pays less, but it's more convenient. There's an after-school daycare here, and I can pick up Andi on my way home when I work."

"Good for you," I told her. I felt good about the corner she had turned. I hung up and went to talk to Chaney.

The kitchen was being redesigned with top-of-the-line equipment. Chaney looked brand-new as he watched the installment from the sidelines.

"I guess I don't have to ask you how you feel right now," I said to him.

"This is going to be off the hook!" He was salivating as he spoke.

"They're putting in everything on the other side, too. You're going to have to step out of this kitchen and come take a look."

"I will in a minute." Behind the counter was where Chaney felt most comfortable. I think it was because food was often what brought people here, and what brought people together. That's why even as owner, he loved taking orders, sometimes cooking, and serving people. It gave him a direct line of contact with the customers.

"Let me get out of here. I know this is your domain, so I don't want to trespass."

"What do you mean *my* domain? What's up with that?"

"Meaning, the kitchen and café is your thing. And the Internet café will be mine. I won't cross the line." I waved no with both hands in front of me.

"I'm not feelin' that. We need to handle everything together. You should know the ins and outs about this side, and I should know that side."

I paused thoughtfully. "Guess I'm not used to that attitude."

Chaney paused, then spoke slowly as things fell into place for him. "Oh, I see where this is coming from. This is residual thinking from that clown you worked with." He laughed.

I leaned on the counter as I reflected and joined him in a chuckle. "He wanted to be the front man. We had 'roles.'"

"Well, there's no dividing here. No 'front man' or 'front woman.' We're in this *together*. Feel me?" He slapped me on the back.

"Gotcha." I slapped him harder. He pretended he was coughing up a lung.

Chaney's hand unexpectedly slipped around my waist.

"You remember that foot massage?" Chaney asked.

"Remember? How could I forget?" My face felt flushed. "I always wondered. Why didn't you try to do anything? Most guys would have."

He smiled. "Why do you think I left the room? I wanted to get with you, but it wouldn't have been right. You were in a relationship. We were friends. You were stressed out. It just would have made an ugly situation worse."

The air was still except for the clamoring coming from the kitchen.

He faced me. "As long as we're on the subject, I do have something to confess."

I tensed.

Chaney adjusted his stance. "I've admired you for a long time. You have the same spirit as my deceased wife. I never thought I'd see that again." He lifted a hand to either touch my hair or stroke my face, but at the last second decided against it.

I blushed, even though I didn't want to.

He continued, "Things are coming together for us here." His eyes wandered around the café. "You know what would make all of this complete?" He continued before I could even think about answering the question. He took both my hands in his. "If we were together. A couple."

I searched his eyes. "Chaney," I said softly.

"Getting back into business is great," he said. "But nothing would be better than to do it with someone I was sharing my life with. To be honest, I didn't think it would ever happen. I didn't think I would find anyone out there like that, because that spirit is so hard to find today. But I see it in you."

His touch was marvelous, but I hesitated. I just didn't want to take that chance again.

"You're a great friend. And I love you, as that. But I don't think I can take that chance again."

"What you went through before won't happen again. I can guarantee you that."

"Funny. That's the sort of thing that Russ said when we got together."

"Please don't compare me to Russ." He shuddered and frowned. "I'm definitely not like that cat."

I looked down and patted his hand. "Let me think about it."

He groaned a little before saying, "I'll take that."

"We have a problem with the audio," one of the workers came over to tell us.

"Go ahead and handle it," I said to Chaney.

"No, let's handle it together," Chaney said as he pulled me by the hand.

"HOW ARE THINGS working out with Mel?" I asked Vlora as we walked through the aisles at the annual Missouri Black Expo at the America's Center. It was early, and the crowd was light. It usually didn't start to get packed until two in the afternoon, so each year, we came as early as possible. We strolled the aisles, picked up information on various local companies, and stopped at the vendor booths to eye services and new products.

"Mel is absolutely wonderful. We have the most perfect relationship." Her eyes beamed.

"What, is he romantic?"

She flipped her hand in the air. "Girl, no. Nothing like that. Mel travels a lot, so I hardly see him."

I wrinkled my brow. "How is that a good thing?"

"He's not around long enough to get up under my skin. And every time I see him," she said dreamily, "it's like the first time all over again." She sighed in ecstasy. "And just when I start to feel a little crowded, boop, he has to go off on a business trip for a week or two. I tell you girl, it's heaven."

"You are one strange sister when it comes to relationships." I lifted a pamphlet called "Stress and What It Can Do to You."

"How is this strange? It keeps the relationship fresh. Plus, I've got work to do and don't have time to have a man all up under me. This is perfect. I just might marry his ass. And live in separate houses."

I laughed. "You are out of this world."

"So, you still going solo?"

I laughed a breathy laugh. "Chaney wants to get with me."

Vlora swung around and slapped me on the arm. "Get the fuck out!"

I rubbed my arm. "Damn, V."

"I'm sorry," she said. Then she smacked my arm again, only lighter, as if to say, This is what I meant to do. "Get the fuck out!"

I smiled a weak smile.

"Oh, don't tell me you don't like Chaney. Now *that's* who you should have hooked up with a long time ago. Instead of that short-ass, beady-eyed, insecure little dick Russ."

"Damn. Tell me what you really think about him."

"Chaney's got it going on. He supports the community he lives in, he helps the kids, he's an entrepreneur who never gives up—"

"I think I know who he is."

She went on. "And he's smart, makes good decisions—"

"And he values my opinion."

"See, there you go. So, what did you say?"

"That I had to think about it."

"Aaauuuggghhh!" Her knees buckled as she smacked her lips and huffed. "You are so unbelievable. Aren't you even attracted to him?"

I twinkled. "Yeah. Even though he dresses kind of hip-hop, Chaney's sexy."

"So what's up then? Don't tell me it's the business relation-ship thing again?" She rolled her eyes.

"That would be it."

"Chaney's different."

"Tell me about it."

"You know him." She tried to convince me.

"The things that happened with Russ are still so fresh, though. But I'm not brooding over him or anything."

"I'd kick your ass if you were."

"I don't know if I want to take that chance again. And have things not work out, and lose the business."

"Chaney's not an asshole like Russ."

"That's what I thought about Russ."

"You hardly knew him."

I sighed heavily and frowned. "I don't know. I just—"

Before we could continue our conversation, we were interrupted by a well-dressed man who stepped out from in front of a booth that was dressed with posters and flyers of a book cover. "Ladies, let me give you some information on my new book," he interjected as he shoved two postcards under our noses.

"This is the hottest book of the millennium."

Without giving us a chance to retreat, he ended our conversation and went right into his spiel and we stood there, unable to get a word in edgewise. Vlora listened. I thought about Chaney.

TWENTY-THREE

I WEAVED THROUGH THE CROWDED CAFÉ AND offered assistance to our new customers. The grand reopening of the Rosebud Café was going great. Jarvis manned the door, as we had already reached maximum capacity, and he let new people in only as others came out. Manny offered complimentary beverages to the line that formed, in hopes of nurturing their patience. Vlora had answered my call begging for her help when we saw that our new staff was overwhelmed. Allie was unavailable, but had said that she would stop by the opening, so I was expecting her to come at any time. I was sure that she would help out if we needed her to.

Chaney supervised employees at the counter and in the kitchen, and joined me for press interviews and working the room. New customers sampled the items that Chaney served while they either chatted, browsed our new book and magazine section, or familiarized themselves with the computers. Old customers ordered their favorites and appeared extremely happy to see Chaney and be in the Rosebud Café again. Support from Mill Creek Valley was overwhelming.

By evening, the crowd slowed down to a more manageable pace. Vlora nearly collapsed with a cup of ice in a chair by the window. I sat across from her.

"Whew! I haven't done work like this since college." She took in as many ice cubes as her mouth could handle.

"Thanks for helping us out. I know you're not on the payroll, but we'll hook you up, of course." I winked at her.

She waved her hand at me. "Nonsense. Consider it a gift. I loved helping out. This place is live." She looked at Chaney behind the counter giving instructions to our new part-time employees, Jarvis and Manny. "So, have you decided yet?"

"On?"

She nodded her head toward Chaney.

"I think so" was all I said as I restrained a smile. I didn't want to say anything to her until I talked to Chaney first.

"Well, you gonna keep a sister guessing?"

"Yes. Yes I am," I said, not budging.

"You're no fun." She threw back a few more ice cubes while keeping a mean-looking eye on me. Then she sat up straight and leaned in toward me. "Me myself personally," she said with a full mouth, "I'd go for it."

"Would you now?" I asked, smiling.

Allie came through with what one might call an unattractive gentleman by her side. Unusual for Allie. They were dressed like they just came from the golf course, but Allie didn't play golf.

"Hey, Naja. I'd like you to meet a friend of mine, Alex. Alex, this is my sister Naja Rodgers and our friend, Vlora Dern."

We shook hands before I told Alex to browse around and help himself to the samples.

"What's with the getup?" Vlora asked Allie, eyeing her clothes.

"We just came from Pevely Farms Golf Club." She twirled around. "You like?"

"Yeah, but you don't play golf," I said.

"I do now. Well, actually, I'm learning. Alex is teaching me."

"Since when have you been interested in golf?" I asked.

"I'm not. But I figured out the secret: Men are. There are some *fine* men on the greens. And wealthy." She leaned in to us to get within earshot. "I keep asking where all the good men are. Honey, they're all out there playing golf."

"Uh, fine?" Vlora asked, looking at Alex. "No offense, but . . ."

Allie waved her hand at Alex's back. "Alex is just the unsuspecting patsy. I met him at a First Fridays, but I was trying to get with his friend. They said they were going to a golfing and networking party, but Alex is the one who asked me out. Don't worry, I'll trade him in for a finer model soon. I'm just trying to see what's available so I can make the best choice without being assed-out." She faked a swing of a golf club. "Fore!" she yelled.

Vlora and I exchanged looks of ridicule and laughed at her.

"I thought you gave all this up," I said.

She used a pointed finger to correct me. "I said I was getting my life together. I didn't say I didn't want a successful man if I can land one. I'm not dead."

Alex looked over at our table and winked at Allie. It was obvious that he was smitten with her. Allie puckered her lips into a fake kiss, took the sides of her skirt in her hands, pulled them outward, and did a curtsy.

The evening was winding down, and Jarvis and Manny were about to debut the new Open Mic Nite. Jarvis stepped onstage and did a mic check. He gave an introduction, then announced me and Chaney as the owners and announced that he and Manny would kick things off. Manny sat at the bongos and tapped out a beat while Jarvis recited a new poem that he had written in commemoration of the grand reopening.

After he finished and received applause, he hyped the crowd by freestyling a few verses about the success of the reopening and Chaney. The customers bobbed their heads to the beat, clapped their hands, and gave them a standing ovation when they finished. He had flows.

Chaney and I broke away from the customers to steal a moment while they set up the stage. We sat at a table with a view of Mooncents across the street. Earlier, Jarvis reported that the owners had been out on the corner all day just standing and watching our activity. Looking at the Rosebud Café and the customers that were being taken away from them.

"This is a good feeling," Chaney said as he watched the owner pace on the corner, staring, but not wanting to venture over for an up-close view.

"Tell me about it."

He paused. "You know what would make it even better?"

"I can only imagine," I said. I knew where he was going.

"I know you're not going to play coy with me, Miss Rodgers, are you?"

"Certainly not." I sat up straight in my seat. "You deserve a lot more than that." I got serious.

Chaney moaned. "Somehow, I'm not liking this vibe I'm getting."

"I thought about it and thought about it. I can't deny that you're a great guy and a good friend." I took his hand in mine and looked into his eyes. "But I honestly don't think I can do it right now. I don't know if I'm ready to take that chance just yet."

Chaney's face dropped to his lap. He had a tight grip on my hands.

"I don't want to push you or try to convince you, but is there anything that I can say?"

I stared down at our intertwined hands. "It's not you, Chaney."

A gush of air escaped him. "Not that speech."

I sat back and looked into his eyes, not letting go of his

hands. "I don't want to be one of those women who go through bad relationship after bad relationship, and get so worn down that when the right person comes along, they pass him by. Because they're bringing their baggage with them. I really don't want to be that woman."

"Then don't."

"But I have to trust my heart. And right now, my heart doesn't want to take that chance again, at least not this soon. I need time."

I still didn't know the answer to the question. The one that Russ asked me more than a year ago: Which was more important to me, following my passion or finding love? If I knew, this decision would have been a hell of a lot easier.

Chaney reluctantly patted my hand and forced a smile. He revealed a perfect set of teeth between his full lips and I was already beginning to wonder if I was making a mistake.

"Then there's the smoking thing," I said, looking for reasons to say no.

Chaney smiled and pushed up his sleeve to reveal a nicotine patch. "I'm clean. Or I'm getting there. What else you got?"

I felt warm inside. I smiled and said, "Let's give it some time, then. And we'll see what happens. I have a good feeling about this." I rubbed his patch.

His smile grew deeper. "I feel you."

I looked at Chaney as we held hands. The gleam in his eye matched the twinkle in mine.

READING GROUP GUIDE

1. Naja had issues with mixing business and personal relationships. Were her fears valid? Do you agree with her reasoning? Can business/personal relationships ever work? In what ways can they work? In what ways can they not?

2. What was the root of the problem between Naja and Russ? What were Russ's views on running a business and on business roles? What were Naja's? Did their views have an impact on their business relationship, personal relationship, or both?

3. Did Russ truly have an impact on Naja's business? If so, was it due to their relationship? Was she able to separate the two? What impact did their relationship have, if any, on her dream of business ownership? Can the line successfully be drawn? Should Naja have handled things differently with Russ? If so, how?

4. How did Allie focus on finding a mate? Was there anything wrong with her strategy? She thought her strategy was in her daughter's best interests. Was it?

5. How was Allie as a mother? What were her strengths? What were her weaknesses? What would Andi be like as a teenager at the beginning of the story and at the end of the story? Would there be a difference?

6.   Did the Rodgers sisters have an issue with loving themselves? If so, how is this evident?

7.   What do you think of Vlora's outlook on relationships (family, friends, and men)? Did she have an issue, or is that just her prerogative? What will her personal life be like when she retires?

8.   Was Chaney truly the man for Naja? Why or why not? What do you think of Naja's final decision? Will she regret it?

9.   Will Naja's business be run successfully? Will that be a result of how she chose to handle her partnership? Will she be able to change the nature of her partnership in the future? Should she?

10.   Were Naja and Russ compatible? Were Naja and Chaney compatible? Could a relationship with either make the business stronger if handled correctly, or should she not ever consider either of them as potential mates as long as they're in business together?

11.   For whom do you have the most sympathy, and why?

IF YOU LIKED
FIRST FRIDAYS,

you'll love Cherlyn Michaels' other novel,
Counting Raindrops Through a Stained Glass Window

PROLOGUE

"Is this what you want me to do?" I remember my father asking as he flung his right leg out of the second-story window of our two-family flat in St. Louis.

August's late-night breeze blew waves into his earth-brown polyester shirt. His narrow eyes were framed by three heavy creases in his forehead. Even from the far end of the makeshift bedroom that transitioned into the living room where he straddled the ledge, I could hear the quick, frantic heaving of his breath. His ashy hands clutched both sides of the white wooden ledge as chipped paint fell to the tattered carpet.

My father continued to hurl fever-pitched words at my mother, who calmly ironed the day's laundry and appeared to be completely unaffected by the unfolding drama. He seemed totally ignorant of my presence at her feet. Or perhaps he thought that a three-year-old brain had not yet developed the capacity for storing long-term memories, and that in a few seconds this scene would be permanently rubbed out of my mind.

"I'll jump if that's what you want me to do. Just say it. Just tell me to jump and I'll jump." Dad leaned his right shoulder outside of the window a little farther. He maintained a secure grip as he straddled the ledge and sustained his balance with his left hand.

I remember dropping the multicolored LEGO pieces that I'd been fiddling with for twenty minutes or so. It wasn't like I could build a masterpiece out of the yellow, red, and blue rectangles. Besides, I thought the little scene that Dad was creating was a lot more fascinating. At the time, I wanted to see him jump. I wanted to see him jump and then see the word "Splat!" in big fat black letters floating up to the window inside a balloon. I smiled at him in anticipation.

"Jesse, come on now," Mom said without looking up. She sighed heavily through her nose as she ironed a bedsheet. When Dad continued, the corners of her mouth curled as her jaws tightened. "Don't you see the baby right here? What you trying to do—traumatize the girl? If you keep on you're going to wake Babysista." Mom gestured with her head toward the open door of the second bedroom just inches behind us.

"Look, I'm telling you that I want to come back. What else do you want me to do? Tell me. What do you want me to do? I'm saying I want to be a father to my kids. To all *my* kids." His beady eyes fixed on Mom's large belly. "I'm trying to do what's right. What you want me to do? Kill myself? Huh?"

Dad's voice grew louder with each word. His breathing got heavier and faster. I saw veins bulge along the side of his neck, and his face dripped fury-laden sweat. Then that entertaining show became scary to me. Somehow, it didn't end as funny as it began.

I looked up at Mom.

She pressed down hard on the sheet, concentrating on one spot for several seconds as the iron emitted puffs of steam. Then she jerked the iron back and forth a couple of times before stopping on another area. Her stern eyes focused on the sheet as her hand choked the iron's handle.

"Tell me, Veda. What do you want? What you want me to do? Huh?" Dad repeated.

Mom had had enough of Dad's tirade. She slammed the iron down in its upright position. It fell over, iron-side down. She gripped it again, raised it to its upright position, and dared it with her eyes to fall again.

"You left, Jesse. You *left*. You left your kids. You left me. For five months! Now all of a sudden you're back? Suddenly you decide you want to come back and just like that I'm supposed to say okay?" She waved her hands and pointed her finger for emphasis. "No explanation, no reason from you, no nothing?" Mom's face crumpled. She gasped, threw her arms in the air, and shook her head from side to side.

"I made a mistake. I said I was sorry. If that's not good enough for you, then I'll jump. Just tell me that's what you want and I'll jump. I'll jump right now." Dad shifted and moved his rear toward the outside of the window ledge. He deftly leaned down and gripped the inside of the ledge tighter. His calculated balancing act was deserving of a Tony Award in this one-man off-Broadway play.

"Jesse, stop it!" Mom finally yelled. I think she started to believe that the fool might actually jump. "Jesse, Van's right here. What are you doing?"

Mom reached down and covered my face for a very brief moment. By that time, I was already clinging to the hem of her dress and tears were on the verge of spilling over the bottom rim of my eyelids. I didn't know what was going on, but I knew it wasn't a funny show anymore. Something had changed. I didn't understand what, but then things took a turn for the worse. I wrapped my arms around Mom's right leg and began to whine. It seemed appropriate. Maybe it would make Dad stop.

"Just tell me to do it and I will. Whatever you want, Veda. Just tell me. All you got to do is say it."

Dad had shifted more to the right and now gripped the bottom of the window ledge with his lower left leg and his left arm. He was confident that he had his balancing act under control.

"Come back in," Mom said. "Come back in and get out

of the window." She pulled away from me and ran toward the window.

A smile developed behind his eyes. Satisfied with the reaction he'd garnered from her, he lifted his left arm to pull himself back inside. As he reached in, the disproportion of his weight across the ledge caused him to slip farther outside of the window. Dad's eyes widened; his mouth opened as if he was trying to call out but couldn't. His eyes now harbored panic. His left arm fell against the inside of the ledge and began to slip upward as the weight of his body pulled him down.

"Jesse!" Mom screamed. When Mom screamed, I screamed, and then, as if to fall in line with the women of the family, Babysista wailed from the bedroom behind me.

I cried out as Mom grabbed Dad's left hand. She couldn't hold it. His hand was slipping from hers. She kept repositioning her hands over his sweaty one, cupping it and trying to pull it close to her pregnant belly, but it kept slipping from her grasp.

"I love you, Jesse. I love you!" Mom yelled. She was crying and panting and struggling to pull him in.

Dad's mouth was open and silent. He shifted his leg back over the top of the ledge and searched for a groove in which to anchor the heel of his foot. His movements slowed as his eyes anxiously searched Mom's for a miracle.

"Baby, I do love you, baby. I love you, baby," she repeated as she repositioned her grip again and again. I wailed as I sat watching from beneath the ironing board. Babysista wailed, too.

Dad stopped moving. Warm air brushed past him, whisked inside the room, and dried my face. Mom moved her hand once more to get a better grip so she could pull him in. As she lifted her right hand, Dad's hand slipped out of her left. Then I didn't see any more parts of Dad at all.

Mom leaned out of the window, speechless. I stopped wailing. Babysista whimpered.

I followed Mom down the long flight of monster stairs that led to the front door. I was usually afraid of them because of the way the entire staircase lifted up to access the basement at the press of a latch. I always expected Herman Munster to come walking out. But this time I held on to the banister and took one baby step after another. I stepped right over the latch and pushed open the screenless screen door.

I stepped out unnoticed onto the warped porch. I stared at the crowd that surrounded Dad as he lay mangled in the bushes below the window while Mom held his hand and stroked his forehead. She whispered that everything was going to be all right and that we were going to be a family once he came back home. She spread his hand over her belly and moved it in a circular motion.

Dad's hardened cold eyes met hers, went down to his limp hand on her belly, then up to her face again. He moaned and his eyes turned empty.

Then I heard Mom profess her love. She sprinkled kisses across the back of his hand and his face as an ambulance drove up. Our neighbor, Mrs. Woods, spotted me peering over the banister and whisked me back upstairs as I began to absorb what I later came to know as a strange kind of love—an inevitably bitter kind of love that surfaced when you stayed with someone long enough. That sick, bitter love that I came to know as the gift of any marriage that lasted beyond seven years. That gift of eternal misery.

ONE

"Okay, we can stay at the Marriott or the Roney Palace again. Or, we can do the Hilton," Alton said to me as he browsed the Internet.

Even though we'd already been to South Beach at least six times and designated it as "our spot," Alton became ritualistic whenever we decided to go again. He'd break out the legal pad and mechanical pencil, park himself in front of the computer, and check out every single hotel on the strip. He'd examine the size of the hotel, parking services, nearby restaurants, attractions, clubs, and whatever else crossed his mind. That was his thing, and I never bothered him. I absolutely loved it. Except for the times when he shook me awake or called me after midnight to check out a hotel room on the Internet. That's when his enthusiasm for the perfect trip made me want to take away his paper and pencils and ban him for life like Pete Rose.

"Honey, really, any hotel is fine with me. You know we never stay in our room anyway," I said from my soft-side bed, where I was sorting through a week's worth of mail—mostly bills. Working ten hours a day and some weekends hardly left enough time for even the essential things that I needed to do, like writing checks.

"Well, what do you think you'll be in the mood for this time? At the Marriott we'll be right on South Beach. If we do the Roney on Miami Beach, we'll have some quiet time. We can always walk down to South Beach when and if we feel like it. The small hotels in the Art Deco district are another option."

"Um, we're not going through this again, are we?" I looked up at him and smiled. Alton didn't even notice. The travel wheels in his head had already started to burn rubber like Evel Knievel. He sat at the computer desk gazing at the nineteen-inch flat-screen monitor, completely mesmerized as he read the amenities of different hotels, all of which he could probably recite from memory.

"Go through what?" he asked.

"Looking at the Internet sites of every hotel on the strip, choosing either the Marriott or the Roney, and then getting there and spending all of our time on the beach, shopping, and at clubs." I chuckled.

"Well, you never know. There could be a new hotel that's opened since the last time we were there. Maybe it's plush, the way you like it, and reasonable, the way I like it."

He put the mechanical pencil between his full lips and used both chiseled hands to type on the keyboard.

Envying the pencil, I plopped the stack of mail on the espresso-colored nightstand. I deviously slipped behind Alton for a Sunday-morning attack and began massaging his massive shoulders as I peered first at the computer screen, then down at him. His solid shoulders were a result of consistent dedication to the gym a few days a week. He had managed to carve out a well-sculpted body that was not too bulky and, most important, wasn't supported by the birdlike stems that seemed to be common around here. I'm sure I loved touching and massaging his body more than he loved feeling my touch. I hopped at any chance to caress his maple skin and soothe his muscles into relaxation.

I moved inward to the base of his neck and used my thumbs to gently knead and stroke from top to bottom. Alton immediately released the tension in his neck, willing his muscles to surrender and let my hands have their way. I moved a hand to each side of his neck and stroked in circular motions. He leaned his head to the right side, which signaled to me that the left side of his neck could use some extra attention. Using both hands, I kneaded the pressure out of his neck and shoulder. He let out a low moan of approval, put the pencil and legal pad on the computer desk, and let his arms fall limply to his sides. His head rolled back and, with his eyes closed, he smiled at me.

Continuing Operation Seduction, I took my thumbs and stroked his right eyebrow first, then the left. Alton has thick eyebrows that add depth to his high cheekbones and ruggedly squared jawline. His brown eyes are narrow at the inset, open abruptly, and end with a slight slant at the outside corners. As I ran my fingers over his eyes, his lengthy lashes tickled my fingertips. He pushed out a long, approving breath through his nose as I traced the sides of his face and caressed his smooth skin. He has the smoothest skin that I've ever seen on a man. Whenever I mentioned this to Alton, he would always laugh and say, "That's because I got Haitian in my family."

I glided my fingertips from his cheeks to his full lips and thought about kissing him. I loved kissing him. I leaned over and planted tiny kisses across his forehead.

"Oh, see, now you know you're trying to start something."

"Uh-huh," I replied as softly and seductively as I could.

"You know that drives me crazy," he said with his eyes still closed.

"For sure, no doubt," I said, playfully using his favorite phrase against him. He laughed when I said it. Alton always used that phrase as his way of saying yes.

I held his head between my hands and continued to tenderly kiss his forehead in random spots.

"Okay, that's it, Vanella. I warned you." Alton stood, picked me up, and gingerly lay a giggling me on the champagne-colored Egyptian-cotton comforter. He straddled me, brushed my hair off my face, and passionately kissed my impatient lips. Alton was a master at kissing, and he knew it. I knew it, too, which is why I loved kissing him. He would start with small, quick teasers, then gently lick, kiss, and suck my lips before completely driving me crazy. He combined slow and medium strokes to enjoy tasting me before allowing me to give his mouth the feel and taste of heaven.

I slowly lifted off his sleeveless undershirt, gave it a quick toss, and ran my hands across his powerful chest while he suspended his five-foot-eleven-inch frame over all five feet five inches of me. Mmmmm . . . he smelled of just a hint of cologne. The fragrances he chose mixed well with his natural scent and always made my body simmer with excitement. Whenever he was at my place, Alton would lightly anoint his body with cologne after a shower. He knew I loved to snuggle against him and let his sexy scent lull me to sleep. I slowly pulled him closer to me and buried my face in the crook of his neck, feeling the crests and depths of his firm shoulder blades and spine. I moved my hands to the back of his head and ran my fingers over his low-cut hair as he worked artful kisses down to my neck.

Now the getting was good. Alton moved his strong hands down my neck, across my shoulders, and began to . . .

The phone rang.

Damn! I hate intrusions. The telephone, doorbell, it never fails. Especially when he's doing it well. Oh, so well.

We both paused and groaned at the same time—Alton, perhaps because he knew he had gotten into a groove and was about to experience one of our most intense encounters of the day, and me because I knew it was probably somebody in the family, which meant nothing but more drama.

Alton grunted. He rolled his luscious body off me and ran the palm of his hand down his face, as if to wipe away the intimate moment and snap his mind into football mode.

"Well, I'm going to shower and start setting up for the game." He pecked my lips, grabbed his undershirt off the top of the headboard, and headed for the shower.

I couldn't resist watching his bare backside as he walked away. Boy was a walking poem. Alton already had a well-built and perfectly proportioned body, but I loved it when planning one of our beach trips compelled him to prepare more by putting in extra time at the gym. The product was simply scrumptious.

"And quit looking at my ass!" Alton said without looking back. He knew me too well.

I pulled myself up on the bed and looked at the imposing phone as it rang for the third time. What is it going to be this time? Who is it going to be about now? Is it my sister, Jaelene, calling to borrow money again? Or is it Kizaar and Dad this time? Dad forever complained and instigated his own hypertension about either something Kizaar said, did, or didn't do. It beat me as to why Kizaar kept trying.

Or was Mom calling to tell me how insensitive Dad had been to her again? She constantly calls to tell me how Dad yelled at her, put her down and demeaned her, missed her birthday or their anniversary, or made a bedroom out of his home office and refused to sleep in their bedroom with her anymore. She told her children about all of these things but she begged us not to say anything to him because she feared that it would only make the situation worse. Frankly, I didn't know how she put up with it. I felt sorry for her, and sometimes wished I could slip her the backbone she needed to stand up to him and his disparaging remarks—and maybe even kick a little ass every now and then.

I picked up the phone. "Hello?"

"Hey, Van. How are you doing?" It was Mom. I knew she wasn't calling to see how I was doing. Mom rarely calls just to chitchat. There's always a purpose. I could have told her that I'd just been hit by a semi; she would have said, "That's nice," then rolled right into the reason she was calling.

"I'm fine. Alton's here and we're gearing up for the Browns-Steelers preseason game."

"The who?"

"We're about to watch a football game," I said. Mom isn't into sports, so there was no use in taking an extra fifteen minutes to try to explain the football teams to her. Besides, I knew she didn't really want me to anyway. "How are you? Is everything okay with you?" I asked.

"Well," she drew out the word with a heavy breath, which let me know that I needed to buckle up because I was in for a long ride. "Your father is refusing to give me money to take that personal-finance class that you told me about, and the class starts tomorrow. He says that since I don't have a job, there's no reason for me to learn about finances and that I probably couldn't learn, so it would be a waste of good money anyway."

I rolled right past the condescending remarks because no matter how much you told her not to take the mental abuse, she would continue to do so without a word. She would be scared to death if we even mentioned telling the man off for the way he talked down to her. Scared like he would beat her or something. I'd never seen any signs of physical abuse and she never spoke of any, but I wondered about that possibility sometimes.

"Mom, every woman should know about finance. At a minimum, everybody should know about bill management, investing, and handling retirement funds. What if something happens to Dad, God forbid? How would you know about handling insurance, income taxes, household debts, and everything else?"

Mom sighed. "I know. I told your father everything you told me. He just said it was nonsense and that I would know what to do when it happened. He said I wasn't going to handle any bills or money, and it didn't matter since he wasn't going anywhere and that I shouldn't worry my thick head about it anyway. Then he left the room before I could say another thing."

As if she would have said another thing, I thought.

"I'm going to talk to him. It's important for all married women to know how to handle finances, even if you aren't bringing an income into the household. This class is important for you. That's why I told you about it. You need to go. I'll talk to him," I said. I knew what was coming next.

"No, no, if you talk to him it would just make him more upset that I talked to you about it. Then things would just get worse over here." She heaved a sigh as if she'd just been hit with the heaviest burden of her life.

"Mom, we go through this all the time. There's no reason you should be this unhappy. I wish you would say something or let me say something for you. This is ridiculous."

No answer.

"Well, look," I said, "I'll go ahead and send you the money for the class." I knew that was the solution she was waiting to hear.

"Oh, would you? That would be great because I really do want to take that class. I really appreciate it."

"Of course I would, Mom. I don't have a problem with that. I just hate to see your life like this, and I don't understand why you want to keep it that way."

"It's not bad. Not as bad as you make it out to be. He's bitter because of James's death."

"Mom, I'm really sick of hearing the excuse about Dad's twin brother. That was twenty-five years ago."

"They were really close and—"

"I know," I interrupted. "They were close, they were inseparable, they were in the Marines together, and they were starting a business together until Uncle James died in a motorcycle accident," I recited. "You know what? I've heard the whole story a million times. Uncle James died years ago and I know it was extremely painful, so I don't mean to sound insensitive, but Uncle James's death over twenty years ago doesn't give Dad the right to treat you like shit today. There's no reason for it, and I wish you'd stop making excuses for him." I could feel sweat beading on my forehead and between my breasts.

Again, no response.

"I'll put the money into our account tonight and you should be able to get it out tomorrow."

"Thanks, Vanella, baby. Well, I'm not going to hold you. Tell Alton I said 'hi.'"

"I will. Love you."

"Love you, too." She hung up the phone.

I put the phone back in its cradle, shook my head, and growled to myself. As I sat on the edge of the bed, I ran moist hands down my thighs, trying to ease away the frustration. I love my mother dearly, but her passivity with my dad drives me absolutely insane. My stomach turns sour, and I always feel a tightening in my throat whenever we talk. I wanted to shake Dad, but mostly I wanted to shake some sense into Mom for allowing him the freedom to trample on her spirits. I didn't understand why any woman today would stay in a marriage with a husband who didn't appear to love her and made her life as miserable as he possibly could. I am far from a proponent for divorce. But I am less of a proponent for sticking around someone who abuses you—mentally or physically, man or woman, husband or wife, girlfriend or boyfriend. I didn't know how long I could grant Mom's wishes and be a passive listener. She had perfected being passive and was damn good at it, but I'm not and don't want to be.

Alton had finished his shower and the aroma of microwave popcorn from the kitchen saturated my condo and made my mouth water. I glanced at the clock on the nightstand, jumped up, and showered quickly so I could be ready in time for the start of the pregame show. Since the Browns were away, I went to my walk-in closet and grabbed my "away games" Browns jersey to wear—and nothing else.

I scurried into the den, where Alton had just finished setting up for our Sunday ritual. He'd changed into his Browns jersey and a pair of drawstring shorts. His legs were looking too good. He had arranged a small spread of finger sandwiches; bowls of popcorn, snack mix, baked potato chips, and fruit; a couple of beers for him; and a bottle of Chardonnay on ice for me.

It was an overcast day in Cleveland. Cleveland skies can be overcast quite frequently, especially the closer it gets to fall and winter.

My three-bedroom, garden-style Shaker Heights condo faces east. On a sunny day, the natural sunlight seeps in and bounces off the cathedral ceiling, thoroughly illuminating my simply furnished unit. Although there was no direct sunlight, Alton turned the blinds down to minimize the soft daylight radiating on the wall-mounted TV.

I stood in the doorway for a second and peered at Alton. I

loved him and our relationship. I didn't want it to change, and I didn't want him to change. Most of all, I didn't want to end up a divorced mess like most of my girlfriends or in a loveless marriage like my parents. I'd grown up watching my mother endure verbal abuse and not being touched or kissed at night—or perhaps at all, for that matter.

I refused to do that.

I looked at Alton and realized that at some point Mom and Dad had to have been right here where we were. Perhaps they started out with a deep love for each other, and somehow, somewhere, through the passing of time, their love evaporated and left the scum of a marriage that it was now.

As I stood there watching Alton, I thought about that and resolved not to let it happen to us.

"So are you just going to stand there, babe? The pregame show is about to come on." He looked around the room. "What? Did I forget something?"

I smiled. "No, you didn't forget a thing."

I headed toward the blue couch, where he was propped up on pillows with one leg on the floor and the other stretched out along the length of the cushions. I took my place between his legs and tucked my legs under me. I grabbed a fistful of popcorn and began feeding him three or four kernels at a time. Alton used the remote and turned up the sound on the TV as James Brown, Terry Bradshaw, Howie Long, and Chris Collinsworth began talking. I turned my head to face him and stared.

"What?" he asked, feeling my vibe.

"I love you," I said.

He squeezed me tight and said, "For sure, no doubt," knowing good and well that his response would not suffice. He held a playful smirk on his face for as long as he could, watching the television and pretending to ignore my stare. I patiently held a steady gaze and waited for the proper response that I knew was coming.

"Okay, okay." He laughed and wiggled his nose into my cheek. "I love you, too. Can I have some more popcorn?" he asked, then kissed my forehead.

I reached over to grab another fistful and felt him rub his hand along my backside.

I jumped. "Hey! The game's about to come on. No time for freaky stuff."

"I'm just checking. After all, it's only preseason." He grinned his devilish, sexy grin.

"Uh-huh." He didn't have to tell me. I knew what I was doing. I was always one step ahead of him.

Vanella Morris is one woman who *thinks* she knows how to hold on to a good thing…

Too bad her man has just asked her to marry him.

HYPERION

CherlynMichaels.com

© CHERLYN MICHAELS

CHERLYN MICHAELS

was the 2003 Shades of Romance Magazine
Best New Multicultural Author of the Year and was
nominated for the African American Literary Awards
Show Open Book Award for Best Self-Published
Author of the Year. She lives in St. Louis, Missouri.